saving
BARRETTE

Saving Barrette

SHEY STAHL

Copy Editing by Becky Johnson, Hot Tree Editing
Cover Image by Sara Eirew
Cover Designer by Sommer Stein, Perfect Pear Creations

❀ Created with Vellum

"Guilt is to the spirit what pain is to the body."
– Elder David Bednar

Warning: This novel contains scenes that might be a trigger for those who have been victims of sexual assault.

Part One

CHAPTER 1

Welcome Home

ASA

JUNE
BOSTON HARBOR, WASHINGTON

I've never liked Washington. Rain, cold, clouds, wind... it's fucking depressing. At least the summers are enjoyable. I prefer my home town of Massillon, Ohio. And though this small-town of Boston Harbor could be considered my home, too, it's not really. I only lived here for six years.

The only reminder or appeal this place holds are the summers. Blue sky, soaring pine trees, and this marina. The one where I met a girl. It always goes back to a girl, doesn't it?

I look out the window to the marina and I can still pinpoint the exact place I met her, between the docks where my dad moored his boat. On the water, kayaks, paddleboards, and boats litter the marina. Amongst them, my dad's forty-foot Fly Absolute yacht stands out.

Way to blend in, Dad.

Laughter floats through the marina, its sound carrying through the open window in my room. I draw in another deep breath. I don't want to be here, but I also don't have much of a choice.

Sighing, I look around my bedroom. Not much has changed since I left, but then again, everything has changed. Boxes line the wall, my suitcase on the bed and in it, hundreds of memories that didn't take place in this town. On my nightstand, a picture of a girl I used to know. The one with haunting gray eyes and a smile that never quite touched her eyes. It's there at times but held at bay for reasons I never did find out.

For the past four years, I've thought about her every single day. It's not an exaggeration either. I think about her now, since I've been back in this town for only hours. It's constant, the memories that is and the pull to see her; it's stronger than anything I've ever experienced. It's so bad that just the idea of her sends my pulse racing and my breathing erratic.

Roman: Dude, get here! We're at my mom's house. I'm savin' ya a ho.

What the fuck does that mean? A ho? Roman's always been the wild child of the group. I'm not even sure I can say group, because when you up and leave two days before high school starts, and return two days after you graduate, you're not part of any group. You're the guy who left. The one who abandoned them.

Part of me knows I shouldn't go, because I know what happens at those parties—they drink and do stupid shit. But when have I ever listened to myself? Never.

"I'm headin' out for a bit," I tell my dad, searching the counter for my keys.

One look at my dad and I can tell you right now that's not what he wants to hear. I don't know him very well anymore so I can't tell you exactly what he's thinking, but I'm guessing by the hard lines forming across his face, he's not happy.

He raises an eyebrow as if to say "Are you serious?"

"Fuck you" is what I want to say. I'm eighteen. I don't have to do anything he says, but I'm not sure I'm ready for that argument just yet. Maybe save it for my second day home.

"You just got home," he reminds me, screwing on the cap to his water bottle. My dad is a health nut. Protein shakes, cross-fit, runs at least three-to-five miles every day and probably hasn't had sugar in over a decade. His body portrays the physically fit condition with lean, defined muscles and veins protruding from his forearms. "Besides, Carlin is on her way home with Livia. I thought we could go for a boat ride. Water's calm tonight."

Ah, yes. Do you see what he's doing here? The dad who abandoned his family and decided to get a new one is making an effort. One day back and I'm supposed to fall right back into his perfect family life he's created. The one where cancer doesn't reside and nothing but perfection exists. That shit, it's not reality. It's superficial. It's a dream, and one day his dream is going to come crashing down on him.

I shrug one shoulder and reach for my keys. "I'm sure I'll see them eventually." Or maybe I'll spend the next month until I move up to Seattle avoiding them.

There's a thought.

"I thought maybe we could get some dinner." And then he glances away and to the bottle of water, then to his cell phone next to it. "Carlin wanted to meet up with us."

"I'm not hungry," I snap, hating the mention of her name.

Dad sighs. He doesn't say anything and I know why. He's pissed off at me. There's one thing Dr. Brent Lawson doesn't like. His plans not going his way. I love my dad, but as a man, I have very little respect for him. My reasoning?

He left my mother when she needed him the most. And now he thinks just because my mom is dead, I'm gonna treat Carlin—his mistress—as if she's my mother now.

She's not. My mom was the best woman in the world. The dirt covering her grave is still fresh, and he thinks I'm suddenly gonna want a new mother. I don't fucking think so. It doesn't work that way. He doesn't get to play this game with me. Not now, not ever.

My dad sighs, again. "Asa, I'm worried about you."

"Don't be. I'm fine. I'm just going out for a bit."

He slides his hand through his hair. "I know you say you're fine, but I don't think you are." He frowns at my expression. "You know what I mean."

"No. I don't know what you mean." If he says her name, I think I'll scream.

The chiseled lines of his face are etched with an emotion I don't understand. Closing his eyes, he draws in a breath and then shakes his head, looking down. "Your mom died, and you got arrested at her funeral."

Right. That. I roll my eyes. He doesn't know the half of it. "Whatever."

His eyes soften, but I can tell he's beginning to panic that I might leave and never come back. "You're raw right now and easily provoked. I just don't think you need to be hanging out with that group at the moment."

"I'll be fine."

He fidgets, his jaw tight and flexing. He's pissed now. I may not have been around him much in the last four years, but I know this look because it's what I do. I think back to the funeral last week and the way he stood stoic in the distance, unmoving, unfazed on the outside and I wonder, did it tear him up inside? Did he feel anything that his first love died so brutally from a cancer that tore apart her life and body?

And then comes the fatherly advice he's been dying to give me since I came home. "Asa, I don't want to hear that you're fine, because you're not. Your mom d—"

"Don't you dare say it!" I shout at him, stepping closer. "Jesus Christ. I know she fucking died. I was there when she took her last breath. You weren't. So don't act like you suddenly know anything about me. I'm fine. And this town isn't the problem. I am."

He knows there's truth in my words, but the dad in him won't let me get the last word. He grabs hold of my elbow. "That's what I'm talking about. You're not yourself right now and it's okay. You've been through a lot, but you have to be smart. If you go out now, with your temperament, it's only going to take one person setting you off and you could lose everything. I agreed by bringing you here that you wouldn't get into trouble. You're already on the NCAA radar and it's not a place you want to be. It's the only way you're not in jail right now, Asa. If you get in another fight, your scholarship to UW is gone."

Lose everything? Ha. I thought I already had.

From the time I was six years old playing youth football, I've had one goal in mind. The NFL. For me, nothing stood in the way of that. Until my mom got sick. I moved to Ohio with her and played high school ball for Massillon High School. For her, I refocused and made the best of the life I now had. For her, I forgot my old life in Washington and did what I needed to do for her. It certainly wasn't easy for a fifteen-year-old boy, but I did it because I knew my mom needed me.

Have you heard about Massillon Ohio? They breed football players. Hell, every baby boy born in Massillon is handed a miniature football. They've had twenty-three pro players, three NFL coaches, and fourteen collegiate all-American's graduate from that school. The Massillon Tigers are one of the winningest high school football teams in the country, and I lead them to the state title this season. They say some kids have talent and others don't. Well me, Asa Lawson, I have the talent, just not the head space most of the time. I obsess. I have anxiety and quite possibly the worst temper you can imagine when pushed over the edge.

Being arrested at my mom's funeral might just be a good example, but it's still early. I'll probably give you another reason why sooner rather than later.

It comes down to this. I should stay home. I should. But the draw to see her is far too tempting.

"I won't get in any fights," I tell my dad in passing, unsure if I will keep the promise.

He mumbles something, though I'm not sure what because from then on out, my thoughts are centered around a girl and the need to know where we stand now, if anywhere.

CHAPTER 2

The Night We Met

eep breaths, B. That's all you need to do to keep from passing out.
He's here. You may not know who I'm referring to,
but if you saw him, you'd know. He's the one who holds
everyone's attention and the target of every snickering girl trying to
draw him their way. He doesn't move from his place beside the fire.
I'm not sure he's noticed me, or even if he remembers me.

My heart thuds louder, a steady, persistent drumbeat. *Shit, stop
staring at him.*

Do you notice the way I hide behind my hair and avoid contact
with pretty much everyone? That's a girl who clearly wants to disappear into thin air.

Laughter and playfulness fill the air beside me. Girls screaming,
guys too loud, too obnoxious in their attempt to be cool. But not
him. He's relaxed, undeterred, unfazed by anything around him.
Standing tall, muscular, rigid, and if I had to guess, his thoughts are
not with the ones around him.

The pacific northwest summer sun beats down on my bare shoulders, the only relief under the thick shade of the pine trees lining
Budd Inlet. There are noises all around me—summer noises—boats,
creaking docks, laughing. I drop my head, my hair falling forward to

conceal my face. My stomach squeezes, ready to vomit the pizza rolls I scarfed down just hours ago. Come to think of it, I've never had a weak stomach, until now. Until I can't draw my eyes away from him. They flicker and then away, only to find their way back again like the pull he's always had on me.

Don't puke, I tell myself. *You don't have a change of clothes with you.*

I don't know what I'm doing here. I hate parties. High school parties, even worse. I guess I've never experienced anything but high school parties and the occasional birthday, and one very awkward graduation party for my cousin Layne. I've never enjoyed anything where I'm forced to interact and pretend I'm comfortable being surrounded by strangers.

"We should be at your house," Cadence says, rolling her eyes at the laughter coming from the water where the keg is. While the party is just getting started, it seems her on-again—more off-again—boyfriend, Roman, is doing a keg stand. "At least there we wouldn't be bothered by anyone."

"Yeah, but I'm sure they have the cameras on to watch our every move," I tell her, knowing they do. "And we have nothing but kale chips and sparkling water to drink."

Cadence makes a sour face. "Your parents are so fucking weird."

"Try having them as parents."

My, shall I say, eccentric parents, they spend the summers traveling without me. Every teenager's dream, right? Believe me, it's for the better. They used to drag me around to all the places they wanted to go, but finally, when I turned sixteen and proved I could stay home alone, they stopped forcing me to go. Besides that, my grandpa lives next door to us. It's not like I'm really left home alone.

"Holy shit. Isn't that Asa Lawson?" Cadence gestures toward the bonfire where I know he's standing. Her eyes slide to mine and it's a waiting game of what my reaction is going to be.

My red cup rests in my hand and I struggle to maintain my "distracted" look I've been practicing. I do that jerky head motion that makes it look like I have Tourette's syndrome. I don't, but it doesn't matter. When I'm nervous, I get jerky and my voice becomes high and shaky. Classic teenage-girl move for sure. "Yeah, it's him." I divert eye contact. See? Did you notice the octave my voice reached? Embarrassing. "Stop looking at him!" I hiss.

She snickers. "I'm sorry. But damn, it's just so hard not to. He certainly filled out, didn't he?"

Believe me, I know. I've been drooling over him long before she noticed. I noticed Asa over an hour ago, but I didn't want to give myself away. I've been watching him the entire time, my heart fluttering with every blink of his dark lashes and the way his golden blond hair shines under the shimmering sunset. He's just as beautiful as the day he left. It should be a crime for a teenage boy to be beautiful. It's unfair to all the girls that work at it and he probably—I know he does—just rolls out of bed that put together.

"When did he get back in town?" she asks, as if implying I should know by the tone of her voice.

Cadence knows our history. I cried on her shoulder for two weeks after he left. She gets it. Trying to play it cool, I shrug. It's easier than telling her I don't know. One would think given our past I would know exactly when Asa returned to town, but I don't. I lost touch with Asa not long after he left.

It happens then, his eyes slowly drifting to mine, meeting my gaze. Only this time, they don't hold. He looks away, as if his expectation of what he thought he'd seen, he hadn't.

Did he not recognize me? Sure, I look slightly different, but just because I have boobs now doesn't mean I'm completely unrecognizable to the girl he used to know.

You know that feeling when a memory hits you and it plays out in your head like a nightmare? That's the feeling I get when I recall the day Asa left and me begging him to take my virginity. Yep. At fourteen I had it in my head I needed my virginity taken and it was going to be Asa Lawson. It had to be as far as I was concerned. Wasn't exactly my best memory of the last four years because spoiler alert, he said no. He said, "I can't take that from you."

Whatever the hell that meant other than, screw you—actually no screwing happened—I'm not having sex with you. And then he laughed, pushed me away and smiled before following up his soul-crushing denial with, "You don't want me like that, and you know it."

Cadence glances over her shoulder at him, and then quickly looks away. "Did you ever hear from him at all?"

My hands tremble at the memories, my heart catching. It stills, tries to understand, but it's something beyond comprehension for me. Dryness seizes my lungs and I swallow, or attempt to. Nothing works. My heart races, my breathing fast and rapid.

Why does he still spark this reaction in me after four years?

Cadence bumps my arm, my drink sloshing in my cup and spilling over the sides. "Hey, did you hear me?"

I stutter, "W-What?"

Her blue eyes snap to his and then back to me. "Have you talked to him?"

"No." I bite the inside of my cheek. Can you hear the way my heart thuds? Do you notice my breathing and the quick hitch to the shifting of my feet in the gravel where the water's edge tickles our bare feet? When you're an eighteen-year-old girl on the verge of everything you don't understand, those are the emotions that drown and suppress words.

I lift my eyes to his and notice the quick glance to mine, as if he knows I'm watching him. To my surprise, he crooks a half smile in my direction.

Holy crap. Look away.

I can't.

He still has that same smile, boyish but serious. It's the same smile that used to instigate my own. And he's beautiful, as always. Me? I'm nothing like that fourteen-year-old girl he left. For a moment, I'm lost in my own head, remembering the smallest details about a boy everyone in this small town worshiped, including me. It's then I realize he's looking right at me.

Shit, he noticed.

And here I thought he seemed completely unfazed by my presence here, or at the very least, unaware. Quickly as I can, I divert my eyes because my face is probably redder than the plastic cup I'm holding. It pisses me off that I'm so easy to read it's ridiculous.

"Roman said his mom died," Cadence adds, a certain sadness to her voice. "That's like, so sad. I thought for sure she'd beat the cancer."

Afraid to risk a glance in his direction, my eyes deceive me again and land on the boy who held my hand for two years through the awkward middle school years, and harshly left me when I needed him the most.

With my cup pressed to my lips, I mumble, "Yeah, she passed away last week." Just because I didn't keep in touch with him didn't mean I hadn't stalked his dad to find out every little piece of information I could about him. His dad? Orthopedic surgeon. I intern at his office doing filing only so I can hear every detail about Asa's life. If that doesn't scream pathetic, I don't know what does. Probably me stalking him on Instagram under a fake account—which I do—but we won't discuss that. Maybe throwing yourself at him and begging him to take your virginity. That's probably one too.

"I heard he has a full ride to UW."

"Yep." Again, I only know any of this because of his dad. It's the same reason I applied there too.

Cadence stares at Asa, eyeing his appearance. I can't really blame her. I do it too. He's wearing relaxed jeans, a black T-shirt, and a hat. Though I can't see his eyes, I'm familiar with their exact color. Dark brown with a hint of green to them. He stands across the fire, solid, strong, a red cup in hand. Is he drinking beer? Vodka? Water? I'm dying to know.

There's a girl beside him, black hair, busty, but his interest doesn't lie with her. He hasn't even looked over at her, but it doesn't stop the burning sensation in my chest or the pinch to my brows as I attempt to melt her with my gaze. I wish I was the one standing next to him, sharing the space and conversation, but I can't make myself move closer to him in fear he'll say he doesn't remember me.

Sliding her sunglasses up, Cadence tilts her head to mine when she hears his laughter in the distance over something Roman says to him. "He seems okay, like not sad."

Not sad? Sure, that's probably what he wants everyone here to believe. I know the truth. Years can't erase that. I can tell by the rigid set of his jaw and the slump of his shoulders, he's not okay. And that laugh? It's the one he uses when he's trying to be nice. I know this because I know everything about Asa Lawson from every single facial expression to the way he smiles when he lies. Time can't erase everything. And I bet if I walked over to him and leaned in, he'd smell the same, a mixture of pine trees, spice, and oranges. It's like Calvin Klein threw up all over him. It sends a familiar tingle up my thighs.

Cadence bumps my arm again, attempting to untangle her sunglasses from her wavy hair. "You should go talk to him." I stare at her as she pulls and tugs only to rip a clump of her hair out with the sunglasses. She winces and rubs the spot. "Damn it."

I know what you're thinking. That I should, in fact, go up to him. I should tell him I'm sorry for his loss or ask him why he never kept in touch. I should maybe ask him how he liked Ohio and if he still plays football. I don't because I know the answers. Instead, I play the bitch card and act like his presence here doesn't faze me.

But I'm a girl and rather predictable at times, and the idea that Cadence thinks I should go over there sends a shock through me. A horrified snort bursts out of me and I slap my hand over my mouth at the same time as beer spits from my nose. It burns. I choke and it's like I've been waterboarded with beer. It's awful.

Cadence rubs my back, laughs at me and guess who is staring at me now because you know damn well he heard me choke? Yep. Asa. And he steps in my direction as if he's going to come closer, but then Roman says something to him and draws his attention back to him.

Fuck you, Roman.

That's when Remy, our friend and Roman's twin sister, practically jumps on top of my shoulders to see him. "Girl, check it out. Asa's back!" Remy yells in my ear while she holds the red plastic cup in her hand to her lips and crawls on my back. I lose my footing with her spider monkey climb and end up falling to my knees, her drink spilling down my back.

Still trying to catch my breath from inhaling beer, I jump up at the shock of the ice-cold beer down my white tank top. "Remy!" I screech, my arms straight out, and heart pounding.

I stand there shocked for a moment before I realize that one, I'm wearing a white, soaked tank top with one of those lace halter tops we think are bras but really aren't.

And two, everyone is staring at me. Either from my scream or the fact that my nipples are saying hello.

"I'm so sorry!" Remy says, her eyes wide. "Let me go get you a shirt."

"Don't bother," I hiss, turning to leave. I didn't want to be here in the first place and now that Asa's here, I definitely don't want to be.

"B, don't go!" Cadence yells after me and grabs hold of my hand in passing. "We just graduated. We need to celebrate." She forces me to turn and look up at her. It's not hard. I'm barely five foot two and she's damn near six feet tall.

Tears sting my eyes the moment I look up at her. I'm a crier. Mad, sad, frustrated, happy, all my emotions end in crying for me. It's quite possibly the worst fault to have if you ask me. I'd rather turn green like the Hulk than wear my emotions on my sleeves.

So naturally, tears surface with my frustration and embarrassment that I'm wearing Remy's beer. My muscles tense, and I pull at the front of my shirt to keep it from sticking to my chest. "I'm not leaving." My gaze darts to the side of Cadence toward the bonfire. Smoke fills the air, guys whistling at me in the distance. One yells, "Take it off, B!"

Cadence flips them off. "Shut the fuck up!"

I close my eyes and fight off the need to punch the fucker in the face who just yelled. I don't know him, but he's standing next to

Roman, so I assume he's one of the football jocks and just as annoying as the rest of them.

Despite the lack of visibility with the fading sun, I know *he's* watching me. It's his glare I'm not expecting. Is he glaring at me? What the hell did I do wrong?

The teenage girl in me glares back. "I'm going to look for a new shirt," I tell Cadence and Remy. Realizing I need a minute, they don't follow me. I didn't drive here, so I don't have my car to search through and I have absolutely no clue where I'm going to get a shirt from. Cadence probably has something in her car I can wear.

I walk up the beach, through the twists and turns of the trail that cuts through the woods leading to the house overlooking Budd Inlet. Throngs of people line the deck and there's no way I'm going up there to Remy's room to look for a shirt. I keep walking up the driveway to Cadence's car hoping there's a shirt in there I can wear.

You know, something told me not to come tonight and I should have listened to that little voice in my head. But I didn't. *Stupid. So stupid.*

Each step becomes more aggravated than the next, and before I know it, I'm stomping up the driveway with such force it hurts my knees.

I can't believe I came here.

"Hey, B?" comes from behind me, and the sounds of heavy foot-steps follow.

Hey, B? Everyone calls me B and it never fazes me. But when it's said by *him*, it's so unbelievably sexy. The sound entices, teases, and leaves my heart waiting for the storm.

I don't need to turn around to know who it is. His voice. It shouldn't make me feel this way, so familiar, so distinct, but it does. It's as if I've been waiting four years to hear it, and I have been.

At first, I don't turn around. I refuse to. I'm afraid to. But I have to because it's *him*.

Are you ready to meet him? Are you ready to have those syrup eyes draw you in and his sharp tongue turn you on? I wasn't when I met him at nine years old. I'm still not, even after all this time.

So I turn slowly, unwillingly. I don't want to face him because I know the effect my heart will have, the reaction reflecting on my cheeks, the one he sparks so easily in me. He branded me with his love so long ago only to rip it away. Why should I turn around? I don't owe him anything.

Curiosity, that's why. I want to know why it was so easy for him to cut me out of his life like I didn't exist at all. I want to know why I wasn't good enough to sleep with, yet Heather Randal was. Yep. First girl he slept with was Heather Randal. The biggest slut around, and he, as Roman puts it, "tapped that" two days before he left.

Why her and not me?

So yeah, curiosity. That's why I turn around. At first, I don't meet his eyes. I think I'm afraid to, but when I finally do, his expression is unreadable. He doesn't say anything. For the length of a heartbeat, I let myself believe time hasn't changed anything. There's a long pause, our gazes locking for a moment. Mine pale blue, his golden.

"What?" I snap, crossing my arms over my chest so he can't see the fact that my nipples are perky and hard.

His lips twitch, fighting a smile, and he hands me a sweatshirt. "Need a shirt?"

"No, not really." I close my eyes and inhale slowly through my nose trying to calm myself down.

He waits and holds it out like I'm supposed to take it.

"Okay, yes. Fine." I groan. My palms tingle. I want so badly to hit him or something to show my anger. "I do, but not from you." Years. Fucking years, I've spent wondering why, only to have him come back here and act like our childhood didn't mean shit.

"Why not from *me*?" He sounds confused, his face serious as his hand falls to his side.

I look at his hands, his forearms, the tan skin and the golden flecks of blond hair covering them. "Because.... You left, remember?" I point out, my voice and stance guarded.

"You know it wasn't like that," he explains. "What was I supposed to do?"

My eyes narrow in on him. "Not leave me. You just cut me out of your freaking life like..." I hiss through my teeth, "...like I wasn't good enough."

He's staring at me incredulously, his face tense and defensive. My words obviously caught him off guard. He stares at me in disbelief. "Is that what you think? That you weren't good enough?" His questioning tone pulls at my sanity.

"What else am I supposed to think?" There's a good amount of sarcasm from my end if you can't hear it.

He matches my tone, spitting out the words, "My fucking mom was dying. It wasn't like I had a damn choice in the matter." It's as if he growls the words, licking his lips. And just like that, I've pissed him off. Easy to do. One thing hasn't changed. Asa's moods flip like a switch.

I want to apologize to him. I knew why he left, but to cut all attachments to the girl he said he couldn't live without, that's what makes me angry. And Heather. So I stand my ground. Only time hasn't changed anything. I still feel his presence deep in my bones. Caught up in the pull he has over me, it takes me a minute until I can move. I step away from him. "I know you left for her, but why not call?"

He swallows, shrugs one shoulder, and then lands those beautiful golden eyes on mine. His brow pinches, his emotions trapped inside his tense stare. He looks away toward the trees when he says, "I thought it'd be easier that way, but it wasn't."

I open my mouth to say something, but no words come. So I close it, and then try again. This time my anger speaks for me. "I don't want your stupid shirt."

Or your dick. But... I leave that part out because of two things: I still want him, and there's no way he's gonna know that.

"Barrette, please. I'm sorry. I really am. I never meant to hurt you." Asa reaches out, his touch unprovoked, a natural reaction. He did it the day he left when I tried to leave his room. Only he walked away that day. I bite my lips, holding the swell of feelings inside. Don't react. Or maybe I should?

His grip tightens and he attempts to pull me into him. I don't go. My hand slips from his. His mouth clamps together, his shoulders stiff and defensive as he glares at me. Anger works his face, his jaw clenching. I quickly look away feeling a blush creep up my neck.

"Just go, Asa."

With a deep breath, I let go and walk away like he did when he left town.

CHAPTER 3

What I wouldn't give

ASA

F uck this bullshit party.

I knew what coming here meant, I did, but I didn't think she'd react like this. I should have, though. Barrette Blake is anything but easygoing. She's stubborn, relentless and never lets anyone tell her how she's going to feel. Above all else, she's beautiful, inspiring, and deep. One look at those ocean eyes and I know I'm in deep already.

Do you notice my breathing heavier, louder, body temperature rising and the tension in my face? It's all an indication that I shouldn't be drinking and shouldn't be here.

I bring the beer in my hand to my lips. It provides no relief. My mind is numb, my actions forced. I'm rooted in a haze of uncertainty. I want to go to her, but I can't make myself follow.

Can you hear the beating of my heart and the skip when *she* walks away? It's deserving. I shouldn't be here, at a party, that is. And while we're at it, back in this town, but I am. It's just another reminder of what I wouldn't give to have the last six months back. Six months can change a lot about a person. Four years can destroy you.

It can take a life, and give you back the one you thought you lost. The one you thought you wanted. I don't know what I want anymore. My thoughts spin and I lift my gaze from the one holding it, to the one beside me now.

"Dude." Roman pushes my shoulder. "Everyone can't believe you're back. They're looking for you."

I look over at him, and then away toward Barrette in the distance. It's his words that rattle around in my head. *You're back.* Those are the ones I focus on. Back here, back in her life, but so far away from her. I don't look at Roman. No, I can't focus on him when she's this close. I watch my reason for breathing walking away from me.

I know, hold up. Your reason for breathing? You're eighteen, you don't know what love is. Fuck you if you think that. Harsh, I know, but my reason for everything is blonde, feisty, and doesn't have a goddamn clue she's the only reason I kept going these last six months when my mom went from bad to worse. Barrette's the reason I made it through the worst time in my life. Like watching my mother die brutally of a disease she didn't deserve.

When I watched my mom's casket being lowered into the ground last week, I had one thought. Actually, two. First was how I was relieved that she was no longer in pain. Second? That I wished Barrette had been there for me. Maybe that's why I snapped and beat the crap out of my mom's boyfriend's son, or maybe it was that I couldn't stand the son of a bitch for a moment longer. Either way, I wasn't exactly in my right mind.

"*That* girl," Roman whispers, letting out a low whistle watching Barrette in the distance. She's hunched over inside a car searching through it, her ass clearly visible in the high-waist shorts she's wearing.

That girl is right. She's the kind that should come with a label. *Cute, tiny, and has the potency to knock you dead with one look.* Underside effects it should say, *May destroy your heart forever.* I want to tell her she's all I've thought about these last four years. I want to tell her I'm sorry I disappeared from her life. But I don't say anything. It's clear by the way she's acting she wants nothing to do with me.

"Is she—" I pause, struggling with the words. I certainly don't appreciate the way Roman says "that girl," like he's had her. The idea, the assumption, it hits me right in the chest like a knife. It takes the breath from my lungs. I stare, contemplating his meaning. Hell, I fucking shake. Clearing my throat, I don't look at him when I mumble, "Is she with someone?"

Roman snorts and raises his eyebrows. "With someone?" I nod, and he smirks. "B?"

"Yes, fucker." I shove him away from me and jerk my chin toward *her*. The impatient part of me needs to know. I don't have time to play around. The teenage boy in me is the one hesitant to know. "Is she seeing anyone?"

He gives me that look. The one that screams, "I wish it was me," but he doesn't say anything to that effect. At least not around me because he knows if he ever touched her, I'd kill him.

"No, not that I know of," he says, smiling. Roman rights his sunglasses on his face, hiding away his expression from me and pulling up the hood of his sweatshirt. "She's off limits if you know what I mean."

Off-limits? I need a second to clear my head, but I don't have it. I snap my eyes to him, drawing in a breath. "Am I supposed to know what that means?"

"You know exactly what the fuck it means." Roman stands tall, his linebacker shoulders stiffening. He's not a linebacker, but he's sure built like one.

I wait for him to continue, but he doesn't. Yeah, I suppose I do know what it means at least on my end, but hers, no, I don't. She certainly wasn't waiting for me, was she?

He flips his shades up, his eyes focused in the distance on a group of guys. "Why are you even questioning it? That girl has been hung up on your ass, for like, *ever*." He slaps his hand to my chest. "She don't pay any mind to any of these fools."

For reasons I don't understand, anger and jealousy surge through me that I left her with guys like this, the ones watching her ass, and that she's been hung up on me the entire time. I should be glad that she is, but the feeling isn't there yet.

I don't know any of the guys hanging around in the driveway, but they're watching Barrette with rapt attention. It sends a jolt of jealousy through me when one approaches the car she's at.

While she's bent over, he makes an obscene gesture toward his friends like he's fucking her doggie style or something.

"What a douche," I mumble, only to have Roman snort. He leans forward, rocking on his heels to see who I'm talking about.

He laughs and then looks at me. "Sounds 'bout right."

In the distance, Barrette straightens up, turns around and faces the guy behind her. She smiles a familiar smile, one she used to give me. I probably don't deserve those smiles anymore, but it doesn't stop me from wanting them.

Roman nudges my arm with his. When I don't look, he slaps his palm to my chest. "Bro, Heather's lookin' for ya."

My stomach tightens, and not in a good way.

"No thanks," I mumble, my eyes fixed on the interaction between Barrette and the guy next to her. "Who's that?"

Roman sighs, his frustration with me evident. "Xander. Graduated this year."

I nod, trying to appear uninterested, and failing at it. I can't look away, no matter how hard I try. I hate when she laughs at something he says, or when she takes his fucking shirt and gives me the stink eye like I did something wrong.

I did, though. I left and didn't call her when she called my mom's house looking for me. I didn't call her back because I felt bad about the way I just left without much of an explanation. I was trying to deal with the turn my life had taken and didn't know how to talk to anyone about it. Not exactly the best way to keep a friend. Especially someone who was supposed to be my best friend.

"C'mon, man. Let's party. It's been a while."

I look back at the house where the party is in full swing, and then at Barrette who's walking away with Xander, his arm around her shoulder. I walk back to the party with him knowing damn well I shouldn't.

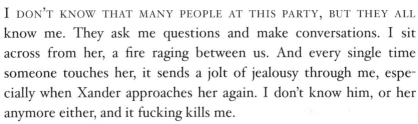

I DON'T KNOW THAT MANY PEOPLE AT THIS PARTY, BUT THEY ALL know me. They ask me questions and make conversations. I sit across from her, a fire raging between us. And every single time someone touches her, it sends a jolt of jealousy through me, especially when Xander approaches her again. I don't know him, or her anymore either, and it fucking kills me.

I know where this is heading. If I stay, I'm going to go over there, and I know what will happen. I'll get in a fight and my dad will be right. I'm emotional and raw and not in my right mind.

That's what the therapist says so it must be accurate, right? Or maybe I'm just an eighteen-year-old kid who doesn't fucking care and has lost everything he loved.

I don't leave. I sit and bounce my knee. I drink even though I know I shouldn't. I bite my nails and obsess over the girl I can't stop thinking about. I don't know anything about her anymore, but then again, I know everything there is to know. Little things like the way she tucks her hair behind her ear when she's nervous or the way she stares at the trees like they hold meaning for her. She's always been obsessed with the forest and the mystery it has.

She's wearing a sweatshirt now, and it's not mine. It's another guy's, and I want to rip it from her delicate body and toss it into the fire where it belongs. She should be wearing mine, and that should be my body she's clinging to.

I breathe in through my nose. It doesn't help. Do you hear my heartbeat? I don't over my breathing, but I know it's probably racing. Do you notice the way my throat tightens every time I attempt to swallow my beer? They're all signs that I'm losing it. I'm hanging on by a thread and if I don't leave, I'm going to cause a scene.

I stand, and I have no idea what I'm going to do next. Knowing I can't be here with Barrette in the arms of someone else, I turn to leave.

"Where are you going?" Roman asks, one arm around a girl just as gone as him, and the other holding beer by the neck.

The smoke from the fire shifts and turns in my direction. I squint at the burn, my eyes lifting to hers. Barrette catches my gaze and then quickly looks away toward the boy who doesn't matter. My entire body fights with the need to rip his arm from her. Running my fingers through my hair, I shrug. "Leavin'." My voice doesn't hold as much conviction as I intend for it. I look over at Barrette with blank eyes.

She looks at me for a moment and then moves to the one she has her arms around.

Roman attempts to hand me another beer. "No, stay. Get shit-faced with us."

Get shitfaced? There's more to life than getting drunk and forgetting your problems.

Rage festers inside me. My jaw clenches and I swallow, pushing the beer bottle away. I pick at the rough skin around my thumb to avoid eye contact. "Nah, I'm good."

And then I leave. If I stay, I'm going to rip that douchebag's arm off her and cause a huge scene. One I promised my dad I wouldn't cause this time.

CHAPTER 4

I thought I knew

He left. I think, no, I know it's what he does.

Cadence shifts toward me, glaring at Xander and shoving his shoulder as he's trying to kiss my neck. "Get off her. You're mauling her like a damn bear." Her eyes lift to the distance where Asa is walking up the hill toward the house. "Where's A going?"

I twist on Xander's lap. Setting my cup beside me, I shrug because I don't know. "I don't care," I mumble, knowing it's far from the truth. I want to chase after him, tell him I'm sorry for ignoring him, but something stops me.

I don't move and instead, look down at my drink at my feet in the dirt. It's beer and I hate the taste but love the feeling it gives in return. I'm on Xander's lap, my arm around his shoulders. I've known Xander since he was three and he used to eat his boogers. He's a year older and we really don't hang out. I've never liked him so why I'm on his lap is probably a testament to Cadence's claim that I've had too much to drink.

Unable to make sense of my actions, I down the beer and retrieve another one.

Cadence notices and reaches out for my hand, tugging me up. I smile and wrap my arms around her shoulders. I pull back and smash my face to hers. "You're pretty."

"And you're drunk." Cadence tries to pull me toward her, her voice rising. "C'mon, girl. It's time for a change of scenery."

I resist and sit back down on Xander's lap. "I'm good here, thanks."

"Seriously, B." She motions for me to get up and dangles her keys in my face. "It's time to go. Now. I'm not leaving you here with these jerks."

It's one of those moments when my vision isn't quite clear, more than likely from the alcohol and the amount of sun I've gotten. I've spent the entire day drinking, smoking, and avoiding. It's come down to this and I don't think I'm ready to leave. Someone puts their hand on my knee. I think it's Xander, but it's not. It's some other guy I don't know. I look down at it, then to Cadence who's still talking.

"You know I need to get home. After last time, my parents are watching me like a hawk. So c'mon. Get up."

I laugh, and it comes out as a childlike giggle. I've never been a mature drunk. "That sounds like a *you* problem. Go home so you don't get in trouble. I'll find my own way home."

Xander glares at her, noticing the tension between us. "Jesus, you're not her goddamn mother." He rolls his eyes, his lips closing on a cigarette. "Back off."

With the glow from the fire behind her, anger works its way to Cadence's voice. "I don't like leaving you like this. You're drunk."

My heart thumps wildly in my chest. I know it's wrong, but I don't move. I'm not sure I can. "I am not."

"Yes, you are." She tries to sound stern but fails miserably.

Her words bounce right off me as anger takes over. "No, I'm not."

Roman approaches us, pulling the black sweatshirt in his hand over his shoulders, hood up. He smiles at me, his arm around Cadence. "Relax. She's fine here. I'll make sure she gets home."

"Yeah, sure you will," she mocks, glancing over me momentarily at the guys surrounding me, and then back to me. "Text me when you get home."

I attempt to nod, but it feels like I've just taken Nyquil and its setting in, my actions, my words, slower. I urge myself to get up and walk away.

Xander pulls me closer, his head buried in my neck and though I know with every ounce of my being I should pull away from him, I don't and let his hands wander up my inner thigh. He smells like smoke and stale beer, not like the spice and summer scent I crave.

A CRACK OF THUNDER ROLLS THROUGH THE INLET, BOUNCING OFF the water in waves. Startled at the sound, I jump and smile. I stagger and wonder where I am because it's different. Nothing looks familiar anymore. "That's scary. Think it's close?" I say those words, but for some reason, they're slurred and take so much effort.

"I'll protect you," a deep voice says. There's an arm around my shoulder. It's heavy. My eyes move to see it's a guy who I don't know. I can't make out his face in the darkness, but his hand, there are tattoos on it.

Maybe you know where it's heading, maybe you're screaming at me to make sense and move away, but I don't.

I look around. I don't see Cadence. I don't see Xander, though I thought he was right beside me. I'm no longer by the fire. I'm in the forest and I don't know how I got there, or how much time has passed. There's rough laughter around me, but I don't think I recognize the voice.

Blinking rapidly, I look at the cup in my hand, the smell strong, potent. I should put it down, but I don't. I think of Asa and his smile, and I drink more.

"Come with me," a voice says, taking me by the hand. You'd think I'd know better. You'd think a girl like me wouldn't follow.

Don't follow, I tell myself, or at least I think I do, but my mind doesn't comprehend the same action, held hostage by something I don't understand. I can't explain it.

I take his hand, but my arm feels strangely heavy, like lifting a weight that's too much for me. I can't see his face in the darkness, but there are specs of light shining through the trees. I look up, lost in the darkness. I'm swallowed whole by the black. It's consuming and unforgiving. It feels like I might be floating, but I dig my hands into the dirt, and I know I'm on the ground. I don't know how I got there.

"I think... I'd like to leave," I mumble, or at least I think I do, but my lips are numb. Every motion feels foreign and forced. "I want to leave."

Why do I feel so strange? Did I really drink that much?

"No," he growls, pressing his mouth to the curve of my neck, "that's not happening."

Before I know what he's doing, it seems too late. I'm held there and my heart rate drops. Fear. I fight against him. Harder than I've ever fought for anything. Every ounce of strength I can muster, I use.

It's not enough. It feels as if nothing will be enough.

I'm being held down by strong hands and I hear the words, "She's a virgin," but I can't distinguish the voice.

There's a reply, a deeper more gravelly voice of, "I hoped she was," but I can't tell who it is.

More than one?

"Stop!" I scream. "Get off me!" I'm pressed into the dirt, a harsh breath leaving my lungs and he's on top of me, panting and sweating, struggling to get my shorts off.

I can't focus. Everything is a blur and just blinking feels heavy. It's as if I'm underwater and my arms and legs are tied to the bottom of a muddy lake. I try to listen to the sounds around me, focus in on their voices, their words, but it's all muted and the sounds, mumbled. It seems like it takes an eternity to form a thought, but when I do, I stare at the sky, the darkness, and I think, do they know what they're doing? Don't they see what they're taking from me? What did they give me?

Then the pain hits me, harder than before. Between my legs burns, aches... and it's more than I can take. "Asa!" I scream, but it's muffled. I don't know why I say his name, but I keep saying it, and I beg and plead for them to stop.

Nothing works.

Pain and wetness hit my shoulder, my neck, my chest. There's grunting and the sounds of leaves crunching, movements and pressure between my legs. The pain, it's unimaginable.

"Hold her still!" a voice growls, the one on top of me.

There's pressure on my wrists, and at the same time, on my thighs. "I'm trying to. How much did you give her?"

There's no answer, at least not one I comprehend.

His breath hits my ear. "Fuckin' stop moving," he grunts in a broken command. "I'll only hurt you more."

I squirm, I think, moaning for them to stop. Intense pressure hits my face and my heart already beating fast, picks up. There's an image that appears in my mind, working its way through the jumbled thoughts. It's him, the one. I hold onto that. His eyes. Not this guy's, but Asa's. I hold onto it like that rope swing when he begged me to let go when we were nine, telling me he would catch me.

He didn't. I belly flopped into the bay and he smiled. This time, I couldn't, wouldn't let go of that one memory keeping me from drifting away completely.

They continue, I fade. I feel things happening to me, but I can't do anything. My arms and legs feel so heavy. Like irons bolted to the ground.

I can't move. I can barely breathe.

Why does everything burn?

Why is my skin on fire?

I try to blink, focus enough to move away from them, but I can't.

Sharpness hits my side, and it hurts. Worse than between my legs. I scream, my plea muffled by his hand. I bite, anything to protect myself. Something hits my face and I fade, the pain too much to endure. I fight to hold on, I do, but the pressure in my head is too much. It's too late. I can't take the pain. I count seconds, and then minutes, and then I forget. The thoughts, they're gone. I leave my body and inhabit the air and the silence in my mind as I stare at the tops of the trees. They're black and I can't make out any shape as the rain hits my face, but it's better than the alternative.

CHAPTER 5

What I didn't do

ASA

Three hours. That's how long I wait. I tell myself, forget it.

Look at me, the one so out of control he can't even stand without moving. I'm clearly not listening because I can't forget her, not ever.

Pain shoots through my jaw from clenching and unclenching it. Drawing in a painful breath, I struggle through emotions I don't understand. This girl, since the day I met her, she's been the one I live and breathe for. One might wonder why I left her then and never called. Even I don't understand why, but I know one thing for sure. That guy, the one obsessing over every single thought and her reaction to him, he shouldn't have left her again.

Listen to my heart, the beating, the shaking of my hands and that tightness in my chest. Do you remember the look on her face? You know what's coming, don't you? Do you feel it too? Something isn't right.

"No, you shouldn't have," I tell myself, running my hands through my hair.

Ever since I was a kid, I've calculated my responses. I've never let my emotions get the better of my reactions. Emotion, fear, anger, happiness, it all starts out the same way. A jolt. And then the reaction. For someone like me, I control them to the point of obsession. I'm careful. Cautious. Maybe that's why I was the starting quarterback all four years at Massillon High School.

Or maybe... I was just in the right place at the right time.

Do you see me pacing the parking lot of Safeway in Olympia? I drive all the way to Olympia thinking it will clear my head enough to make a rational decision about anything, but it doesn't. I'm left with one final thought: I shouldn't have left her.

Breathing in deeply, I attempt to clear my thoughts, but nothing makes any sense. I straighten my body and look at my cell phone. Leaning into the side of the car, I stare up at the black sky, and then back at my phone. I don't have her number.

"Fuck this," I mumble, sliding into the seat and starting my car.

My mind races through thoughts about what I'm going to say to her. That I'm sorry and I shouldn't have left her, or that I should have called. Knowing Barrette, headstrong, and determined to be her own person, she won't forgive me easily, but I have to try. At least then I'll know I did what I needed to do, and I can leave for college in August with a clear conscience and not worry about her. But then again, if she denies me, tells me to fuck off, then I'll wonder why I hadn't called sooner or made an effort.

Remember when I said I was obsessive? You're starting to see the truth behind it, aren't you?

It takes me a half an hour to get back to Roman's house, and by the time I do, it's pouring outside and the party is still in full swing. I search, but I don't see her, but I do see Xander sitting by the fire, passed out with a beer in his hand.

I want to go up to him, ask him where she is, but I don't. Something stops me. A thought. She never cared much for him. Had she been doing it to make me jealous?

I search the lawn, by the fire, the driveway, but I don't see her anywhere. I look for Cadence, Remy, Roman... but they're nowhere to be found. Has she left the party already?

I think about giving up when I notice the sweatshirt she was wearing by the water where the forest meets the shore. It's dense over there and usually where couples go to fuck. I remember that much from my time here at Roman's house. His dad used to find couples out there all the time.

Making my way over to the edge of the water, I look down at her sweatshirt, and then to the tree line. Did I want to go look for her? What if she's out there with some fuck and I see that? I'd kill any motherfucker who has the nerve to touch her, in that way, but then again, what right do I have to feel that way?

My pulse quickens, the sounds of my heavy breathing and the waves lapping at the shore fill my thoughts. Rain hits the water making a popping sound. Swallowing over the lump in my throat, I say to myself, "Fuck it," and walk toward the trees. Worse case, she's with someone. Best case, she's reading a book? I don't fucking know. Christ.

Shaking water from my hair, I trudge through the dense salal lining the base of the large pine trees. It's dark and I have to use my phone to guide me. For what seems like hours, in reality, it's probably minutes, I vaguely make out a prone figure on the ground. The white stands out. A white shirt.

Barrette.

My heart races, my breathing ridiculously labored as I attempt to make my way over to her. My first thought, she wandered out here and tripped. She's never been very coordinated. As I get closer, reality sinks in. She's not moving. A trickle of fear punches my stomach.

"Barrette?" I yell, hoping she stirs. I'm about twenty feet from her now, everything around me dark, silent, deserted.

I look up to see if there's anyone else around, whirling my phone's flashlight around. It hits nothing but trees. As I get closer, I swallow over the tightness in my throat. Two feet from her, I see the blood. Have you ever heard the saying "my entire world crumbled?"

I used to think it was bullshit. How can the world crumble?

Two weeks ago, I thought I had an idea.

And now... I know exactly what people meant when they said it. Everything ceased to exist and turned to a crumbled version of reality. One where I knew my next step might mean I find her not breathing. Not living. Not being.

Everything moves in slow motion when my knees hit the ground. I scramble through the leaves and broken branches around her. Gently, I turn her over. "Barrette? Are you okay?" A gasp leaves my mouth when I see her face. Is she okay? No, not even close. There's a lot of blood coming from her face, cheek, her hair matted to the side of her face. Carefully, I touch her hand, scanning the rest of her.

I shake my head, swallowing down the anger pulsating inside me. That's when I notice she's naked from the waist down. I start shaking, hard, and I think I feel my chest moving, beating, and it stings. It fucking boils, bursts into flames. Only... it's not beating fast enough. It can't keep up with my breathing. It's so bad it knocks the air from my lungs, and I gasp, a muffled cry from my lips. There's so much blood, everywhere. It's all I see. Red. In rage, anger, blood... it's everything I can do to not scream and find every male at the party and integrate the fuck out of them until they tell me who did this.

I glance at my phone thinking I need to call the police, but something inside me tells me to take her myself to save time. It'd take them as much time to get out here as it would to take her myself. Every movement I make is too slow, as if I can't make up my mind what I should be doing. I touch her hand. "Barrette, I'm going to pick you up and get you out of here," I tell her, unsure if she can hear me.

"Asa," she breathes as I cradle her head. "You stayed?" She looks at me then, her eyes swollen and red, bruises forming already.

Relief washes over me that she can talk, but I hesitate. I stayed? Did she think it was me who did this to her? No... she means came back for her? Right? I don't say anything because when I lift her head, she curls into herself and screams in pain. And turns her head to the side and vomits.

"I'm so tired," she whispers, closing her eyes. Her breathing's low and drawn out, the word slurred through a sigh.

Did someone drug her?

Rage rolls through me again. Who could have done this? I saw Xander... he was asleep. Did he have any part of this? Who else did? One person couldn't have done this, right?

The smell of vomit hits me, and beer. She's soaked in it or maybe this isn't the first time she's thrown up. She mumbles something, her eyes opening and closing. Her hand squeezes mine, just once, and I look down and look at her hand. It's hard to see with the harsh darkness, but a twinge of relief hits me. If she can squeeze my hand, she's going to be okay, right?

Harsh breathing escapes me in gasps. I can barely keep from falling beside her. I have to get her out of here. Ripping my shirt off, I manage to wrap it around her waist and then as carefully as I can, I pick her up. Her breathing is shallow, strained, and my hands keep slipping on the blood.

I don't know how I manage, but I carry her to the edge of the water, notice a group of people not far from me, and then scream for help. They rush over. "Holy shit, is that Barrette?" one asks.

I eye them suspiciously and nod. "I uh... she's hurt. Help me get her to my car." I motion them forward and stop one of them, my hand on his chest. "Give me your shirt."

He gives me a strange look, arching his eyebrows. "My shirt?"

Heavy exaggerated breaths and uncontrolled actions overtaking me. "Yes. She's naked. I don't want everyone seeing her this way." I hold her tight in my arms, her head pressed against my chest.

Without questioning, he does, and it takes three of us to get her to my car. I lay her down in the front seat and turn to the two guys who helped me. "Do you know who did this? Who was with her last?"

They both look at me, and then each other. "Last time we saw her she was on Xander's lap." The taller one says, burying his hands in the pockets of his jeans. "I hadn't seen her in a couple hours."

Frustrated, I run my hands over my face. Wetness hits me. It's then I realize it's Barrette's blood on me. I turn to look at her when she moans. She bends to the side and vomits again. Her labored breathing brings me back.

My heart pounds, blood raging with nowhere to go. Breathing in deeply, I pinch the bridge of my nose. "Fuck."

"She was with Roman for a little bit," the other says, shrugging one shoulder and wiping blood from his hand on his wet jeans. "He left though, so I don't know either. He's with some chick in his room."

A good part of me wants to rush inside his house and ask him what happened, but I know if I don't get Barrette help soon, it could be too late.

Rushing around the front of the car, I slide into the driver seat. Gravel and dirt spray up from my tires as I peel out of the driveway and head to the hospital. A drive that should take thirty minutes takes me fifteen. I park in front of the building and rush around the front of the car to the passenger seat. She's not awake, either passed out or sleeping. I scream for people to help me. No one does at first. It's nothing like in the movies. A few people stare as I carry her inside, and then they jump to life and bring a wheelchair toward me. "She's in bad shape..." is all I manage to say.

They take her from me immediately, her body limp and unresponsive, doctors surrounding her as they wheel her through the emergency room doors. They say nothing to me at first. Until a woman in blue scrubs approaches me. "What happened?"

"She was... *raped*. I think." I run a shaking hand through my hair, then down the front of my face, trying to clear my thoughts. "I don't know for sure. We were at a party together. I left and then I came back and couldn't find her. I went searching and found her in the woods."

She scans my face, the blood, my face... all of it like she's doing inventory. Sizing me up like I did this. She thinks I'm lying to her.

"I didn't do this," I bark, anger lighting my face.

Her lips press together. "Sit over there. I'll come get you soon." She points at my face. "Do not leave the hospital. The police will be notified."

The police? Fuck. If they call my dad... or worse, the NCAA finds out, then what? Is my football career over because I did the right thing? I shove my hands in the pockets of my jeans and stare at the emergency room doors, my heart pounding in my ears, searching for an answer. Someone raped her. It's obvious. The word, the meaning, it tears at me. It fucks me up in more ways than I can comprehend. Pain and adrenaline punch my stomach, it sits, finds a resting point, making me nauseous with each thought.

In my head, I picture everyone at the party. Xander. Roman. There's no way Roman would do this to her. But, fuck, I don't know a goddamn thing about Roman and his friends anymore. I let my face fall into my hands and slide my fingers back into my hair. I pull until it hurts.

I hunch over, my hands on my knees for support. I breathe in as fully as possible.

And then release it.

I do it again, but it provides no relief. I lean into the wall again. A nurse asks me if I'm okay. I can't answer. I'm spinning out of control, the room with it, enclosing around me. My stomach burns and my throat feels like it's on fire. Images of Barrette's body lying in the woods rush through my mind so quickly I can't see them, but they're there. It's flashes, and each one makes me sicker than the next.

I find a garbage can and throw up, and then realize I'm sobbing and curled up on the floor. I lay there, I don't know for how long, but the next thing I know, there's a nurse rubbing my back.

"Asa?"

I lift my head, unable to focus on anything other than the stark white floor.

"She's asking for you."

I stand, move as if my body is doing things my mind can't quite comprehend. Maybe I'm in shock. I swallow excessively, trying to clear the lump in my throat. It's fire, and nothing soothes the pain. I run my hand through my hair. "Is she okay?"

No answer. At least not to that question. The nurse with wide brown eyes blinks and helps me up. "I'll take you back to where she is."

With shaky knees, I stand and follow her. Through the doors, they lead me to a room in the back corner with glass doors. A curtain is up, shielding her from the sight of others on the ER floor. The nurse looks back at me, then slowly opens the curtain. "She's a little out of it at the moment. The last of the Rohypnol is slowly coming out."

I tip my head, and squint, unable to focus. My eyes burn so badly in the harsh fluorescent lighting. "The what?"

"We ran some blood work. Her blood alcohol content is .32 and we found Rohypnol in her system. It's commonly referred to as the date rape drug."

Someone drugged her? Nodding, I don't say anything. Inside, my heart beats harder, my body tensing. I can barely keep from falling to the floor.

My eyes land on Barrette, a thick white blanket covering her from the chest down. Bite marks cover her shoulders and neck. Deep ones that leave blood and bruises. With each pass over her body, my hands shake, hell, my heart fucking shakes. It's the worst imaginable pain I've ever felt. It's worse than watching your mother die slowly because at least with that, I knew eventually she'd find comfort in death.

Seeing Barrette like this... nothing is taking this pain away. These wounds are forever. I can't imagine what this is going to do to her.

"You can sit with her, but the police are going to want your story."

She motions behind her where two cops stand outside her room, watching me.

Sitting in the chair next to her bed, I stare at Barrette. The bruises, the marks, it's too much. "I found her, that's all," I cry, tears rolling down my cheeks before I can stop them. "I have no idea who did this."

Removing the gloves she had on while checking Barrette's vitals, she nods slowly. "Where are her parents?"

"I don't know.... I can call them...." I stop speaking because... I don't know, seems irrelevant. I don't know her parents' number, or even if they're still around. I don't know anything anymore.

She hesitates, like she doesn't know whether or not to believe me. "We'll take care of it. A doctor will be in shortly."

And then she leaves me alone with her.

"You're okay," I whisper, brushing my lips across her temple. Clearly she's not okay, but I said the same thing to my mom hours before she died. I didn't want her to suffer and I thought if I said she was fine, she would be.

For two hours, I sit beside her. I call my dad and explain where I am. Another hour goes by and Barrette's parents haven't shown up, but from what I can remember of them, they were never very involved in her life.

They give me a shirt to wear since I used mine to cover Barrette up, and it smells like medicine. It reminds me of the nights spent in the hospital with my mom, begging for a cure that wouldn't come.

A sexual assault nurse comes in and tells me I need to give them a blood sample. I do without question. I have nothing to hide. The police question me, twice. I don't think they believe me, but it's up to Barrette to give her side, if she can.

And then I sit and recalculate the night, try to decipher the looks she got from the guys at the party. I try hard to pinpoint who it could have been and come up with nothing because I don't know any of them anymore. Four years can change a lot. And then I think to myself, I don't know anything about Barrette either. I have no idea if she was a virgin. Not that it matters, but it crossed my mind many times in those two hours.

I watch her, surveying the marks, the bruises, it's different under the harsh lighting of the hospital room. Reality sinks in, and I begin to understand whoever did this was angry with her. They had to be to inflict this kind of pain on her.

It's another hour later before Barrette comes around. She looks at me and says nothing. She doesn't ask what happened, she doesn't ask why I'm sitting beside her... nothing. No words. Tears flow down her cheeks and she reaches for my hand.

I hold hers, breathing out slowly. I won't talk until she's ready.

The doctor comes in and sits next to her. Her eyes drift to his. "Barrette, you're safe here. Nobody is going to do anything you don't want them to, but I need to know if you want him in the room while we discuss this?"

I look to Barrette for her reaction. She reaches for my hand and holds it.

I swallow and lift my eyes to hers. I don't know how to react.

The doctor goes on to explain that she was drugged, and though her wounds are nasty, nothing is life threatening. Her cheekbone was crushed by what they think is a rock given the jagged edge and dirt, and numerous cuts will require stitches. He stares at her, watching every reaction as if it's another clue for him. "Do you know why you were brought in?"

She nods.

"Do you remember how you got here and who you were with?"

This time she answers with a shake of her head, no words.

I swallow before I speak, because I don't know if my voice will shake, or if the words will crack and break the rest of the resolve I'm holding onto. "Was she raped?" My question comes out in a whisper, afraid she'll hear me. She does, but there's no reaction.

Deep concern is embedded in his features. Maybe because he thinks it's me. "Her injuries indicate she was." He presses his lips together and darts his eyes to Barrette. "We will need to perform a rape kit examination, if she agrees."

I nod slowly, still staring down at the stark white floor with drops of her blood. I suck in a rush of air and lift my eyes to Barrette. I wait for her answer, but it doesn't come.

There's a noise, a bang in the distance where a surgical tray hits the ground with a ping. Barrette jumps at the noise. I notice her eyes aren't focusing on anything. They're moving around the room and then to me, searching for truth. Any truth. I know by the way she's looking at me that she has no idea what this means.

Her life will never be the same again.

Mine won't.

CHAPTER 6

The night I don't remember

Have you ever had a cold and taken medicine for it to sleep? You know that groggy feeling you get when you wake up and you can't remember how long you've slept, let alone where you are?

That's how I feel. It's as if I'm trapped in a fog and can't seem to find my way through it to form a thought or words. Everything from the voices around me to the movements I make are excruciatingly slow.

Turning my head, I look around the room, trying to make sense of where I am. My head throbs with the motion, muscles seizing, blood rushing to my ears in a thumping rhythm. I squint at the onset of the pain, but it only makes it worse.

Raising my hand, I touch my face. It's puffy and tender. One thing surfaces above everything else. Pain. It's intense. So much so I fight to not cry out and scream.

Someone touches my hand, and though I don't want anyone near me, I know that touch. There are three people in the room with me. A woman, a man, and *him*.

My heart stumbles. My eyes lift to his. I don't say anything. Asa.

I try to recall how and why I'm here. I flip through thoughts, but nothing comes. At least not right away.

I remember the smell of the rain, the dirt, and the way the wind felt hitting my face. I remember the pain, the plea to stop. The excruciating pain... I remember standing in the driveway with Asa, and the beer. And him leaving. But that's where the memory ends for me.

Nothing before, nothing after.

The male doctor sits next to me. "Do you remember anything?"

I breathe out, but no words come with it. My chin shakes, a rush of emotion hitting me. Asa holds my hand and doesn't say anything.

It's the woman standing at the foot of my bed who whispers, "I want you to know you don't have to tell us anything." And then she continues with, "Your wounds are consistent with someone who has been sexually assaulted. We would like to talk to you about performing a sexual assault evidence collection kit...." Her words hang there, as if I'm supposed to jump at the chance to report it.

What exactly am I reporting? That I don't remember being raped? That I got drunk and had no regard for those around me?

"What does it involve?" Asa asks, his words so broken, so damaged like my body. I can't imagine what he saw, what he went through to get me here.

I know I should be concerned with myself, but in those moments as he holds my hand and comforts a stranger to him, I think to myself, what kind of homecoming is this for him? First his mom dies, and now he's here, in a hospital comforting his childhood friend he hasn't seen in years.

I want to tell him I'm sorry, but I don't know what for. That I got myself in this position in the first place? That I drank and left myself vulnerable? I think I said no, but I don't know for sure. Did I say it?

"The exam can take up to four hours, but in that time, you give us your best description of what you remember, then you undress and we survey your injuries and take photographs. We collect samples of DNA, take swabs of your genitalia, fingernail clippings, your clothing is taken to be examined and tested, and then we can treat you for your injuries, STDs, pregnancy, and then, you have a choice whether to report it, or wait. You don't have to decide anything right now."

I stare past the doctors, their words floating around me and they're just that, words. They hold no meaning to me.

"We can start the process and you can tell us to stop at any time," the woman says, as if they're trying to convince me. She has a name, and I know she's told me, maybe once or twice, but I can't remember. Everything is still so foggy.

Could I report it? Would I? My words, my denial had gone unheard tonight, I think, but now I'm given an option? I turn to the woman peering down at me, concern on her deeply wrinkled face. My answer lodges in my throat, unable to slip past my lips. What would this mean?

The male doctor reaches for my other hand, "You have injuries that need to be treated, but if we prep you with an antibiotic solution, evidence is lost. This is your time to at least start the process. It's up to you to decide what you do with that evidence, but at least you have it."

My eyes wander over my hands, my forearms, the blood underneath my fingernails, everywhere I look there's evidence that someone had used my body for their needs and left me to die. My first response, the words I chose to say is when I look at Asa. "I don't want that." Just the idea of the act, of what was done to me feels like I've been dropkicked in the stomach. I don't want to remember any of the details.

I can see the disappointment on his face. It's etched in the crease of his brow and the way his jaw clenches. "Yes, you do. You have to report this, Barrette. They need to pay for what they did, and the only way is for you to report it."

"She doesn't have to do it," the female doctor says, touching my hand. "It's *her* decision."

I glance at the doctor. She's glaring at Asa and he's not backing down.

He dips his head forward, catching her eyesight. "I know it's her decision. I'm not forcing her to do anything, but she should know if she doesn't do this now, the likelihood of them ever finding out who did this—and them paying for it—are slim to none." He motions to my body with a flick of his hand. "This is evidence. Evidence that will hold them accountable."

The male doctor clears his throat. His hair is buzzed close to his head, his arms covered in tattoos. None of that matters, but I find myself looking at him for some reason and the ink on his arms. "He isn't wrong."

"No, he's not, but no one should convince her of anything. It's her choice," the female doctor says, her arms crossed over her chest. I notice her name tag finally, my eyes narrowing in on her. Lucy. Her name is simple. I've always liked that name.

Something happens to me when I'm looking at her name tag. She doesn't know. She's never seen me before tonight, and this will probably be our last interaction and here she is, sticking up for me. Giving me a voice I'm not sure I have.

I look over at him, strain perceptible on his face. "Can you stay?" I ask Asa, unsure of my own request. His eyebrow rises, like he's wondering if he heard me correctly. I glance at the woman doctor. "Is that allowed?"

She nods. "If you want him here, he can stay." She waits, studying my face. And then her eyes focus on Asa.

He shakes his head. "I don't have to." He swallows, his jaw clenching. "It's private. Maybe you might want to be alone?"

"I don't... want to be." Tears flood my eyes. I don't want to be alone, my mind screams, but I don't say that to him. I squeeze his hand, unable to separate myself from him. "Will you stay, please? Don't leave."

His jaw clenches, works back and forth. He swallows twice, his eyes clouding over. "I'm not going anywhere." He speaks the words slowly and precisely, as if he needs me to believe them no matter what. He reaches for my hand. "I'm staying."

The doctor clears her throat. "You understand that if you're in the room with her, you will be called to testify as a witness should she press charges."

"Will it go to court?" he asks, the vulnerability in his words so raw, so real. "If she presses charges?"

"It will. It's her choice if she wants to have the evidence tested and prosecuted."

My choice. They keep saying that.

Would a jury believe me? If I tell them I drank, I flirted, I left myself vulnerable, would they believe me that I didn't want this? I meet Asa's gaze, and the moment I do, my mouth goes dry. I've put him in this position and now what will it mean? At my reaction, his mouth clamps together. His shoulders stiff and defensive as he glares at me. "Don't you dare, Barrette. Don't do that. I'm here because I want to be and you need to report this for you, not me."

Leaning forward, I bury my face in my hands, each breath more labored than the last. I suffer at the pain deep within my body. It aches and radiates with every movement.

"Barrette." The doctor waits, studying my face as she speaks the words, her hand on mine. "It's just an exam. You can tell us to stop at any time, but you have to tell us you want to continue each step of the way."

I nod and look to Asa.

"You have to say it, Barrette," the female doctor says. "We can't continue until you do. You have to tell us you consent to the exam."

Tears roll down my cheeks and all I taste is the salt when I cry out, "I want to continue." My vision focuses on Asa and the way his face reflects every emotion from relief to anger.

"You're making the right decision, Barrette. Lucy is going to take it from here." The male doctor excuses himself. "I'll come back later to take care of that laceration on your face and we can discuss further treatment of your injuries."

Before he leaves, he talks to Lucy. She nods to everything he's saying. I don't look at them any longer, and instead, I obsess over details in the room. The table, the camera they bring in, and then my gaze finds Asa because I don't know what else to do. I do not want him to leave the room, and the death grip I have on his hand is unhealthy, and I have no idea where these feelings of attachment are coming from. But the thought of being alone now terrifies me.

"I won't leave," he assures me, seeming to know where my thoughts are.

I draw in a heavy breath as Lucy sets a box on the counter. I read the label. Sexual Assault Testing Kit. Never would I have thought I would see that. Up until now, I was a virgin. The girl guys ignored and classified as the prude. But I wasn't. I just didn't want any of the boys at our high school. Is that why this happened? Because I was the prude? Was it retaliation for something I didn't do for one of them?

"Were my parents called?" I ask, looking to Asa, and then Lucy.

His worried gaze moves to hers, his grip on my hand remaining strong and controlled but underneath the hold, I can tell by the sweat and the tremble to his fingers, he's just as scared as I am.

Lucy opens the box and pulls out a sheet of paper that's on top, her pen in her hand. "We called, but there was no answer. We haven't been able to locate them."

I swallow over the lump in my throat. "They're in Spain for the summer."

She nods. "We will get in touch with them."

FOR HOURS THE DOCTOR POKES, PRODS, SWABS, AND TAKES pictures of my body and assesses my injuries. They undress me in front of him, to keep evidence intact and run a blue light over my body. They measure bruises, cuts, and abrasions, evidence of the brutal beating I took not only psychologically, but physically. Dozens of bruises cover my arms and every inch of my body.

Through all of that, I focus on one person. Asa. He doesn't react, he doesn't look when I'm naked in front of him. His eyes never stray. They simply hold mine and reassure me that he came back for a reason. For me. He brought me here and without a doubt, saved my life. They ask questions and expect answers I don't have. They record my responses. They want to know if I have any enemies? Did I suspect anyone? I have no memory of the night, other than drinking.

What's the use? Would anyone believe me?

And then it comes down to, what do I do next? Do I report it to the police and hope that they believe my story? Hope that if they do find out who did this, they are in fact held accountable? You see it on the news all the time. Sexual assault victims pleading their case only to get nowhere after years of exhausting themselves both mentally and physically. I didn't want to be a rape victim, let alone publicly known as one. As far as I'm concerned, nobody outside of this room will know about it.

"Would you like us to report this to the police?"

That's when it hits me in the chest that it's real. Sure, the exam made it feel real and a complete invasion of privacy. They photographed me completely naked! I cried through the entire exam thinking that if I hadn't drank—none of this would have happened. None of it.

I shake my head. I shake it because I don't know if I understand the meaning. "I... don't want to report it," I tell them, clinging to the blankets covering me. I want to hide under them, away from the world. I don't want anyone to see me or hear my words.

Asa doesn't say a word but by the look in his eyes, the flash of anger that hits them, I know he's upset with me.

I squeeze my eyes shut because the confusion and pain are unbearable.

Lucy rubs my shoulder, and Asa stands, his chair screeching against the tile floor before hitting the wall with a bang. I jump, my breath catching, and I look at him. He gasps. "I'm sorry." He sighs heavily and runs his hands through his hair, gripping the back of his neck.

Lucy, who glares at him, then shifts her eyes to mine. "You have time to decide. This was the first step and gives you a longer statute of limitations to report it."

I stare at the wall, past the doctors to the window. It's morning. The sun's streaming through a window in the upper left of the room. A memory hits me, but then fades just as quickly. It's the one of Asa walking up the driveway, leaving last night, but now he's here, holding my hand through a night I don't remember.

CHAPTER 7

What she didn't do

ASA

She isn't going to report it. All that and she isn't going to fucking report it? I thought I knew anger when I found her, but the idea of whoever the son of a bitch was that did this, is going to run free, well, take a look at me. Do I look fucking calm?

It's only when Barrette is being treated for STDs and given the morning after pill that I'm alone with my thoughts. She's given a sedative to get some rest after they stitch her forehead up. I excuse myself and punch the wall in the bathroom.

I scream, I cry, and argue with her doctor that she should force her to do something. "You need to force her to do this! She has to report it!" I yell at him, my breathing out of control, my emotions all over the place. I can't control my words or my actions.

He pulls me aside, caught off guard by my temper tantrum in the ER. I can tell by the slow turn of his head to Barrette's room and the way he narrows his eyes at me that I crossed a line. The vein in his forehead protrudes as he attempts to hide his irritation with me. "You think forcing a victim of sexual assault is the right thing to do? You don't think she's been forced enough?"

It's his use of the word "forced" that resonates with me and I begin to understand by the way his jaw hardens, he did that on purpose. My stomach leaps at the word. "But they're going to get away with it if she doesn't."

He shakes his head, as if I'm just not getting it, and in a sense, I'm not. "This is her choice. And if you're really her friend, you're going to leave it as her choice." His voice lowers and he leans in. "Barrette was raped. Brutally raped. Her denial, if there was one given her state of consciousness at the time, meant nothing to them. You forcing her to do something leaves you just as guilty as them."

Before his words made sense, I think about hitting him. It'll make me feel better, for sure, but with my luck, he'll sue me and I'll be in more trouble than I was back in Ohio. That scholarship to UW will be gone and I probably won't see Barrette again because, well, I'll be in jail. Hitting him won't solve anything. Finding the mother-fuckers who did this will, but then again, his words held meaning.

Forcing her to report this makes me just as guilty as them, and I know there has to be more than one. In my gut, I know it and regardless if she reports it, I'll find who did this to her.

Reluctantly, I return to the room where Barrette is. It's the middle of the afternoon, Cadence has been calling me nonstop. I didn't realize she had my number, but it got out. Remember the guys who helped me to the car? Well, the rumor mill's started. Everyone knows she's been raped.

Barrette stares at me when Cadence shows up. She freaks out. "Who raped you?"

I've never wanted to hit a girl until now, and it's Cadence because the moment she says the word rape, Barrette shuts down. She refuses to talk, eat, look at anyone, or respond in any way other than she wants to leave and wants me to take her home.

I pull Cadence aside, much like the doctor did to me, only this time I'm not as subtle as he was with me. "Nice going," I mumble, leaning on the wall.

"What the fuck happened? I left her last night, and she was drunk and sitting on Xander's lap. I'll fucking kill him if he had something to do with it."

I draw in a breath, trying to calm myself from doing just that. "I don't know if it was him. When I found her, he was passed out near the fire."

She tucks a strand of her dark hair behind her ear and then crosses her arms over her chest as if she's cold.

"Who else was with her after I left?"

There's panic in her eyes, an emotion I don't know whether to question, or appreciate. "Nobody that I know, but I left not long after you."

"What about Remy?"

Tears flood in her eyes. "She passed out before that in her room." She gasps and the tears slip past her cheeks. "Asa, I... I'm sorry for what I said in there. It's just... I don't know what to do for her, and I just sorta freaked out."

I lean into the wall with my shoulder. "You and me both. I nearly punched her doctor."

"You've always had the worst temper. I still remember when you decked that kid for taking her lunch money in the fourth grade."

"He had it coming," I grumble. You're starting to see a pattern, aren't you?

She laughs, but it doesn't touch her eyes.

"How did you get here? Did she call you?"

"No. Something told me to go back so I did. When I didn't find her by the fire, I wandered down by the water and I noticed her sweatshirt. I found her in the woods."

Cadence takes a tissue and wipes her eyes. "I'm so glad you came back."

It's then I wonder what everyone's saying because maybe then I'll get some insight into who was there. "What's everyone saying?"

"Nothing really, just that it's fucked up someone would do that. Roman said he didn't see anything, but he was in his room all night. The last thing anyone remembers was her walking away from Xander and standing by the water."

Okay, so it wasn't Xander. But maybe he was pissed off she denied him. The questions eat at me. I can't stop my mind from trying to piece together everything and nothing at all because I wasn't there. I have nothing to go on and the one person who can potentially connect the dots can't remember anything about the night either.

THEY RELEASE BARRETTE ON SUNDAY, TWO DAYS LATER. I DRIVE her home because she refuses to let Cadence, who meets us at Barrette's house with food.

Barrette stares at the food, her favorite, Chinese, and won't eat. She hasn't eaten anything in two days. I can't say I blame her. I have barely eaten myself.

My dad calls me, wants me to come home, but I tell him I'm staying the night with Barrette. Her parents? They haven't even made flight arrangements to come yet. All of these things, they make me angry, hell, livid, but I control my emotions around her.

"We have to get her to eat something," Cadence says, picking out the egg roll she set on a plate. Taking a flake from it, she rolls it up into a ball. "She doesn't look good, A." Her eyes follow Barrette down the hall to her bedroom.

"I know." Sighing, I look around the house. Pictures of her parents' adventures line the walls, some with a younger Barrette, years I missed, and most of them without her. Her parents are hippies. That's the term my dad gave them at least. They're free-spirited, eat everything from the earth, and make their own soap. I never really knew them all that well.

I stare at a photograph taped to the fridge of them holding Barrette on her first birthday. My jaw clenches at Barrette's bright blue eyes and the big smile she's wearing. I don't know where that smile is and if it's ever going to surface again.

"I'm sorry about your mom," Cadence says, drawing my attention toward her.

I nod. "Thanks." Something else catches my attention. A letter beside it from the University of Washington. An acceptance letter to the same college I have a full ride to.

You didn't think it was coincidence that I accepted the least likely college to attend after getting offers from Ohio, Michigan, Texas, and Yale? I chose Seattle for a reason. It was closer to Barrette.

I look over my shoulder at Cadence, her attention still on the uneaten eggroll as she mumbles something about staying the night with her. "Is she going to UW?"

"Who, Barrette?"

"Yeah?"

She smiles and straightens her posture. "Yeah, we both are. I heard you're the star on campus though, Mr. Full Ride."

"I don't know about that." I motion toward the hall. "I'm gonna go check on her."

Cadence straightens up. "I can."

"No, I will," I insist.

As I walk down the hall, I hesitate, my steps heavier, as if I'm trying to walk through mud. The kind that sticks and holds you in place. Maybe she doesn't want me to bother her, but I have to know she's okay. She hasn't said anything to me today, other than holding my hand as we left the hospital.

I stand in the hall, my head pressed to the wall, waiting. "What the fuck do I do?" I mumble to myself. I hear a noise coming from the bathroom, a sob, and I know the sound. I press my ear to the door, wait, and it gets louder. She's crying.

"Do you need anything?" I ask, my voice a shaking whisper. I have no idea how to comfort her, but I know how to be there for someone. I know how to let them vent and cry and hate everything in life. I know what it's like to wish for death to ease the pain and through all that, I think, no, I know I can be there for her. Maybe it's me trying to make up for lost time, but I do it without question.

The door creaks open and takes my breath with it. She's standing there, the shower running behind her, completely naked, her clothes a pile at her feet and she's sobbing. "I hate them," she cries, staring at me like I'm the answer, the one she needs. "Why did they do this?"

For a moment, a split second, I'm not at all sure what to do. I think I shouldn't be in here, seeing her like this, but then again, I don't want anyone else with her. The bruises are darker, the bite marks more pronounced and evident. The marks on her neck, red and swollen. And her face, her fucking face, it's bad. That's the only way I can describe it. Surrounding her beautiful blue eyes are deep purple bruises. I have no words for what was done to her other than horrific.

Steam rolls through the bathroom and I reach for her, unsure what else to do and catch her when she falls into my arms. Closing the door, I hold onto her as tightly as I can and I kiss the side of her face, because I think it's what she wants. The moment my lips touch her skin, her sobs come harder, faster, and it's as if she's going to hyperventilate if I don't do something to stop it.

Maybe I shouldn't have done that? My mind races for something to say or do to make this better for her. But what do I do?

"It's okay," I soothe, running my hands gently around her back, unable to stop my body from trembling. I'm shaking so bad, I'm not sure who's more of a mess in those moments, her or me. Taking her hand, I place it on my chest so she can hear my breathing and heart-beat. "Breathe with me. Slow deep breaths."

It takes her a minute, but she does, her hand gripping my shirt in a fist. "Don't let go of me," she pleads, her words broken and desperate.

"I promise I won't." I let her cry, because I don't know what else to do. The need to protect her and make sure she knows my inten-tions are only pure takeover, and I don't look at her body. I keep my stare on the shower.

"The warm water might help."

She doesn't move and clings to my body, every inch of her pressed against me as her arms wrap tightly around my neck. She cries, harder, every ounce of her frustration pouring from her.

With slow steps, I open the shower door. "Let's get you in here."

She won't let go of me. So I step inside there with her, fully clothed and hold her under the spray. Pulling back, I cup her cheeks carefully and make her look at me, my clothes clinging to my body. Her blue eyes lock on mine. "I... I don't want to be alone."

"I got you, okay." My jaw clenches, my breathing increasing. "I'm not going anywhere, and I'll stay with you as long as you need me. Whatever you need."

Her crying slows and I think she understands that I'm here for her. Even if that means getting in a shower fully clothed because she doesn't want to be alone.

Cadence knocks on the door. "Is everything okay?"

"Make her leave," Barrette whispers, laying her head on my chest.

I stroke her wet hair and kiss the top of her head. I know I haven't been in her life in years, but everything seems so natural around her, the actions, the love, the need to protect her, all of it.

Clearing my throat, I yell, "We're fine. Why don't you take off?"

"B, are you sure?"

Barrette lifts her head from my chest. "Yes," she tells her, raising her voice over the sounds of the shower.

"Okay, I'll call later to check in on you."

"Thank you," she says, but she's looking at me when she says it.

I help her wash her body, my eyes never straying anywhere but her face and shoulders. I'm not a creep and though, yeah, the guy in me wants to look, she's been through something so horrible it makes me sick to my stomach to think about it.

When she's done, I stare at my clothes and think about how awkward this is now because I have nothing dry here. There's no way I'm leaving her to change. I did that yesterday and when I returned to the hospital, they'd had to sedate her again.

Wrapping a robe around her body, she stares at me. The white in the robe makes the marks on her more pronounced. "My dad has some clothes you can wear."

Smiling, I strip off my shirt and jeans and leave them on the floor of the shower. She hands me a towel. "I can get them if you want."

"Okay, or I'm sure I can find them if you want to get changed." Panic rises in her face, a flush to her cheeks and widening to her eyes. "I won't leave. I'm just going to change."

Nodding, she tightens the strings on her robe and places her hand on the door. I watch her leave the bathroom, and then I make my way to her parents' room. I'm able to find shorts and a T-shirt to wear and then place my clothes in the dryer. When I'm finished, Barrette is curled up on the couch staring out the window. Their house is right on the Budd Inlet, much like my dad's house, only their home faces Tacoma.

I sit next to her and like it's habit, she moves closer, curling into my chest. And then she begins to cry again. I don't know what to say, or if I'm even supposed to, so I hold her. That's all.

Four days ago I was packing up my life in Ohio, unaware of what the next twenty-four hours would bring, but never did I think this would happen. Ten days ago, I was holding my mother as she took her last breath, and now here I am, holding the girl who's forever owned my heart, and praying she makes it through this.

I don't know if I'm enough, but I'm here and I'm not letting go. Not ever.

Part Two

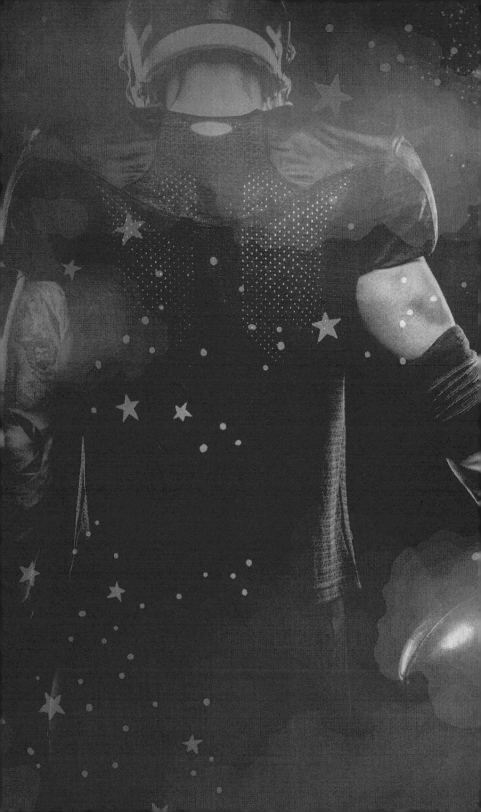

CHAPTER 8

Living in darkness

BARRETTE

November - 17 MONTHS LATER
University of Washington
Seattle, Washington

Washington in the fall is my favorite time of year. It's still sunny, pumpkin spice lattes return, and the leaves on campus burst to life in vibrant orange.

I'm never vibrant anymore. I'm a dull shade with dark thoughts.

Sitting to the far left of the classroom near the windows, I stare out at the leaves beginning to fall over the bright green grass with specks of brown, yellow, and red. I envy the colors in the leaves.

I look around the classroom. There's only me and two other people. I don't know them, and I definitely don't make conversation.

It's rare I'm at this 9:00 a.m. class. I personally don't think classes should start until noon. I'm not even sure why I took one this early, but I needed this class and it was only offered at the ass crack of dawn. Okay, it's not dawn, but it's early for me. These days I prefer to sleep during the day, for many reasons.

This class, it's Neuro 501: Intro to Neurology. The official course description from their website is "the survey of molecular, cellular, and developmental neuroscience, including gene regulation, the cytoskeleton, protein sorting in the secretory pathway, growth factors, and neurotransmitter receptors."

You're probably wondering what the hell all that means, and even I don't know. All I know is I need it as one of the requirements for a bachelor's degree in physiology.

A door opens, closes. I jump at the sound and settle back into my seat, the rush of heat from the ventilation hitting me. Sipping my latte in my hand, my eyes follow a girl who walks in with her hood up over her head. I recognize her. She's a freshman cheerleader this year, and while I don't know her, I've seen her at the games and with the players. She sits on the opposite side of the room, her dark hair attempting to shield the bruises on her face and the cut on her lip. But I know those markings. I've had them myself.

I imagine the worst. I put myself in her place. Was she beaten like me? Was she raped like me? Does she remember the incident?

My hands shake while my heart thumps wildly in my chest, and that ever-present lump in my throat thickens, takes over, and I fight to push it down. If you were inside my head to see the nerves firing, the reactions I'm withholding, you'd think I have so much control over myself. Maybe you'd even be proud of me for how good I am at it, but it'd be a lie because reactions, words, promises, they can be deceiving.

I look away from her. I don't know her story, and honestly, I don't want to. I want to pretend I didn't see it. I want to believe maybe she tripped and slammed her head into a door or took a dodge ball to the face. But this isn't elementary school and the likelihood that her face just magically ended up like that isn't a coincidence. Someone did that to her. Someone took something that wasn't theirs.

Sound familiar?

I've told myself to forget the night. You don't remember it so why dwell on it? It's times like this when the reminders surface and I realize that just because I don't remember the night, doesn't mean it didn't happen.

The professor walks in, his monotone announcement ringing through the room.

I divert my eyes to the window again.

This last year, I became interested in psychology and how the brain works. What interests me about the human brain is why we remember certain parts of our lives and why we purposely forget others. I can't tell you much about that night, probably because I was drugged, but still, I wonder how much I would have remembered without the drugs? Would I have blocked it out as a traumatic event? All I remember is right before on the beach, the fire, Asa, and then nothing else. I woke up in the hospital with Asa beside me.

I know there's more to the night. I see it in my dreams, but to actually remember every minute detail or faces, I don't.

For that reason, I chose psychology.

After that night, it was weeks, even months when the heavy reality of what happened hit me. I'd wake up in the morning and think to myself, just smile. You don't need to be sad about this. Forget it happened. Move on with your life. And when I couldn't— when I couldn't find a reason to smile and move on—I couldn't understand why people tried to force me to. I wanted them to just let me be.

At times, I ask myself why can't I appreciate what I have now and ignore that pain? I'll tell you why. It feels wrong. If I accept it, it makes what happened okay, and it's not okay. It's fucked up and I can't ignore it. No one asks or deserves to be raped. Yet here I am, a year and a half later, still blaming myself.

I've never said to myself, you're a survivor. I can't use that term because I didn't survive. I simply lived through it, and now I'm in the after part.

I'm not sure I'll ever *survive* again.

I NEVER WALK ALONE AT NIGHT ON CAMPUS. INSTEAD, I RIDE A bike. Like somehow being on the bike will allow me to get away quickly if needed. I'm five foot two and barely a hundred pounds. The wind could knock me over if it wanted. But on Tuesdays at seven thirty, I attend a support group for rape victims that's across campus and I don't walk. I hate going to the support group because it's another reminder of something that was taken from me. I hate even being in the same room as others who have been through it because it's a reminder that this happens to so many people.

I didn't want to go to support groups. I didn't understand the purpose to them, but I have met two friends while attending them. Joey, a girl who might just be my soul mate, and Waylon. Waylon, he's... gay. Not that it matters, but when I think about being raped, the naïve part of me thinks it only happens to women. That's not the truth. It doesn't matter who you are. There's no demographic that's targeted despite what people make you believe. Yeah, the majority are women, believe it or not, there is no specific gender or race that's targeted. It can happen to anyone.

Joey, she proves that size doesn't matter. The man who raped her... he didn't care that she was a size eighteen or that her hips and stomach were covered in stretch marks. She was an easy target. As he held her down with a knife to her throat, he told her, "You should be begging me for it."

Rape doesn't happen to the prettiest, skinniest, or most likely. It happens in the wake of weakness.

The therapist who leads the group sessions is Maggie. I kind of like her. She's blind in her left eye. Her rapist took her sight with a rock. But still, she's here, giving us support. She said to us once that her boyfriend at the time told her, "You're sick and you need help," when she couldn't have sex with him. They're no longer together, but she went on to say, "Being raped isn't a sickness. It's a circumstance. A torn page from a chapter I'd like to forget. But I can't because it's my book and part of my journey. It's not his, it's mine."

I lean into Joey, who's beside me. "Do you ever think to yourself I'll never be whole again?"

She smiles. "No, not really." She cups her double-D breasts with both hands. "I feel pretty whole."

"You know what I mean."

Joey rolls her eyes. "I guess I do, and no, I probably won't be. But I'm too stubborn not to try."

Laughing, I think about what Maggie said. *It's not his journey, it's mine.* Immediately my thoughts drift back to Asa. You're probably wondering about him, aren't you? You'll see him soon, I'm sure, but it's her words that resonate with me. This, my life now, his, it might be my journey, but he's just as much a part of it as me. He was there. He held me through the panic attacks and the nightmares. Never once did he leave my side the months following the incident. Until he had to leave for football camp, but until then, he *stayed.*

Outside, Joey smiles at the poster of Asa on the walls of the building. It's the one of him throwing a touchdown in the championship game freshman year. "What's with you and Lawson?"

I smile. "He's my friend." And I'm in love with him. I leave that part out because she already knows it.

Teasingly, she bites her lip. "I'd be his law-abiding citizen any day."

You'd think someone who went through a sexual assault wouldn't say things like that, right? Not Joey. She uses humor to deal with the pain. She'll laugh, joke, even tease about her attacker as a way to overcome it. In her eyes, they didn't win. She did because she lived through it.

I stare at the poster, thinking about her words and wishing I had Joey's confidence. And then I let my thoughts drift to Asa and how good he looks. He looks like a king up there and I'm never going to compare. I'll never be his queen. I'm the sad girl in the shadows of his greatness, forever tied to him by one night.

Waylon offers to walk me back to my dorm after the group session. He claims he doesn't want me walking alone.

"I brought my bike," I tell him, smiling.

He shrugs. "I don't care. I'm walking with you."

Waylon is on the football team with Asa. He's become a good friend and it makes me sad to think that if this hadn't happened to me, I wouldn't have met him or Joey. They're part of my book now. A journey I never thought I'd find myself on, but slowly navigating through it.

"How are you doing?" he asks, walking beside me as I peddle slowly.

"Fine, I guess," I assure him, trying to appease him. He knows I'm lying.

"Are you though?" He shifts his eyes to mine.

"I don't think I'll ever be fine again." The cool crisp fall air hits my face.

The longer we walk, the more my mind drifts. We pass by Madrona Hall where Asa lives. I check the time. Nine. He's probably home.

When I count over from the far left to find his window, I see his light is on. I let my mind drift as I inhale and sit down on the concrete bench outside. I kind of feel like a stalker for a half a second.

Then I remember why I do this. I miss his smell and the warmth of his body. I miss *him*. It's hard to say why I can't let him go. It's because I need the connection. After that night, I was lost in more ways than one. I'll be the first to admit a part of me died on that rocky shore and the other part, she might as well have.

Waylon touches my shoulder. "C'mon. I'll walk you home."

"It's fine. You live here." I motion toward Madrona Hall and then place my hand on the seat of my bike. "I'll be fine. Got my bike."

He's hesitant and gives me a nervous smile. "I sorta promised I'd make sure you got home, and the last person I want to piss off is Asa."

I snort, hanging my head. Staring at the peddles of my bike, my heart thumps wildly in my chest at the mention of his name. My gaze travels lower from my ripped black Pearl Jam T-shirt to the black jeans that fray at the heels. "Fine. Walk me home."

"He's just looking out for you," Waylon adds. "He loves you."

Asa's never told me he loves me, and though I see it in his eyes, he's never said the words. Neither have I, but I went through something pretty damn tragic and he was there to help me through it. I love him. There's no escaping that. Without a shred of doubt, I'm completely in love with Asa. But still, I've never said the words either. There just seems to be too much that goes with it.

I love you, but I'm fucked up.

I love you, but you don't have time for me.

I love you, but you won't report the rape.

It's the truth. Asa hates that I still haven't reported the rape.

Why haven't I? I still haven't come to terms with it.

"Waylon?"

"Yeah?" He glances over at me, his hands buried in his pockets and the whites of his eyes shining brightly under the street lights. I look at his skin, dark as the night, and then I wonder how he deals with it. He's African American, gay, plays football, and secretly in love with their tight end. All of that doesn't really matter, but then again, it does. He has a lot going for him with his future and announcing to the world he's gay, well, that's not something he's willing to do. I can't say I blame him. Most know. He's not obvious about it, but he hasn't been seen with a girl, ever, so a lot of people just assume. Waylon always says it's none of their business.

His story? He's a junior this year, and freshman year he was raped at a party off campus. I haven't talked to him much about it, but now I'm curious. "Did you report it to the police?"

He holds me captive with his stare for several seconds until his gaze slides over my shoulder to the passing halls. "I did...." And then his words hang there.

"And?"

His jaw tightens. "It's still sitting on a shelf with the Seattle Police Department waiting to be tested."

We keep walking, our steps intentionally slowing down. "Really? They didn't do anything about it?"

He runs his hand over his face, sighing. "I mean, yeah, they took the test when I went into the ER, but three years later, nothing. Every time I call, they say they're working on it. Out of every thousand instances of rape, it's something like only thirteen get referred to a prosecutor and only seven lead to a felony conviction." Waylon shrugs one shoulder. "Those aren't great statistics so I don't exactly have my hopes up that anything will come of it."

He's right, nothing may become of it, and I think in some ways, I haven't reported it yet because of that. I'm also not sure I'm ready to deal with it if I know who it is. Right now, I can pretend they have no face.

Waylon stops walking and looks over at me. "Barrette?"

My eyes lift to his.

"I'm not going to tell you to do something you don't want to, but I can understand why it bothers Asa so much."

"Why?"

"Because he watched you go through something horrendous and he wants justice. It's only natural, and until you report it, there will never be justice."

Again, he's right, but I'm still not sure I'm ready. Or if I ever will be.

CHAPTER 9

Downward spiral to nowhere

BARRETTE

I have a habit of staring at nothing. It's calming to get lost in thought, only now, it's not. It's like I'm nervously waiting for something bad to happen. On the edge and unattached to everything around me. I'm sitting at my window, smoking weed I got from Roman, staring out it at nothing in particular as smoke drifts through the small crack. I don't usually smoke, but I recently found how calming it can be for me. It certainly helps when I can't sleep at night because I'm afraid of the nightmares.

My phone dings beside me and I notice a missed call and a text from Asa. It's not often that I see Asa during the normal hours of the day. As the starting quarterback for the Washington Huskies, to say his day is busy in the fall is an understatement.

Asa: Dinner?

I stare at the text for a few minutes. We haven't been to dinner since freshman year. Then I remember a comment he made the other morning when he was leaving my dorm room that I needed to eat more.

Me: Trying to make me fat?

Asa: I like something to grab.

Me: Sure. Where?

Asa: Well I like to grab your ass. You know that.

It takes me a minute to reply, shocked he's flirting with me so openly.

Me: I meant dinner.

Asa: Lol, I know. Be there in a minute.

We're flirting. We have been for probably the last year. It hasn't led to anything yet, but we flirt and tease, and sometimes I provoke. Let my hands travel over his body to see what he does. Every single time, he reacts and holds me closer. It hasn't always been like this with us. It's just sort of evolved into this. Freshman year, even after everything that happened, we actually went on dates that summer before college started but never classified anything as "dating." Once college started, it became harder with school and his crazy football schedule.

When he knocks minutes later, I move toward the door and notice Cadence in her room through the bathroom that separates our dorm. She keeps her headphones on and smiles. We're room-mates, but my friendship with her will never be the same again. I can't tell you why, but I pulled away from everyone but Asa, Joey, and Waylon. Cadence has some resentment over me hanging out with Joey, but school keeps her pretty busy. She and Roman broke up again. I honestly can't keep track. He's like the campus whore these days, and I know it bothers her to see it. I know it would if I saw Asa acting the way he does.

My heart beats a little faster knowing Asa's on the other side. There's a fraction of a moment before I open the door that I imagine our lives to be different. I imagine we're together again and that night never happened. I imagine *they* didn't ruin our lives. But then I open the door and I see his eyes. The golden hues that meet mine changes things for me. It's adorable in ways only Asa can be. When I look at him, that light hair sticks up in the front, those dark, brooding eyebrows that crease when he's nervous, that's when I know that everything is different and nothing will ever be the same again. Because of me. Because of a night I can't change.

Asa smiles softly, stepping inside my dorm room. Smiling and waving at Cadence, he sits on my bed flipping through my *History of Motion* textbook that's on my pillow.

"I'm failing," I tell him, shrugging.

"That sucks. Need help? I took that class last year because I thought it was interesting."

"That's okay." The last thing I want is for him to feel like he has to do this. "You're busy with football."

He nods, his eyes on the floor, seeming to know I don't want him to help me and not pushing the issue. "Dinner?"

I bite my lip, my arms wrapping around my stomach. "I really should study."

"It's just food." He nods again and then looks up at me standing near the window as if he knows that but he's wanting something from me. "You'll feel better if you eat. It's a proven fact that food and... well..." He pauses and winks. "We'll start with food. Food helps you concentrate."

I want to beg him to tell me where he was going with that, but I know he won't tell me. "Fine." I roll my eyes sarcastically. "I guess I gotta eat."

He laughs, throwing my sweatshirt that's beside my bed at me. "Don't sound so enthused to go out with me."

This time I laugh. "It's like going out with a celebrity."

Once outside the door, he slings his arm around my shoulder. "It's not that bad."

Just wait, I think to myself. He really has no idea the trance he has everyone on campus in. Including me.

WHEN WE ARRIVE AT THE PAGILIACCI PIZZA, I'M REGRETTING IT already. It's never easy seeing girls instantly hanging all over Asa, regardless of how *undefined* we are. But it's the way it is with us lately. Like a Taylor Swift song, I'm always in the shadows and he's center field where he belongs.

He walks in ahead of me but reaches for my hand when we get to the door. I feel safe when he touches me like this, warmth enveloping my body instead of the all-encompassing cold I live with daily.

Just before he opens the door, a group to our left calls his name as they sit outside in the green plastic chairs reserved for outside dining. Asa gives them a nod, never letting go of my hand as we're led to a table in the back, his eyes on the televisions that line the wall above the bar.

When he lets go of my hand to take a seat, that's when I feel the warmth leave me.

Everyone stops by to congratulate him on the game against the Oregon Ducks. They won 38-3. I watched the entire game, so I have an idea of what they were talking about. Asa threw for 204 yards and ran with two touchdowns himself.

"That's amazing!" one tall brunette says to her boyfriend when he tells her about the yards. She has no idea what he's referring to, but she's impressed by Asa and smiles, her eyes never meeting mine.

Asa is low-key. He's always modest when it comes to his playing ability, and though he's the captain of the team, you'll never hear him say he's the best player. He doesn't believe that even for a second.

"It's pretty cool," he says, giving the guy standing beside him an autograph on a beer coaster. He and his girlfriend take a photo with him and then they leave.

Tonight isn't any different than it ever is with him. Since his freshman year here, he's been this school's superstar. They worship him. It isn't too hard to be a superstar back home, but at a university where tens of thousands of students and faculty know your name and high five you randomly walking around campus, yeah, that's a big deal. What they don't see is what he has to give up because of it. When most college kids are home for holidays, Asa is at practice. Summer? He's in summer classes trying to keep up, hitting the weight room, and pushing through two-a-days.

What's the reward?

Big Ten title? NFL contract? College degree?

If you're lucky, yes, but it's not a guarantee.

A cheerleader comes by. I don't like any of the cheerleaders. Not to say they don't have talent, but I hate the way they look at Asa. Like he shouldn't be with the tiny depressed girl. This one, her name is Eva, her hands lingering over the chest I lay my head on and watch the night fade to morning. Her dark hair is perfect, her body toned and eyes bright. So different from me with the messy hair pulled back in a bun, baggy clothes, and tired eyes fighting an internal battle even I don't fully understand. I feel like when I see him like this, surrounded by people and girls who pine for him that I'm in the way. An obligation he feels entitled to watch over.

Sometimes I wish he wouldn't bother with me.

Sometimes I wonder why he does.

Sometimes… I'm thankful he does, because if I didn't have Asa in my life, I'm not sure I could have kept going.

"Nice game, Asa." Her pretty brown eyes flutter to mine. She knows Asa doesn't belong to me, but she'll never understand just how much *he* and *I* control each other.

Asa looks up at her, winks and smiles. "Thanks, Eva."

He's always polite. I don't think he knows anything else.

I shift my gaze from them. I don't want to see this. It hurts to see it firsthand, but I have no say. I've created this monster, fed it. My unwillingness to move on from the past keeps this monster's viselike hands around me. The longer I watch him and the endless flow of students congratulating him and talking about the game, I see what kind of person he is.

Asa is different than most college football players. Even Waylon, and he's definitely nothing like Roman. Nothing rattles him like it should. He's extremely focused on the field. Off the field, he has a 4.0 and still manages to be the star quarterback. Naturally everyone looks to him wondering where the fault lies. We all have them. Some just hide it better than others.

He has one. And it's me.

I'm the disease slowly killing him.

Eva turns away from him. "See you in class."

Great, they have classes together. Even better.

Asa turns back to me. "Sorry about this."

I shrug. "It's okay. I know what it's like going out with you." And then I freeze at my use of "going out with you." Our eyes meet. "I mean, being seen with you."

"I knew what you meant," he says, but there's a different edge to his words. It's almost upset. I can't place it.

Picking at a slice of pizza, I avoid eye contact with him when I mumble, "Are you having sex with her?"

I can't believe I just said that! It's a bold question, I know, but I ask it anyway. Caught off guard, Asa looks down at the bill on the table and then up at me. He doesn't say anything.

I reach inside my pocket and pull out a twenty. "You don't have to pay for me."

Asa doesn't answer. He watches my reaction to his silence and slides the money back at me. "No," he says, taking a drink of his water and then gives a nod at the door.

"No, what?"

"No, I haven't slept with her."

I'm relieved somewhat. What if he did? How would I feel about that? We're not dating. I have no ties to him in that way, other than when I'm really sad, he's there for me. He can't go his entire life just being there for me. Surely he has needs and desires, and it doesn't involve the girl he saved.

We're walking back to the dorms, and I slip off the sidewalk and into the street where I lay down between the center lines.

"Do you think of dying, Asa?"

He looks back and sees I'm not behind him. "Come on, Barrette, get up." He jogs over and reaches down, grabbing my hand. "Don't mess around."

I don't move. Instead, I stay in the street, letting the rain hit my face as I look up at the sky. "Just lay here with me," I say, looking over at him.

"No." He turns away and walks to the sidewalk. "Get out of the street."

Asa doesn't like to think of that night. When I talk about dying, it reminds him of it. I can feel his body tense from where I lay on the street.

"Why is everything with you so planned?" I get up and walk the five steps it takes to reach him on the curb. He stares down at me as I speak, searching my eyes for the answer to my crazy ways. "Don't you ever just want to live right now?"

"I am living right now." He turns again and starts walking back to the dorms. "If anyone is living for right now, it's me and you."

I think I know what he means by that. We're stuck in this weird transition of needing to move on and being unable to make the steps to do so. Our steps crunch the falling leaves, the cool fall night slaps at my face with a spray of mist. I like the rain. I'll even get up in the middle of the night to go walk in it just so I can feel the water on my skin.

It's refreshing.

It's calming.

It's also a reminder. That's one of the only things I remember from that night. The rain. I think about that night all the time. And why Asa was there. I also think about why up until that night, I hadn't heard from him in four years. "Can I ask you something?"

Asa nods and darts his eyes to mine. We're walking side by side, our shoulders touching every so often. "Anything."

Part of me doesn't want to ask this, but I know I need to. "When you left to live with your mom, why didn't you ever call me?"

His jaw flexes and works back and forth. He draws in a breath, his chest expanding with the motion. And then he lets the breath out, his words filling the space between us. "I was afraid if I did, I wouldn't be able to stop myself from coming back to you, and I knew my mom needed me."

I think about everything his mom went through and it makes me sad to know she died after fighting the cancer for so long only to die regardless of what the doctors did for her. "I'm glad you were there for her."

Another breath, then a nod. "Me too."

We return to my dorm. Asa walks me up to my room. I glance up at him. "Thanks for dinner."

He searches my face and then stares at my lips. He swallows, blinks, and then finds my eyes. "I'll gladly buy you dinner every night if I know you're eating." Running his hand through his hair, he leans into the wall beside the door and then drops his eyes to the floor. "I worry about you."

I struggle with his words, the meaning, his selflessness toward me. He gives and gives and what does he get in return? Certainly not what he deserves. I fidget with the hem of my sweatshirt. "You don't have to."

He lifts those beautiful dark eyes to mine. "I *want* to." What I wouldn't give to hear him say he wants me.

"Is that why your offensive lineman walks me home every night?"

He nods, his eyes narrowing, watching my reaction. "I don't want you walking alone, and you know that."

Sighing, my heart drops. "Because I can't take care of myself," I deduce, feeling like his charity case.

Asa closes his eyes and exhales. Twisting, he presses his back to the wall. With a heavy sigh, he turns his head to look over at me. "You know what I mean."

Nodding, I stick my key in my door. "I know. Thanks again for dinner."

He stops me though, his hand on mine and then I notice he's placing something in my hand.

"What's that?" I look down. It's Sour Patch Kids. My favorite.

I smile, my chest aching. I wish I could be normal for him. "Thank you."

Backing away, he winks. "Enjoy. Save me the red ones."

I want to invite him in, but something stops me. I grant myself one more glance and let the sight of him wreak havoc on my heart. He's beautiful, sinful, and everything I need but won't allow myself to have completely.

And I leave him outside my room. I don't want to be his charity case he can't let go of. I want to be more than that, but he seems so caught up on protecting me nothing ever becomes of it. So yeah, I leave the dude standing outside my room.

I sit down on my bed and look over at my iPad on the nightstand. I think of Asa, again, always. Opening the package of candy, I sort through them to pick out all the red ones and place them in a baggie I find next to my books. It's then I remember I should be studying. I have to write a five-to-eight-page paper reviewing a journal article on any subject that deals with cognitive psychology. I knew I was going to do the paper on False Memory Syndrome. I don't have the energy to do it now.

I look out the window. No stars, only darkness. And though I know I can't sleep, tonight I allow myself to dream without fear of a time when I'm no longer a shadow of my past. I'm borderline obsessed with the addiction of him.

CHAPTER 10

What I wish I could save

ASA

I toss and turn at night. Every night. Nothing helps. All I see is my phone staring back at me and I wait to see if she's going to call. Sometimes at 3:00 a.m., she calls and wants me to come over because she can't sleep. I do without question. Now it's created a habit of sorts where I constantly wait to see if she needs me.

I look at the clock beside my bed instead.

12:16 a.m.

Turning over toward the wall, I stare at the chipped paint where I threw my phone at it the trying not to call her in the middle of the night when I wanted to see if she made it back to her dorm.

I look at the clock again, watching the hours count down.

1:29 a.m.

With my hectic class schedule and football, I need my sleep. I do. So why can't I get any? Barrette.

2:18 a.m.

She's destroying me. I hate to say it, but she is. She's all I think about when I'm not on the field, and sadly, it's spilling over to the moments I am these days.

Rolling on my back, I throw my arm over my face. When that doesn't work, I roll on my stomach and squeeze my eyes shut until they burn. Maybe if I squeeze them hard enough, I won't see images of her or look at my phone.

Doesn't work.

My hands slide up the bed and under my pillow, wrapping around my head. Maybe if I suffocate myself, I won't call either?

There's an idea.

I don't. I look at the fucking clock instead peeking one eye open. 3:04a.m.

I hate this. I fucking hate it. You know what I hate most? She still hasn't fucking reported it to the police. Seventeen months have gone by and whoever destroyed her, he's still out there, probably destroying other lives.

I see a therapist once a month. Football coach demanded that I do, for obvious reasons. You know what he told me? The therapist that is. He said rape destroys boundaries. Think about in terms of football. You're at the ten-yard line and you fumble the ball and give the control to the opposing team. That's what rape does to victims. It takes someone's ability to control the world around them and gives it to the opposing team. He told me I shouldn't insist she do anything. I should listen.

But at some point, she has to make a decision to want more. From life, school... and me. She's gone in the sense that she'll never be the same. But I can't let her go no matter how hard I try. And no matter how much I try, I can never forget the night that changed us forever. I can't stop seeing it. It's a horrible nightmare that we will never forget. When I have nightmares about it, gasping and struggling to breathe, I feel like that breath I need is never granted.

GETTING UP AT 5:00 A.M. FOR MOST IS TOO EARLY. FOR ME, MY day starts at three most mornings, watching Barrette finally fall asleep. From there, I go to the gym with the rest of my team. Most days I'm running on very little sleep, but that's nothing new. I'm a disaster in more ways than I can say.

I'm playing football at the University of Washington and the starting quarterback for the Huskies. Some think I'm this golden boy with the perfect life who is living the dream. Sure. They can say any of that, but I have to disagree. And sure, I've been on the cover of *Sports Illustrated* my senior year of high school and offered a full ride to any college I wanted, but if it was so damn good, I'd have the girl I want and someone behind bars.

I'm none of that. I *have* none of that. What I have is right now. Barrette asked me last night why I don't live for the moment. It's all I do. At this point, I don't know any other way.

I take my time getting over to the stadium. It's unreal the facility we have here and it makes me feel like I'm playing for a pro team every time I step foot in here. We have everything from state-of-the-art training equipment to personal iPads to flat-screen televisions everywhere, and even a barbershop.

A barbershop.

It's insane.

As I'm changing into my shorts and T-shirt, I hear bits and pieces of conversations around me. I'm the quiet one on this team. I don't talk much because all these guys are talking about is pussy and football. Sure, I'll talk football all night long but not pussy. It's none of their fucking business. And sadly, I'm not getting any so there's nothing to talk about.

Once in the gym, I'm a little on edge listening to their bullshit and lifting weights relaxes me. I'm exceptionally tense these days. There's this nagging feeling in my gut since the season started. Maybe it's the pressure getting to me. It's Wednesday and we have a Friday night away game against the Bears.

Coach Benning, the offensive coordinator for the Huskies, takes me aside. He immediately starts going over plays while I continue to lift; it leaves little room for confusion or questions. He's thorough and I appreciate that. I never have to guess, and he trusts me on the field. There's this saying that coaches make decisions, players make the plays. I believe that. They let me do what I do, and I respect them enough to do what they ask.

I train a lot with the other two quarterbacks on our team and it's clear I'm the tallest of the three, 6'2", and I think that gives me a good advantage over the other two players. My height lets me see more of the field. It's definitely held some advantages for me because I was the first freshman to start in twenty years at this college as a quarterback. I've been the starting quarterback ever since. I'm watched by the NFL, talked about as being nominated for the Heisman Trophy and contacted by teams as well as promised the world.

If I play well.

If.

That's a lot of fucking pressure for someone who isn't even twenty-one yet.

Playing college football is different from high school. Everything is more pressure, harder hitting, and fast-paced. Even with all that, I led our team to a 12-1 season. I threw 2677 yards on 230 of 336 passing attempts. I threw for thirty-two touchdowns with only six interceptions. Yeah, it was a good season and I'd earned the team's respect. We're four games into our season, and for the most part, we're looking pretty good.

I spend the rest of the hour on the treadmill before needing to leave to make it to my classes on time. Besides the very early start, I enjoy these morning workouts because for once I don't have to think.

When I'm finished in the gym, I take a quick shower and I'm on my way to my cell biology class. I'm dragging ass so I grab a coffee on the way there. Once in class, Terrell is already there, staring at the board and then his book.

"You're going to hurt your brain staring like that."

He looks over at me and flips his hat up. "I think I forgot about the test."

I smile and hand him the coffee I brought for him. He smiles too and takes it. "You know the way to my heart, sugar." Terrell, or T-Bone as we sometimes call him, is our center on the team which means he and I spend a lot of time together. He's also one of my roommates.

"Anything for you, cupcake." I wink at him as we continue to tease one another.

A chick walks by and Terrell bites his fist. "She has a nice fucking ass. The bigger the better."

I look. He's right.

I smile. "You have a nice ass too."

He winks at me. "You touch it a lot too." Being the center, it's a given that my hands are near his ass a lot. Unfortunately.

This class is intense. We not only have to know everything about anatomy and physiology as well as biology at the cellular level, we also have to think like a crime lab and be able to process a crime scene. Why I agreed to take this class as my science requirement is beyond me. But, then again, I think I know why I took it.

A few girls walk by and smile at us. I give them a nod but not much else. I smile, knowing I'll probably see one or two of these girls back at our dorm room later. I've had the same roommate since freshman year, and it's worked well between us. He never cleans up anything, but we're football players so it's not really a top priority for us. And he's the only person I know who can make twenty dollars last him an entire week for food. I think I spend that a day in coffee.

"Careful, you're drooling," I mumble, opening my textbook and tucking my phone away.

He laughs. "I'd drool all over an ass like that."

Terrell Wilson gets a lot of pussy. Like a lot. Every fucking night it seems. He also has a porn stash, and a pretty decent one at that. I'm actually impressed. And a little jealous. Though it's rare we have any classes together because of his accounting major, Terrell, a 6'4" center who most would assume is dumb as a fucking rock, is fucking smart as hell.

My major is in humanities. Everyone asks me what the hell a humanities degree would be good for and my response, "It's going to serve me well when I'm a first-round NFL draft pick."

My passion is football, plain and simple. I had to declare a degree when I accepted the scholarship to play football and this seemed like the easiest route. I had no idea what I'd be up against with the amped-up level of football that is played at the college level. School was important, but I knew what I was here for. I thought it would be an easy degree. Man, was I wrong.

Declaring a humanities degree as my major requires me to study everything associated with literature, art, religion... basically the humanities over the centuries. I do a lot of reading, even more writing, and a ton of research and staring at artwork, paintings, and sculptures by the great artists. And by sculptures and paintings, I mean *lots* of naked women. One more bonus point for this major.

Terrell bumps my shoulder, finally lifting his eyes from the girl with the nice ass. "You should get her number."

Every player on our team has tried to set me up. Aside from Waylon. I don't know what it is about society, but they see it fit that every guy needs a woman to fuck. I don't see it that way. To appease Terrell, I look over my shoulder at her, then back to him. "No thanks."

"Ya picky, man." And then he smiles. "What's with you and B these days?"

I shrug.

"C'mon, man, I know yous beatin' the meat to that pretty little face."

If you're wondering what the hell all that means, just ignore it. It's Terrell, and most of what he says is like trying to read braille. If you know what it means, as you can see, I'm not exactly denying it.

I don't answer him, and he knows me well enough to know I'm not talking about it with him anyway. It's nobody's business that I'm in love with a girl who just might be incapable of loving me. I know that, but still, I stay.

I stay because she's fucking worth it, and I'm going to make her see it even if it takes me a lifetime.

LIKE ANY OTHER DAY, I MOVE FROM CLASS TO CLASS, STUDY MY ASS off before practice, head over to the players' lounge directly after that, relax for a few minutes and have a protein drink, and then it's practice for three hours.

It's clear when you look at the college football stadium and training center, all the money goes into this place and pretty much anything you want. I'm in the players' lounge with an iPad in my hand, a bottle of water in the other, watching films from the Bear's last game trying to see any advantage we might have.

I'm trying to get an idea of the defensive line. But like any other day, my mind isn't on the films like it should be. Instead, it's on Barrette. It's hard to focus on anything but her most days. There are times when I can't think about her, like at football camp because they run you into the ground. Other times, she's someone I can't seem to shake.

I worry about her. I feel like if I didn't have her in my life, in some way, she would slip away completely. It's far from pity or sympathy that I feel for her. What we had is so much more. Hell, what we still have is so much more.

An hour later, our team is on the field and split by position, each of us working on specific plays and strategies. By the end of the week, we're in scrimmage games and heavy-hitting, though I'm usually off-limits for hitting. Surprisingly, I love the roughness of football. Hard hits don't bother me one bit.

I trust these guys on my team and we've played well together the last two years. Who I don't trust is Codey Jackson, our tackle. He's sloppy at times. Like today. When he leaves me open for a sack and I'm picking grass out of my faceguard.

College football is so much more intense than high school ball. Nothing is the same. Every hit is harder and with every play more is on the line. I don't like to be sacked. Ever.

Codey laughs, throwing out his hand. "You good, bro?"

I hate that word "bro." It's fucking cliché.

"Fuck you," I answer, casually picking myself up off the ground. I brush past him and get back into huddle as we call the next play. I feel Roman's eyes on me, but I don't look at him, especially not after the word "bro" is said to me by Codey.

When I look at Roman, anger gets the better of me. I hate that he was there that night and didn't keep an eye on her. Barrette's his sister's best friend. Or was. He should have been looking out for her and he wasn't. For that reason, our relationship changed.

We break apart from scrimmage and run plays. Sometimes the same one over and over again until we get it right. Roman struggles. He can't seem to get to the ball or he overruns it. Just like every other practice. It pisses me off when I watch him. He's by far our best wide receiver, even better than Demarcus Witten, the senior he beats out for the starting position each week.

Roman never gives 100 percent and it irritates me. We're a team that's supposed to be tight and trust one another, yet he can't even give us the gratification of knowing he gave his best. A total slap in our faces.

Roman catches up with me. "Sorry, A. I'll get it."

Yeah, right. "Late nights?" I grumble, knowing damn well he stays out too late, drinks too much and fucks all night.

He doesn't say anything and runs back to the line.

We bust ass through the rest of practice, and I watch Roman bullshitting with Codey and the other running backs. They're talking about some cheerleader they all had the other night, and it makes me fucking sick that they treat sex like it's some kind of game. It also drives me mad to think about them treating sex like it's some kind of status. Believe me, I wish Barrette and I were having sex, but it's not like that with us. I'm not sure it ever will be after seeing what she went through. Because of that I can hardly stomach half the shit said by the players on the team in regards to women and sex.

The idea that the guys who did it to her were probably bragging like this send rage through me instantly.

I leave the locker room without talking to any of them.

CHAPTER 11

Distractions

ASA

It's late when I get back to my dorm room, probably around nine or ten. I'm not feeling like much of anything, nor do I want to study. I have to though.

During the week, we don't usually party. At all. Unless you're Roman. We're too busy with practice and school. Although tonight, as I'm studying, Terrell has some kind of open house going on. Our dorm room is open, as is the door leading into the bathroom that connects our room with two sophomore running backs who play with us.

For over an hour, it's an endless flow of girls moving in and out. Some make their way to my side of the dorm where I'm studying, others don't and stay beside Terrell.

Sometimes I want my own room, but we room together because of the unity. It's important in football. I'm reading the same passage over and over again, only the giggling is louder. When I turn my head, Terrell has a girl on his lap, his chocolate skin standing out against the fair-skinned busty redhead straddling him.

Smiling, I look away.

Like I said, Terrell gets pussy. There have been a few who show up when he's not here and try to test their luck with me. I'm not really into the whole "hook-up with whoever" thing, as I said before. It's not that I wouldn't mind the occasional one-night stand just to satisfy the urge, but it's not my thing.

I came here to play college football and that's what I'm doing. I'm not here to fuck around but, yeah, there's the temptation to do that. I can if I want. It's all around me. It's easy. I wouldn't even have to try. I can go to a party, and there's three or four who will meet me at the door. Ready and willing.

I want a girl who isn't emotionally or physically available. I wish it wasn't that way.

It hurts that we can't have that.

It hurts like a son of a bitch.

It just... fucking hurts.

Eva makes her way over to me. She's a cheerleader and tries every day to get my dick between her legs.

"Homework is boring." Her hands move to my chest over my heart, her dark hair sweeping over her shoulder. "I can distract you, if you'd like."

I crave the blonde hair and ocean eyes, and this girl isn't any of those. I look down at her hand until she removes it. "I'm studying."

Good thing about these girls is they don't like to be denied any more than they want to be humiliated. They'll try again, another night, but they give up easily and move to the next willing guy. I've heard girls say how desperate some guys are in college, but I think that's a fucked-up phrase. I've seen more desperate girls than I've seen guys. Maybe because they're thrown our way, or they simply hang around like leeches waiting on their next meal.

Maybe.

When the girls leave, Terrell notices I never gave any the time of day. "What are you doing? Eva wants ya, A."

Terrell knows about Barrette and what she went through. He also knows my obsession with her. "I'm not interested."

"Are you still holding out for B?"

I shrug one shoulder, knowing he's not going to judge me.

"Are you sure?" His lips purse as he runs his dark hand over his face. "I mean, I just... I don't know, man. I hate seeing you like this."

Nodding, I bite the inside of my cheek and shake my head, pushing my book away from me. "What do you mean like this? This, me now, this is all you've ever known of me." Turning in my chair, I face him.

He nods and slaps his hand over my shoulder. "I know, ya pathetic fuck."

Barrette isn't okay. I see it in the tears she hides and the dark circles under her eyes. She tries so hard to cover it up. Sometimes I don't want to believe it. I don't want to know how bad it is. How far gone she is. Some might venture to say, why bother?

I bother because I can't not. I have to. Her parents don't. Her friends don't, but me, I fucking bother. I check on her. I make sure she's eating and has someone to sleep in her bed when she's sad.

I'm really good at portraying indifferent and never letting her know that it's fucking torture to lay in her bed with her and not touch her in all the ways I want to.

Love makes people do stupid shit. Makes them look past lies and see a truth they believe is there.

Only it's not.

I see what I want time and time again with the hope that she might change. That our situation might change. That someday, somehow, she'll open her eyes and see I'm still there, waiting. She controls me. She takes my fucking breath and she suffocates me with just one look.

Football players have playbooks. We're expected to memorize them and know when and how to play them. Quarterbacks call the plays based on the offensive coordinator's call, and then sometimes we look at the defense and we change it when we see how they are positioned.

We call an audible. We change the play on the line of scrimmage.

She's my audible. I changed the play at the line that night and there was no going back on it.

I FALL ASLEEP AT MY DESK THAT NIGHT, DROOLING ALL OVER MY
research paper.

When I wake, I sit back in the chair, turn off my lamp and then
run my hands over my face. Terrell is asleep, snoring as usual and I
notice that redhead he'd been with earlier, her hair is draped over his
pillow and tucked in his arms.

Reaching for my phone, I look at the screen to see Barrette sent
me a text an hour ago.

Barrette: You up?

Me: I am now, sorry. Fell asleep.

She replies instantly, letting me know the night is still holding her
captive.

Barrette: Can you come over?

Me: Be there in 15

It's three in the morning, but I shower then head over to her
dorm just like I do every other night she needs me. Some might ask
why I do this. Wait for it.

I knock lightly, twice, and she opens the door, smiling, but there's
tears in her eyes. But do you see that smile? That relief? That's why I do
this. I get up at the ass crack of dawn even if it's just to see a little bit of
relief in her hopeless eyes. In the blue dawn of the morning hours when
the restless night begins to give in, and she's consumed by despair, she

doesn't want me to help her. She doesn't want my comfort. She doesn't want me to tell her everything is going to be okay. She wants me to lie beside her with her head on my chest. She wants to find comfort in my presence with the salt of her tears stinging the wounds I can't see. And I do that. For her. Until she's ready to let me help her heal. Until the shards of her heart are stitched together. I'll sew them myself. I won't let her fade into grief.

Setting my backpack on the floor, I reach for her, my hands around her waist. "Rough night?"

She nods. Her face is blank. Still, there's some emotion there and her heart's beating against my chest. Letting go of me, she moves back to her bed and motions me forward, lifting up her blanket and waiting.

My heart beats faster when I see she's not wearing any pants. Only my jersey. I turn my head to look over at the bathroom door. Luckily, Barrette has her own room. Her and Cadence's rooms are separated by a joined bathroom.

I fight the urge to not follow her to her bed. I shouldn't. I know where this leads. She's not wearing pants and I know exactly where my thoughts are going to go, because I'm already there. Running my hand through my hair, I kick my shoes off and reach over to shut the bathroom door. My heart is in my fucking throat, and my steps slow as I make my way over to her bed.

Don't touch her, I tell myself. And I think I can handle that and knowing damn well I won't. Heaviness in my chest halts my movements, and I look down at her, the only light in the room the faint glow from outside streaming in through the window above her bed. There's an expression on her face, one I haven't seen before, and I can't decipher its meaning.

She smiles and I know I can't deny her. Never stood a chance. So I swallow, try to breathe normally, and get into bed with her. Immediately, like I knew she would, she curls into my side, my left arm around her, her hand on my heart. It's beating like crazy and I know she feels it. Hell, my entire body trembles, unprepared for where this might be heading.

And then her hand moves lower, to my stomach. My breath catches, and I want to stop her, but I don't. I wait to see what she's doing.

"Asa?" My name comes out shakily.

I don't say anything, but I turn my head to look at her. The street lamps outside light up her face in orange. I swallow hard. I want to kiss her like I want my next breath. I feel the pull, but I'm fucking hesitating. It's not like me. On the field, I operate on instinct and I'm always right. But with Barrette, I'm always unsure what comes next. I'm not the one running plays here.

Her hand lowers to the button of my jeans and something else is immediately hard. I feel like I can't breathe, and suddenly my chest is shaking. My stare drops to her soft pink lips, and I want to know their taste.

She doesn't close her eyes. She meets my gaze head-on. Propping herself up on her elbow, her other hand moves to my head. Her fingers slide through my hair. Unable to pry my hands away from her, my fingers skim down her hand that's on my stomach, holding her at bay.

"I want you," she whispers, her face inches from mine, her eyes burning. Her breath blows over me, and weakness claws at me.

I shift away from her, only a fraction of an inch to roll on my side. Excitement shoots through me. I want this. I do. "I'm here," I assure her, knowing that's not what she wants to hear, but I say it anyway because I don't know what else to say. We've been in this position a few times. We've even kissed and got close once last year, but I pulled away. This time I'm not sure I'm going to have the strength to do so because I fucking want this so badly.

"I know you are, and I want *you*." Her leg moves, hitching up over my hip and my erection I know she has to feel straining in my jeans. "Right now."

I shift involuntarily when she brushes against my dick again, and my eyes flutter closed at the incredible sensation that shoots through my entire body. My hand moves from my side to her thigh and I fight the urge to roll her over and kiss her like I'm dying to do. "I... don't know, B. Are you sure? I mean, what if it's too much for you?" I shouldn't even be considering this, but damn it, it's fucking unbearable being this close to her and not being able to have her in the ways I want.

She moves her hand from my stomach and rests it against my cheek. "It's always too much, but with you, it's better." And then she leans in and presses her lips to mine. Part of me knows why she's doing this. A distraction. The man in me doesn't fucking care at this point. At first, I'm gentle with the kiss, unable to make sense of it, until... something happens inside me. Without question, I slide my tongue into her mouth. I forgot how good it felt to be this close to her, until she reminds me.

The tip of her tongue strokes mine and I moan and pull her closer. Chest to chest, body to body, heart to heart, I want her. So badly.

She pulls back, breathing heavily. "I forgot how good that feels with you."

One of my hands remain in her hair while I slip the other to her shoulder. I stare down at her, our bodies pressed together, there's no space between us. I know she feels me, there, against her and when she lets out the moan against my lips and moves her hips against mine. I lose any self-control I had to deny her.

My hand brushes down her neck where her pulse thrums against my fingertips and across her collarbone where the bubbled skin from the scars she has there are. Bite marks. She has permanent reminders of that night, and now she wants me to give her new memories. Good ones. Can I do that?

I swallow again, my throat dry. "If I hurt you, tell me to stop," I tell her, rolling on top of her and deepening the kiss. Like it or not, my mind is on the after. What this will do to her. Will it bring back memories she doesn't want?

She senses my hesitation and reaches for the hem of the jersey she's wearing. She works it over her shoulders by wiggling around, and I realize she'd been completely naked underneath it this whole time.

She tugs at my shirt. "Your turn."

I smile and sit up, barely able to tear my eyes away from between her legs. I remove it and reach for the button of my jeans. I look at her, waiting for her to stop me, but she doesn't. So I take them off and with it, my boxers. She doesn't look, her eyes are on mine. This time, my eyes slide over her body. Usually, I never let them stray in fear if she catches me watching her it will scare her. But this time, it's different. She's instigating this.

She's perfect... fucking perfect, soft, warm. I want to worship her like she deserves, and admit I love her.

Don't do that.

Instead, realization hits me in the gut when Barrette starts stroking my dick. "I don't have anything," I admit, feeling defeated. I didn't even think to bring a condom. Obviously.

She shrugs and reaches for my shoulders. "I'm on birth control."

I nod, unsure, still. I mean, obviously I trust her, and I haven't been with anyone. Ever. Not this way. My eyes shift, taking in the way her breasts look pushed against me. Do I even know what the fuck I'm doing? Sure, I know the basics of it all, but I have no idea what to do next.

What a fucking pussy. Get it together.

My chest feels heavy, like she stabbed me with the way she's looking at me and slowly, just like her, I'm bleeding life. My heart may beat, but it's beating for her. In the moonlight, her eyes catch mine, and I see the tears streaming down her face. Without saying anything, I kiss her forehead and press my chest into hers, but I don't make an attempt to move between her legs.

Her eyes slowly drink me in, drifting over my face and lingering on my chest. She tugs at my shoulders. "I'm not crying because I'm sad, or scared, I just... I want *you*, Asa. I always have and they took that from me. I want to give it to you, so please let me."

My hand goes to her back and strums along the bare skin of her shoulder. The reminder that they took something from her, the anger, it hits me hard, but I don't let it faze me in front of her. I won't let her see that side because like I said, I'm really fucking good at being indifferent, and the last thing I want to do is hurt her in any way.

Barrette reaches between us, her hand wrapping around my erection. My hips automatically shift toward her, seeking out her soft hands. My mouth finds her shoulder, her neck, and then back to her mouth.

"Please try," she whispers against my cheek, kissing along my jaw before finding my lips.

Emotion shifts inside me and I try, fuck do I try to find the courage to give her this, but will it be too much? Touching her face, I trace the line of her jaw. "Barrette..." I begin, and then my breath catches as I move between her legs and forget what I was going to say. My muscles tense, my kisses deepen, full of meaning and love. I don't know if she knows it, but I try to assure with my touch that this means everything to me.

She watches me, stroking my cheek in the process. I've never felt so alive as I do now, burning with nerves, excitement, and fear of what this will mean. But then her hips move, rubbing against me, searching for more and I nearly go insane. It feels so fucking good I can't stop myself.

I position myself between her legs and watch her reaction to me. Will she tell me to stop? Nothing. I wait. Still nothing.

I draw in a ragged breath, unconvinced.

She notices, her hand on my cheek. "I trust you," she says, without uncertainty.

I brush her cheek with my fingers and nod, blowing out a slow breath. At least she does because I have no clue what's going to happen. I push against her opening and fucking moan. It's embarrassing. But then her knees spread wider and she bites her lip. It doesn't look like it's from pain. It's pleasure and written all over her.

As I finally enter her, the connection I feel with her is indescribable. "Jesus," I pant, pressing my forehead to hers, trying to catch my breath. My arms shake as I hold myself above her. I'm careful not to give her my full weight; she's so tiny I'd crush her.

The moment I'm fully sheathed inside, her entire body tenses beneath me. Her thighs squeeze around my waist, and her back arches as if her body is recoiling from the contact. I stop immediately, panic, and pull out completely. "I'm so sorry." Even in the shadow that conceals my expression, I know she can see the fear radiating from me.

"Don't stop," she pleads, gripping my shoulders and trying to pull me back inside. "Please, Asa."

I didn't want to stop either, but if I was hurting her, no way. Holding myself above her, I look down, my brow furrowing with uncertainty. "Did I hurt you? You're shaking." She's shaking, but I think I'm shaking harder.

She places her fingers to my lips. "Please... I'm begging you. Give me good memories. I'm shaking because I want you so much." She kisses me then.

Part of me doesn't like that she wants me to replace her memories of something that changed her life, and mine, but then there's a good part of me that wants to. If I can show her that sex can be so much more than someone using your body, then maybe I can heal her? Maybe we can have more.

Taking in a shaky, nervous breath, I enter her again, pull my hips back, then again. It's almost too much to go slow, but I do, for her.

Unfortunately, I admit to her, "I'm really fucking sorry, but I'm not gonna last long."

"It's okay." She breathes a quick jagged breath. "It feels good."

Well, shit. I nearly came just off the idea she's enjoying this.

I move faster, this time sliding with ease. My breathing is all over the place and hers is about the same. My arms tighten around her body, pulling her into my movements. I'm not forceful, but I'm not as gentle as I want to be.

She never gives me any indication I'm hurting her. No, she clings to me, desperately clutching to anything I give. Time ceases to exist. There's only Barrette surrounding me, and me, inside her.

"Asa," she whimpers, her voice hardly recognizable, but I know it's from pleasure.

"I'm gonna come," I pant, my movements slowing, trying to hold off. "Do you want me to pull out?"

"No," she gasps, refusing to allow any space between us. Her hips shift and allow me to slip deeper inside. It's too much. "Come inside me, please. I want every part of you inside me."

Fuck. I don't know what to make of her words, or even how to process them. My face presses into her neck, chasing my need and then I come, unable to hold it off any longer, my hips jerking forward in erratic movements. I groan through my release in her ear, holding her tighter then I want, but never hearing a complaint.

It's all over in a matter of minutes, and I realize this probably wasn't very good for her. So much for replacing her bad memories. What an asshole. Jesus.

Rolling off her, I run my hands through my hair. "I'm sorry. That probably sucked for you," I say quietly, shifting to the side. She blinks rapidly and I think maybe she's fighting tears. I watch her, apologetic and full of regret. Had I hurt her? Had this been too much for her?

The corners of her lips pull up, her cheeks flushed, like she's holding back laughter. "It was great."

"You're so full of shit right now." I laugh breathlessly, my bare chest shaking with the movement. I lift my hands and scrub them over my eyes. "I need redemption," I say, reaching for her. This time I move my hand between her legs and make sure she's taken care of first. Watching her come apart at my touch is pretty close to perfection.

And then we do it once more, this time slower, kissing passionately.

"Was that better?" I finally ask, holding her to my chest as we stare up at the ceiling.

"Yes, perfect." She closes her eyes, a small smile tugging at the corners of her perfect lips. My fingers reach out to run across her collarbone. She lays her head on my chest, curling into me. "That should have been my first time."

The words hang in the air. My heart beats rapidly while her breathing's erratic.

There are a thousand things I can say, most of which are completely cheesy, but instead, I say nothing. I stare at her. *Take my heart, honey. Rip it from my chest and write your name in my blood because I don't want to live without you.* I wanna tell her that, but I don't.

Some people can't help being sad. Then there's some who want to be happy, like Barrette, but something inside them forces them not to be. Shoves them to the edge of darkness that lurks in the corners, waiting to destroy their light. That's what happened to Barrette. She was pushed.

Being sad doesn't just happen either.

Neither does depression.

You can't ignore it. It won't let you. It's in your words, your will, and your unwavering control. It stays there, infecting you until it takes over and consumes you.

I know because I know the girl who's being destroyed by it.

Barrette's eyes find mine, tears in hers, I don't know what's in mine when she whispers, "I wanted you to be my first. I'm sorry they took that."

I kiss her temple and hold her tighter. "Don't ever be sorry. They didn't take *you.*"

I love you through it all, even our darkest moments.

CHAPTER 12

Lost in the light

BARRETTE

I watch him sleep, fascinated by the way his face looks when the morning sun hits the gold in his hair. I want to live in this space, the warmth, the comfort, forever. In our tiny bubble inside this room, we're perfect.

I knew what having sex with Asa would mean. Losing myself and weighted by emotions that chained me to an existence of filling voids. What I didn't know was how unlocked I would feel. A smile no longer forced. Yearning so badly to be whole, I cram my space with his kisses and let him heal me, completely exposed and vulnerable.

And he did. I saw his face, the love, the planes of regret, but would he ever know what he gave me? I'm not sure I could accurately express it to him, so I don't even try.

He stirs beside me, his lips brushing my forehead. "I have to get to practice."

I nod, blinking slowly, sleep finally weighing heavy on me. I don't have class until ten today and I'm looking forward to getting some sleep without nightmares. "Thank you," I whisper, my hand lingering on his as he sits up.

Smiling, he looks back at me, his hair messed up, eyes sleepy and soft. "I should probably be thanking you."

My heart thuds in my ears, wanting so badly to whisper what I really feel, that I love him, but I'm afraid to let the words slip out so easily. Neither of us say anything, but there's tightness around his eyes. He looks so serious with the planes of his face etched in an unnamed motion. "Are you okay?"

I bite my lip, holding back the swell of feelings washing over me. "I'm more than okay." I nod, my emotions clogging my throat.

He closes his eyes and then opens them again. "Call me later?" he asks, his voice torn as he swallows.

I smile and nod. "Yeah, I have class at ten. Meet for lunch maybe?"

He shoulders sink. "Can't. Team lunch to watch films and then we have our team dinner before the game tomorrow."

I knew that. Every Friday night before the Saturday games the team had dinner together and stayed off campus at a hotel to ward off any temptations the players might have to party before the game.

"There's always Sunday."

"Okay." He runs a hand through his hair. "I'll call you when I'm done. Probably won't be until eight though. Maybe later."

"I can wait."

He studies me and lets out a sigh as his eyes drift back to my naked body. "How am I gonna make it through today thinking about this?" His hand moves to my hips, gripping the sheets covering my lower hips.

I giggle when he lays back down with me, his mouth trailing over my neck. "You're gonna be late," I remind him when he's trying to crawl on top of me again.

His forehead rests against mine. "I know."

We stare at one another again and the emotion surfaces, my words on the tip of my tongue. I want to tell him I love him. His arm gives way and he settles his weight on me, all of it, every hard line. I've never felt like this before, so alive it bursts through me in a shock wave, residing deep in my bones, aching for more. But I knew what I was keeping him from. Practice. Obligations. A life without me in it.

So I let go, pull away and smile. "You should go."

He nods and inhales a rushed breath. Pushing back, his hand moves to the back of his neck, fighting the urge to return to the bed. And then he frowns. "You're making it hard to leave."

I snort and then start giggling when I notice the bulge in his jeans. "Good luck tomorrow."

Picking up the pillow that fell off the bed earlier, he tosses it at my face just before he picks up his backpack on the floor. Unzipping it, he pulls out a mason jar that's glowing purple and gold. I stare at it. "What's that?"

He sets it on my nightstand. "It's your own starry night."

I'm constantly searching for stars in the sky, and in Washington, in the fall, it's damn near impossible. He made me my own. Sitting up, I gasp and reach for it, twisting it in my hands. Taped to the side is a quote.

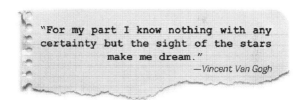

"For my part I know nothing with any certainty but the sight of the stars make me dream."
—Vincent Van Gogh

I smile. Asa looks nervous, biting his lip. "You like it?"

I nod. "I love it. How'd you do this?"

He shrugs a shoulder, shifting his weight to one foot and burying his hands in the pockets of his jeans. "Glitter and a glow stick."

"Crafty." I stand up on my bed and lunge myself at him. "Thank you. I love it so much."

And I love you.

I'm still naked, and he sighs, wrapping his arms around me. "Great. Now I'm hard again."

I laugh and slide my legs to the floor, effectively rubbing myself down his erection.

He tosses he head back, groaning. "Goddamn it." And then he's kissing me again, laying me on the bed and grinding himself into me.

"Asa?"

"Yeah?" he grunts, attacking my neck and shoulder with heated kisses.

"You're gonna be late."

He sighs, shaking his head but pushes himself away. With a frown, he covers me with my blankets. "Stay there." He leans in and kisses my lips, just once. "Don't move and I'll be back in a few days."

I laugh. "I'm not staying in bed for two days." It wouldn't be the first time.

He grumbles something, but I don't hear what before he slips out the door.

I can't stop the smile that surfaces. Sleep hangs over me as I stare at the glittery mason jar on my nightstand. I can't believe he made that for me.

If I hadn't already been in love with Asa, I would have fallen completely this morning. Even in my relaxed state, a rush of fear pricks my skin when I think about the torment on his face as he made love to me. I say make love because it didn't feel like sex or fucking—there was love present in every touch we made. Years of waiting had led to that, and I knew, deep down, I was filling a void I didn't understand. One I might never understand.

CHAPTER 13

My heads not in it - Asa

ASA

Since I was old enough to pick a football up, I've loved it. I wanted to be at the center of it all. I didn't want to be the running back and the tight end, or even a lineman. Let's face it, I'm not built to be a lineman. What I am is the guy in control. When I call "hut," everyone moves. I'm where it's at. The play doesn't start until I give the okay.

"Ready?" Terrell is watching me, waiting for an answer. We're halfway through the fourth quarter and he knows I am; he's just checking. I nod and we move to the line of scrimmage.

Am I ready? Probably not. I'm not ready to call the play. My mind is obsessing, contemplating, going over and over what yesterday meant. Was it too much for her? Should I have stopped it? Should I have told her I loved her?

I wait for the snap. My heart pounds rapidly in anticipation, my mind working to strategize and see the play before it happens. I clap my hands, the ball snaps, and I spot Roman midfield, but he's tied up with a defender. I fake to the left and then spin around to the right and throw across field to Dem. He doesn't gain any ground. He's tackled at the ten-yard line.

I have two options at this point. I can run the play myself or throw the ball. I run the ball myself, stiff arm a guy and then lay myself out for the touchdown. Coach hates it when I do this, afraid I'll get hurt, but when I see an opening, I take it.

We win the game against the Bears 38-7. I surprised myself with big numbers there too when I threw for over 290 yards and rushing thirty-two times for 178 yards despite the wind and rain. It was relentless, and the ball kept slipping out of my hands. The field was a swamp after the game.

It's a big win for us. Part of me isn't feeling it. Since it's a home game, we're looking to get rowdy and party, but my mind isn't on the game, or the win. It's on her. It's on the girl I can't shake. With the way my schedule has been, I haven't been able to see her since the other night when we had sex. I have no idea what her feelings are, how she's feeling, and it fucking kills me.

The guys find a party at a nearby frat house that serves us just fine with an endless supply of beer. I don't drink much. And though I don't want to be at a party, I want to be with Barrette, I welcome the distraction for a couple of hours. I texted her, but she hasn't answered yet.

Terrell stands from his spot beside me and then leaves, finding a place near the keg. A minute later, he comes back with four beers and a bong. I get up and leave. I've smoked before, but not during the season. It's not worth it to me to get caught. The NCAA takes that shit seriously and performs random drug testing throughout the season. I don't understand the guys who smoke during the season, or even before a game. Why? What's the point? They all know we have a bowl game coming up and they'll random test us, but it doesn't seem to bother them. Especially Roman and Codey. It's like they have no regard for rules.

I'm sitting on a couch, well away from the guys smoking and I'm about ready to leave. I need to go check on her.

"Hey, man, is Barrette Blake your girl?" Codey asks, sitting beside me with a fresh beer in his hand. He reeks of his bad decisions and vodka. We've played together for two years now, but I don't talk personal shit with him.

"Why?" I ask, my glare changing his expression real quick. He's scared of me. He hands me a beer. For some reason, I take it, thinking maybe I might want to dump it on him.

"Just curious." He leans in, his shoulder pressing to mine like we're fucking buddies. We're not. "She's a hot little piece of ass." He raises his fist as if I'm supposed to fist-bump him over his derogatory remarks. "Ya feel me?"

Ya feel me? You're about to feel my fucking fist in your teeth you piece of shit. My entire body bursts into flames and I'm sweating. I look over at him, so many violent images surfacing. I want to smash his face into the ground and make him eat his goddamn words. I've always been protective of Barrette but now, since the other night, it's worse. It's uncontrollable and I don't know how to handle it.

And then he has the nerve to ask, "You share?"

I lose it on him. Tossing the beer aside, I watch as it hits the floor with a thud, the liquid splashing over the carpet and I twist violently, my eyes wild, my intentions unpredictable. Even I don't know what I'm going to do next.

He looks to the beer, then me. His hands rise, his eyes widen. "I didn't mean anything by it."

I stand, and without thinking, I grab him by the front of his shirt and lift him up to eye level, my knuckles white, my breathing harsh and barely controlled. Flashes of Barrette's broken bloody body flood my mind and suddenly, I can do something about it. I could take it out on Codey. "You even fucking mention her name again and I will break your goddamn jaw. Ya feel me?"

He swallows, fear evident and blows out a quick breath. "Sorry, man."

I let go of him and he flops back against the couch, our teammates rushing over to us. Terrell grabs me by the shirt. "You good?"

Annoyed, I roll my head to his. "I'm out."

Terrell sighs and glares at Codey. "Now look what you've done."

I intend on leaving, but I see Barrette come in the house with Joey. It's not unheard of for her to be at a party. It's not like I expect her to stay in her room all the time and it makes me feel better to see her with Joey.

I watch her for just a moment, no smile, no awareness of anything around her. She scans the room, but she hasn't noticed me yet. My heart thuds louder in my ears.

She walks by and finally notices me. Relief floods her eyes, her adorable smile contagious. I move toward her, waiting to see what she'll do. Without hesitation, she wraps her arms around my neck. "You won."

"I won more than the game," I whisper, holding her close. "I texted you."

"Sorry. My phone died during the game."

I draw back looking down at her. "Were you at the game?"

She waves her hand around. "No, we watched on my phone, which is why it's dead."

I laugh and pull her back toward me to kiss her. In front of everyone, I kiss her. I wonder if she realizes this is a first, but then again, I don't think I care what anyone thinks. Technically, it's just a kiss. But it's so much more now. More meaning, more feelings, more impatience on my part for sure because I'd rather be anywhere but here.

Joey gags beside us. "You guys are gross. You're making me sick to my stomach."

Roman approaches, smiling and hands Joey a beer. "Hey, JoJo." He's clearly drunk, obnoxiously so, and snakes his arm around her shoulder. "When are you going to give me some honey bear?" Though his question is meant for Joey, his stare lingers on Barrette.

Joey laughs in his face. "You couldn't handle my honey."

There's probably some truth to it, but something bothers me about the way he has his arm around Joey. She doesn't look comfortable with him. I know what happened to Joey. Barrette told me one night, with Joey's permission of course, and then months later, Joey opened up to me. I hated knowing there are thousands of women out there going through the same motions Barrette is.

A heavy bass thumps throughout the house, shaking the windows and my chest. Barrette leans into me, her body curving into mine. To the ordinary eye, we look like a couple though we've never talked about what the other night meant.

She pulls at my hand, leaving Roman with Joey. "Dance with me."

I can't deny her. My nerves are still on edge, but I do as she asks because this feels so normal, and I want normal so badly.

She moves closer. I watch and move with her. My breath hits her neck and she curls around me, melting against me. Her heat becomes one with my heat. Thoughts of our time together the other night flood my brain and it's everything I can do to keep my excitement in check and not be obvious. I can't draw my eyes from her hips when she brings them forward and back again to the beat of the bass.

My eyes move from her hips to over her shoulder where I see Eva watching with curiosity, and then to where Roman is watching. He's not looking at me. No, his eyes are on Barrette's ass that my hands are on. I look away from him. If I don't, I'll break his fucking jaw for watching her like this.

Barrette looks at me, her face inches from mine. I see it then. I'm comfort for her. She can fall to pieces before me and I'm holding it all together.

"What are you doing to me?" I whisper in her ear. She could stab me in the heart at this point and it wouldn't hurt as much as it does to know this might not work. It might be too much for her at any time and I'm going to have to pump the brakes. In my fucked-up sense of reality, a world without her in it isn't worth living. So I'll do anything she wants.

Her eyes water and I hold her closer. I want to fucking kiss her in front of everyone. I want to fuck her against the wall in front of this room just to let them know she's mine. And I hate that I'm thinking that way because she deserves better.

"What?" she asks, her breath hitting my skin. It sends shivers through my chest.

My face is close enough that I smell her sweetness, the coconut of her shampoo, but she smells like me too. She smells like my sweat. My scent is all over her and I like that. "*You.*" Pulling back, I watch her reaction, feeling her chest heaving against mine, her heart beating wildly against mine. "What are *you* doing to me?"

She hesitates to answer. "I don't... I don't know what you mean?"

I curve an eyebrow at her, she stops moving. *I love you. And in a sense, I hate you.* It's harsh, I know, but the hate I have isn't for her, it's our situation and the future that might not be. Because of them. Because she won't report it.

She waits for me to say more, to put words to my expression. I don't and I study her face. I see a broken girl dying inside and I'm going fucking insane. She's trying to be brave when all she'll ever be is a shadow of the person she once was.

We're standing together, no longer moving and her hands slip from my shoulders. "You don't want this, do you?"

"I didn't say that. I'm just not sure you're ready for it."

Her eyes narrow. "You don't get to decide what I'm ready for, Asa." And then she turns to leave. I try to reach for her, but she's at Joey's side before I can get to her.

Damn it. They leave and I let them. She doesn't need me to follow her and demand to put a meaning on this. She needs Joey and I need to let her.

My mind races with thoughts when Roman approaches me. "Put in a good word with JoJo for me," he says, his arm around my shoulder. He's high, his pupils so dilated you can no longer see the blue in his eyes.

I stare at him, anger pulsing through me. "Why, so you can treat her like shit when you're done with her?" Joey is nothing like the girls he fucks around with. He goes for super skinny, tan, and blonde. Joey's tall, thick, with jet-black hair.

"It's not like that."

"With you it always is." I know what he puts Cadence through. He offers her a few nights, maybe a month of his time before he fucks it up and he's screwing around on her. He puts that poor girl through hell.

WHEN I'M BACK IN MY DORM, I STAND AT THE SINK WITH THE water running. When it's cold enough, I splash the water over my face and then stare at myself in the mirror, wondering what the fuck my problem is.

I read this quote by Plato the other day in my philosophy class, and this jumble of feelings I have for Barrette jumped up and started screaming at me when I read it. "We can easily forgive a child who is afraid of the dark; the real tragedy of life is when men are afraid of the light."

That's where we are right now. Everyone's afraid of the dark, afraid to emerge back into the light of the living.

I LOVE HOME GAMES BUT PLAYING ON THE ROAD MAKES ME FEEL like I'm going somewhere. Like I have more to offer than just college ball. The week following that home game, we travel to eastern Washington to play the Cougars.

Four times that week I find myself in Barrette's room and though I don't intend for it to lead to sex every time, it does and it's good. We're good, even if we're hiding from reality. I fight with myself to demand more, and just as easily, I tell myself it's enough if it's what she needs.

I sit next to Terrell on the bus and use his shoulder to get some sleep—something I don't get during the week. He lets me until I drool a little down his shirt sleeve. He pushes me off him. "Dude, gross."

I laugh, my phone finding my attention. There are two texts from Barrette wishing me good luck and one of her sending me a kissing emoji.

I'm tempted to blow off the game and rush to her dorm. Fuck football if I can't have her, but I know that won't solve anything. Maybe time away is what we both need. Unfortunately, since I had sex with her, something changed between us. For both of us. I knew it would happen too. I knew it, and I did it anyway so I can't place blame on anyone but myself. The problem is the change for me is fucking obsession. I want her, all the time, every minute of the day and I'm afraid the attachment I have to her is bordering on unhealthy.

We arrive at the Cougars stadium and it's our usual routine, pregame rituals, praying, taping ankles, talking to the offensive coordinator and the starting offensive line and going over plays. It's a good couple of hours before we take to the field. When we do, it's all business. There's usually very little joking around and game faces in place. College football is way more intense than what you would think.

I know what I can do on the field. I know where plays can happen and where they can't. I know the strong guys, and I know the ones who tend to get caught up. Roman's strong, he rarely gets caught up. I can trust that if I throw to him, he's gonna be there. Same with Dem. I know where both of them are at all times and, yeah, I favor them on the field because of that.

I'm having an amazing game throwing for over 366 yards so far. My passing is spotless even though the guys I favor on the field are covered a lot. In the first and second quarters, I've run the ball three times already.

Halfway through the third quarter, I call the play, looking left, then right, seeing the boys poised and ready. The ball snaps I take two steps back, then another. I see Roman midfield but then I'm jarred from the left, blindsided, feeling the reverberation through my skull. Right before my head snaps back, I see Codey on the ground when he should have been blocking me. My helmet goes flying and then the next thing I remember is about twenty guys are around me.

If I could have kicked Codey's ass right then, I would have. That one knocks me pretty good. I can't even stand up without seeing stars. They don't let me off the field without strapping me to a backboard. I do see Codey as I'm being hauled into the locker room and make him come closer to give him a piece of my mind. I grab hold of his jersey. "You need to protect me in the pocket."

He says nothing.

Fucker.

Blinking, I try to focus. It does nothing and I still can't see. The coaches swarm around me after that, as does our team physician. I don't care for our team physician. He doesn't know what the fuck he's doing half the time and the fact that he asks me, "What happened?" proves my theory. Had he not been watching the game?

I'm fine. But I'm also bleeding from a cut above my eye. I think it's making me a little loopy.

Once they have me in the locker room on that fucking backboard that I find completely unnecessary, our team doctor is in my face asking me all kinds of questions, but I have no answers. I can't even see him let alone answer him. Everything's blurry.

Coach Benning pats my shoulder. "Let's get you checked out, kid." He smiles when I squint at him. "Just precautionary."

Yeah, right.

They make me take a ride to the hospital and it's uneventful. At the hospital, they ask me questions I didn't know before the game.

They do some scans, X-rays, and a neurological exam. It's decided pretty early I have a slight concussion but nothing more.

I don't remember the bus ride back to Seattle. At all. I apparently slept the entire way on Terrell's lap. He treats me good as long as I don't drool.

When we pull up to the stadium, he shakes my shoulders. "Time to get up, Sleeping Beauty."

I sit up, noticing the bus is nearly empty. "Did we win, Coco Puff?"

Terrell laughs. I call him Coco Puff sometimes. Actually, only when I'm drunk. Or obviously when I'm concussed. "Yeah, we did." He stands and reaches for my hand. "Now, am I gonna have to throw you over my shoulder and carry you home?"

Sitting there for a few minutes, I sigh when I see that we are in fact the last people left on the bus. He nudges my knee. "I have to piss, man, get up."

We head inside to the locker room retrieve our bags and then head back to the dorms. It's around two in the morning.

Terrell is in charge of keeping an eye on me and making sure I get some rest. When we get inside our dorm room, he's talking about the game and how Roman and Codey got in a fight in the locker room. I don't care. My mind is not on that game any longer. It's on Barrette when I look at the clock. I start feeling like I need her.

Why her?

Why can't I leave her alone?

Because.

I think I can save her.

I lay in bed and wish for sleep. I do for a while and then stare at the clock as the minutes go by.

2:58 a.m.

3:05 a.m.

3:16 a.m.

Around four, I reach for my phone and see she texted me four minutes ago. It gives me hope she wants and needs more.

CHAPTER 14

A new reason to be happy

BARRETTE

My mind won't stop hanging on everything Asa did and said to me. It was everything, and so much more. What he gives me, his tenderness, there's no way I can even express what it means to me.

Did you know the name Asa in Hebrew means physician or healer? It also means he's optimistic. Enthusiastic. Humorous. Intelligent. All things he is, and I don't know where I fit into any of those.

I watch every game Asa plays. I may not go to the games always, but I watch them. Crowds make me uncomfortable, so I usually stay in my dorm and watch them, or go to the pizza place on campus and watch them with Joey.

I watch the game, my attention on him. The cameraman flashes to Roman first, chewing on his mouthpiece, looking like his mind is far from the game. Three feet down, they show Asa, and his numbers for the game pop up on the screen. He's there with an iPad in hand and the offensive coordinator hovered over him pointing out specifics.

It's sometime in the third quarter when the crowd goes wild. I jump and my eyes snap to the screen when I see the concern in everyone's faces. Asa is sacked on the play but he doesn't get up.

He doesn't move.

For over three minutes, he doesn't move.

I cannot breathe.

They show the replay and his helmet comes flying off and then the snap as his head smacks the turf. My stomach knots but eases when he moves his legs up and rests his feet flat on the ground and then rolls to his side. Breathing a sigh of relief, Joey grabs my hand. "He's okay."

But is he? He doesn't look like it.

Seeing Asa transported off the field on a stretcher is not easy on me.

I ask Joey to leave. I can't watch any more of the game if he's not in it. As we're walking back to my dorm, I send Roman a text knowing he'll reply to me when the game is over.

"Are you gonna be okay?" Joey asks, waiting outside my dorm room. She lives two doors down with a girl who eats tuna fish every single day. Her room smells awful. "Because I could stay and cuddle. I have plenty of fluff for you to lay against," she teases, winking at me and doing an hour-glass motion with her hands. "I might not be all solid lines like your boy, but I'm definitely cuddle-bug material."

It's tempting and wouldn't be the first time Joey helped me while I feared sleep and the ghosts of my dreams, but I resist. "I'm okay. Thank you."

Just before she leaves, Joey pauses and looks over at me. She has the prettiest brown eyes that remind me of chocolate syrup. "Don't push Asa away. I know it's hard, believe me, I know. I seldom let men in because why would they want me?"

I lean into the wall. "Jo, don't talk like that. You're beautiful."

"Gurl, please. I know this." She laughs and tucks her dark curls behind her ear. "But being beautiful and having the body men want, that's completely different. And I'm fine with that. I love myself and I'm not trying to be what they want. But you, my friend, Asa Lawson is one hundred percent in love with your tiny ass and you're constantly giving him an out. You're convinced because of what you guys went through, he can't give you what you want, or that you're incapable of receiving it. That's not the case."

It's not that I'm incapable of receiving his love. It's that he's scared to give it to me in fear of what it means. "I think he's scared."

Joey nods. "He probably is. The biggest hurdle to get over in a relationship is sexual trauma. You have to set new boundaries, reevaluate them often, and make changes as time progresses. But Asa Lawson, babe, he'd follow you to the ends of the earth and back again."

I have no doubt she's right.

When Joey leaves, my room is filled with an all-encompassing quietness as I sit on my bed clutching my pillow. I think about the brown in his eyes and the way he looked moving above me the other night. I put my hand to my face and remember the sensations that follow when he touches me, the imprint of him pumping through my veins.

Joey's right, we do have to set boundaries, but with Asa, I don't want to follow the rules. I want that reckless, unforbidden love that tempts me, and is it so bad that he gives it to me? I'm tired of editing my thoughts and censoring my words because I'm afraid I can't give him what he needs. Or at least, I think I can't give him what he needs.

What if I can?

Roman texts me back and tells me Asa was transported to the hospital and released with a concussion. They're already heading home.

I sigh in relief, holding my cell phone to my chest.

I'm alone in my room for a few minutes when Cadence knocks on the door to the bathroom and peeks her head in. I look up at her and wait.

"Have you heard from Asa?" she asks, concern on her face. "I saw that hit. Looked brutal."

I nod and hold up my cell phone. "Roman said he was okay."

With the mention of Roman's name, she frowns and steps back.

"'K." And then she disappears back to her room without another word.

Sometimes I get the urge to talk to her, but then I remember our last conversation when she got upset with me that I wanted to spend more time with Asa than her. *"You're choosing him over me when I'm the one who was there for you when he left and you had nobody else."* That's what she said to me, and I knew our friendship would never be the same again.

For a long time, I tried to put myself in Cadence's shoes that night and if it had been her, falling down drunk, would I have left her with those guys?

No. Not a chance. I would have stayed there until she passed out and then I would have taken her home. I would not have ever left her alone despite what she told me to do. And no, I can't blame her for anything that happened. I told her to leave.

It doesn't stop me from wishing we would have remained friends.

I SIT AT THE WINDOW FOR HOURS WATCHING TO SEE IF I CAN SEE any players returning to campus. I should text him or maybe call. *No, don't do that.* He's probably busy and me calling will just make him panic and think something is wrong.

I calculate how long it will take for them to get back to campus before I can text Asa. Another hour later, I see the steady trickle of players come in, Codey, Terrell, then Roman.

I wait another few minutes before I send him a text just before two in the morning, knowing he'll more than likely be up.

Me: You ok? I saw that play. It looked like it rocked you.

He replies within a few minutes.

Asa: I'm good. You up? I could rock you.

My cheeks warm, my smile automatic. I love when he's playful and flirty.

Me: I'm up.

Asa: Be there in 15.

HE'S RIGHT. HE'S HERE IN FIFTEEN MINUTES. I LOOK UP, REACHING out to touch the mark on his face. "Are you okay?"

"They say…" he stumbles a little, "I'm concussed."

I laugh when he falls into me. His fingers reach down and wrap around mine, and he begins to pull me toward him. My pulse races. He reaches for me, cupping my cheeks in his hands and draws me closer. Closing my eyes, I lean in.

"I missed you." He kisses my forehead, and then my temple, breathing in slowly. "God, I've missed you. This football schedule is crazy." And then he kisses me deeply but pulls away just as quickly. He lays down on my bed with me and I curl into his arms just like we've done time and time again. Only now, since we've had sex four other times this week, I wonder if that's what he wants. I do. I *definitely* do. Those nights, though the nightmares that followed were hard, I don't regret them. Not in the least. In some kind of weird sense, all I've been able to think about is having him inside me again. I crave it.

My hand slips under his T-shirt, feeling his smooth, hot, rigid muscles. "Do you want to?"

Taking my hand that's on his stomach, he moves it lower to between his legs. "I'm up for anything," he says. His voice is a tender whisper I find endearing and I can tell he's still on the pain pills they gave him.

My heart thumps wildly in my chest. "Clearly," I tease, palming his erection through his jeans, my words coming out scratchy, like I have a cold. It's because I'm swallowing back emotions I'm afraid to let him know.

He groans, his lips finding mine again before he rolls and presses his hardness into my thigh. I want him between my legs. Now. He cups my cheek again. His hands shake slightly, a grunt falling from his slightly open mouth when he grinds into me. "Fuck, you're all I've been able to think about."

I nod, never parting my lips from his. "Me too. I never thought it could be like this, to want you so badly." It's the truth. When I thought about sex after my assault, it made me sick to my stomach, unless it was Asa. I've only ever wanted him.

Asa brings his mouth to mine, just as eager as me. One hand cups my face, his other tight around my waist, holding me closer. His mouth, it's hard and all-consuming, a newfound edge to his passion. I spread my legs wider, wanting everything he's giving me.

Suddenly, he pauses and rips his shirt off, then mine. And when he returns, I lock my legs around his waist because I don't want any space between us.

With his forehead against mine, our bodies fuse together as one with him rocking into me, our breaths mixing as one. We stay in a rhythm, our eyes on one another and it's obvious we want more, but he's not rushing just yet. He seems strangely focused on something... words maybe?

Holding the side of my head, he keeps his forehead pressed against mine. He's looking into my eyes, searching for something. I'm not even sure what. His jeans are on, as are my panties and I think at any moment he's going to make the effort to remove them, but no. He's staring at me like he wants to say something. That or he hit his head too hard tonight.

"What?" I finally ask, smiling softly.

Sighing, he kisses my forehead and closes his eyes. I tuck my head against his chest, but I hear it. The words "I love you, Barrette" are whispered in my ear.

I let the words sink in, find roots and dig deep inside me. I breathe and squeeze my eyes shut. He didn't say it, did he? Had I imagined it?

He doesn't wait for me to say it back. He's on his knees, unbuttoning his jeans. I lay there, trying to comprehend what he said, but I really want us naked for no other reason but as a distraction. I love him. I do. I love him so much it hurts, and when I tell him, he's going to feel the words like I just did.

Tears I hadn't prepared for roll down my cheeks. They're not tears of sadness or regret; they're happy-in-the-moment tears.

Asa lifts his eyes to mine, notices the tears, the smile, and slowly leans in to trail his fingers down my stomach to my hips where he slips my panties past my thighs. Tossing them aside, he places his palms on the mattress and hovers over me. I reach up and touch his face and notice the stitches above his eye. Unfortunately, he notices my tears then.

"Why are you crying?" he mumbles.

"They're good tears."

His brow pinches together, and he nods, but there's no smile. His body shifts and he draws me closer, our chests touching. "I didn't say it to hear it back." His words tremble with the shake of his body. "I said it to make sure you knew."

"I love you," I whisper in his ear as he enters me, filling me with so much more than himself. "Not because of this, but because of you," I tell him, my mouth moving across his shoulder.

His body shudders, his movements halting. He pulls back slightly, his eyes finding mine and then his mouth. It's not the same kisses as before. These are slow and consuming. They promise and assure.

I'm the first to break away from the kiss, and when I do, Asa's mouth finds my neck. "Fuck," he pants, his movements slowing. "I love you so much."

And I say, over and over again, that I love him, even when it doesn't feel like the words will ever be enough to convey my feelings for him. He holds me close, cradling my head in his hands, his chest sliding against mine as he rocks against me. The friction, the pressure, it's just enough that I think maybe I know what's coming if he keeps this slow but precise motion up.

He smirks, and I think, yeah, he knows what he's doing.

I grip his shoulders tighter, my hips squirming, searching for just the right spot. And when we find it, he's staring down at me with such intense need it makes my entire body heat to levels almost unbearable.

"Fall apart for me," he begs, rocking into me.

I shudder beneath him at the same time his hips jerk forward faster than before. "Don't stop," I moan, praying he doesn't in the middle of what I think is my first orgasm while having sex.

"I won't," he promises, keeping his movements sure and steady. He grunts against my lips, "Kiss me."

His words, the tone, the way they course over my skin, salty and ragged, I kiss him. God, do I kiss him. I kiss him like he did to me, promising, assuring, and trying to convey everything he means to me. When I do fall apart beneath him, it's everything and so much more.

I wrap my legs around his waist, tighter, holding on to him anywhere I can. His movements speed and just as mine ends, his begins, jerking inside me, groaning as he rides through his. He holds himself up on his hands, pushing into me and shudders, his eyes heavy-lidded, emptying himself into me. It's everything, and I think he's giving me everything good inside him. It's seeping into my soul, bringing out the good in me.

He rolls off me and to the side, his breathing still heavy. That's when the darkness creeps in. I only feel whole when he's inside me, and I know just how unhealthy that is, but I can't stop it. It traps me there, tightens my chest and holds every other emotion hostage. I breathe in and stare at the jar on my nightstand Asa made for me. My very own starry night. It's fading, the light not as bright but read the quote on the side again.

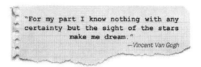

"For my part I know nothing with any certainty but the sight of the stars make me dream."
—Vincent Van Gogh

Asa kisses my shoulder, his breathing slowing. I look over at him and he seems so content I smile. Even if my mind won't stop, at least I have this. Someone willing to see me through the darkness.

CHAPTER 15

The night I can't shake

BARRETTE

I'm studying with Roman for our statistics class. I don't usually study with him, but we're taking the class together and I need desperate help. We're sitting on my bed with our backs against the wall, our feet hanging off the edge. There's a pizza box between us, and he's telling me about Cadence and him and how they can't seem to stop fighting, but yet, he can't walk away from her. Their situation is very much like mine and Asa's, only completely different. As couples, we're wrapped around each other in a lot of ways, holding onto memories from the past.

Asa and Roman were friends first when we were younger. They met playing youth football. I actually dated Roman for a short time. If you can call a third-grade romance dating. We legit thought we were too. Serious stuff back then. Anyway, when I noticed Asa Lawson, I let Roman down gently in a note that said: "I'm breaking up with you. Sorry."

Roman being Roman, gave me a cocky response. "Cadence is prettier."

He's always been a dick.

After Asa left, Roman looked out for me, but I'll admit, my relationship with everyone I know, even my parents, has changed.

When I look over at Roman, he's staring at his textbook, a slice of pizza in one hand and a beer in another. "I just don't get it." Roman groans, drawing me from my thoughts. I feel bad, but I've missed what he was just saying. "She fucking acts like my mother at times."

He's talking about a fight he had with Cadence the other night. Believe me when I say everyone on the floor heard them in her room. I don't have much I can offer him that he doesn't know already. "If you'd stop cheating on her, maybe she wouldn't be so untrusting. You've brought this on yourself."

"I never told her I was going to see *just* her. That's just crazy thinking I can be held to those standards in college," Roman says conversationally, never breaking his eyes from the textbook in his lap.

"You're such a pig." I roll my eyes as he reaches for another slice of pizza. "Who's that cheerleader you've been with again? I think the whole floor heard her name a time or two."

He knows what I'm talking about. He cheated on Cadence with Lydia. I've never seen Lydia, that I know of, but I've definitely heard of her now. "It is what it is, B," he says, angling the slice of pizza into his mouth. "Women love me because I have a dick and I fuck like a boss."

"That's disgusting, Roman. You're so crass." I level him a serious look and smile. "You've got nothing on Asa."

Crap. Why'd I just say that?

Roman huffs, lashes fluttering, closing in annoyance. His jaw works back and forth in what I can only assume is irritation. He hates it when I mention Asa. They got in a huge fight after that night because he claimed Roman should have been looking out for me. "Whatever." And then his eyes shift to mine, narrowing. "How would you know?"

I shrug. "No reason."

"Bullshit. You fucked him, didn't you?"

I slap his shoulder. "Don't be nasty. I'm not telling you."

"Though I can't believe you gave it up to that fool, I'm not surprised if you did." Roman twists his head, his eyes wander to mine. "You know, he's never with any other girl. *Ever*. Even the cheerleaders. Never touches them. Guess you got him pussy whipped."

I shove his shoulder. "Stop being gross." Though I know I have absolutely no say in anything Asa does, it's refreshing to know he's not interested in anyone. Especially girls like Eva or Bethany, two cheerleaders I know who are obsessed with him.

I think about Roman's words. *I can't believe you gave it up to that fool.* They used to be friends and I don't know how or why the shift happened. In my heart, I know it has to do with me and that night. "Why are you so mean to him? You used to be friends."

"Mean to him? This isn't kindergarten, B. It's fucking life, and he's the one who acts like a king around here. And yeah, we were friends before he pushed everyone away. You're just too nice to remember he did the same to you."

"He does not act like he's king," I defend, my heartbeat quickening. Yeah, Asa pushed me away when we were younger, but I can't forget that he was taking care of his mom. He was fifteen and his mom was dying. He wouldn't have been Asa if he didn't give 100 percent of himself to helping her. He's the most selfless person I know. "He's nothing but humble."

Roman snorts, smiling. "Yeah, humble, sure. I gotta say though, I'd probably be the same way with you."

"With me?" My words shake, and I fidget with my pillowcase. "What are you talking about?"

"You know exactly what I'm talking about. You're Barrette Blake. Every guy's wet dream for sure." His eyes lift to mine and there's a sudden edge to him I've never seen before. "Remember when we made out?"

Nausea rolls through me and I laugh around the feeling, trying not to look as uneasy as I am. "Don't remind me." I want him out my room in an instant. My throat tightens and tears sting my eyes. I breathe in through my nose, then let it out slowly, trying to rid the feeling inside my chest. The ones that scream and suffocate, the ones that tell me to withdraw and hide away from everything.

Roman lets out a gruff laugh and pushes the pizza box away, his mood lightening a touch, but there's still a change in his demeanor. "I can't believe I ate two pizzas."

I pick through his pieces of crust he never eats and nibble on one. My stomach rolls when I take the first bite. My body isn't craving food. It's craving Asa and I hate that he's not here, and Roman is, but I have to pass this class.

Roman reaches for the beer he brought over with him. "Do you remember it though?"

"Yeah, I remember." I look over at him tossing the crust back in the box. "Why?" I remember the night. Sophomore year of high school. I was so confused and had no idea what I was doing. I remember thinking to myself, I should feel something when a boy is kissing me, right? I felt nothing.

Roman takes a slow drink from his beer, his eyes heavy on mine. "Why did you stop me?"

"Your sister was in the other room."

"So?" he presses, still watching my every reaction. His eyes slide from mine to my lips.

Fear pricks my skin and I tremble. "She walked in on us."

"If she hadn't, I would have tried to fuck you," he says, point-blank.

It feels like a bullet hits my chest with his words. Something about them doesn't sit right with me. My hands start shaking and I don't know why. I look at the clock, then my phone on my desk and think of Asa. I look at the door to the bathroom and think of Cadence on the other side of the room. We may not be much of friends anymore, but I hate what he puts her through and now here he is working on me. And then my eyes drift to the mason jar on my nightstand and Roman's use of the word *try*. I don't like it.

Roman's quiet beside me and I wonder if he's fallen asleep when I glance over at him. His eyes are on his beer. He's concentrating, deep in thought with the way his brow is scrunched. "Would you have let me?"

I raise an eyebrow, curling my legs up and wrapping my arms around them. "Have sex with me?" I don't like this conversation or how it makes my stomach ache.

"Yes."

"That's a weird question to be asking me."

"Answer it," he demands, his voice harder than before.

I blink, unprepared for his harshness. "Answer what?"

"Stop avoiding the question." Roman stares at me, his expression completely serious as he draws his brows together, piercing blue eyes narrowing. "Would you have let me?"

I draw in a quick breath and then slowly exhale, trying to make sense of his mood and my reaction to it. "No, I wouldn't have."

"Why not? Because I'm not Asa Lawson?"

My hands shake, my voice wavering. "Because I've never felt that way about you."

He nods, a smirk on his lips. "Is that so?"

"Yes, I wouldn't lie to you about that. We're friends. We should just keep it that way."

He shifts slightly, his eyes searching mine when he asks, "If I were to kiss you now, what would you do?"

"Tell you to stop." My words are shaky, the nervousness in my stomach rolling. "I... love Asa."

He snorts and twists his body away from me. "Everyone loves the golden boy. Their favorite football hero."

I don't reply. I don't think he's looking for a reply. I do think, jealous much? It's a known fact Roman has always been jealous of Asa. He's not the only one. I swear in middle school, if there was ever a poll for most loved, and most hated, Asa topped both lists unanimously, and was feared by just as many. To me, he's always going to be the boy who saved me, but to others, they see him differently. He's that guy, the one with the intimidating presence yet the smirk that draws you in and teases, tempts, only for him to ignore you completely. I know very well the clout he has around school. I just don't see that side of him. I see the one holding me in the early hours of the morning and promising to see me through it regardless of what I can't give him.

We're quiet after that. Roman concentrates on his phone and then looks at me. I glance at his phone. He's texting Codey, but all I focus on is the last reply from Roman that says:

She's not up for... it I tried, bro.

What? He tried what? My eyes drift to his. He's breathing heavily and I notice he's lifted his leg, his foot flat on my bed. I don't know why, but my stare hits his hands. My heart races, my stomach twisting. It's one memory I have of that night. The man's hand next to my head. I remember he had a tattoo on his hand. Roman doesn't have any tattoos.

With an aggravated sigh, Roman leans forward and tucks his phone in his back pocket. Standing, he tugs at the front of his jeans. My throat feels tight, knowing why he's doing that. Had our conversation made him hard? But why? That's weird, isn't it? "I gotta head out. Practice first thing in the morning."

I nod, and he leaves without another word. When he closes the door behind him, nausea hits me. I reach for my pillow and curl my arms around it. The idea of Roman wanting me, I don't like it. I feel disgusted with myself and angry for no reason. I'm glad I didn't have sex with Roman back in high school. I know I would have regretted it.

My skin crawls to the point I start itching my skin obsessively.
She's not up for it I tried, bro.

What did that mean and why didn't I have the guts to call him out on it?

I take a shower thinking it will help, but it doesn't. I sit on the floor and cry, unable to stop the depression from taking over. You don't realize how much strength it takes to pull yourself out of a dark place mentally, and tonight, I don't have it in me.

I want Asa here, and I want so badly to tell him what Roman said to me, but I know if I do, he'll go after him. He can't. I can't let him ruin his career over me. If he knew Roman had been in my room, alone with me, he'd be angry. Furious. And maybe even betrayed, though it meant nothing.

It's 4:00 A.M. I know Asa has his workout at five and him still being here means he's running late. He texted me an hour ago and said he couldn't wait another minute to see me. After what happened with Roman, I knew I needed him here more than anything, erasing the uneasiness with his body next to mine.

His breath expels in a gasp when I arch my back against his chest. He's gripping my sheets and whispering words I can't make out but sound like fuck and something else. With him cursing in my ear, I don't feel dirty. I feel complete and needy, sexy and irresistible to him.

I push the palms of my hands to his face and bring his kiss to my lips. I'm searching for comfort and he's the arms I need. I bleed and he tries to compress the wound. I crash, and he catches me, trying to hold the weight of the world on his shoulders.

"Jesus." He grunts. Sitting back on his knees, he brings my legs over his shoulders, his hands on my upper thighs driving me into each thrust.

I cry out in pleasure, pleasure only he gives me.

Asa's body slumps forward. My legs part and his forehead rests against mine, sweat-covered and panting, we make eye contact. "I never want to go three days without you again," he whispers. His thrusts come faster now and he's louder than before, panting and grunting with each movement, his chest sliding against mine.

I can feel when he's close, but he stops for a moment, attempting to hold himself off but he can't. He comes, unable to stop, the sudden fullness inside me as he swells, twitching as he releases. But he doesn't pull out; instead, he mumbles against my lips, voice like gravel ripping my wounds open, "One more..." and goes for another.

I want that too. I want more I just don't know how to give it, so I wrap my legs around him, drawing him in deeper. He groans at the position as his lips finally find mine. "Does it hurt?" he asks, always concerned if he's hurting me. "I'll stop if it hurts."

I shake my head, my hands threading through his wet hair. "No. Don't stop. It's so good."

A shiver works its way through me when he gives me more of his weight, his hands moving to under my bottom, driving himself into me a little harder. "Still okay?" He breaths heavily against my lips, his voice trembling.

I nod. "Harder."

"What?"

"Do it harder," I beg.

His body goes rigid, every muscle tensing. His eyes lock on mine. "No," he says, sternly.

Tears flood my eyes. "Please? I know you want to." My words are broken and frantic. I don't want to lose the connection we have, but I need him to do this. If I was ever going to be okay, I had to have this. Or at least I thought that. If I had the good inside him, maybe the bad consuming my thoughts wouldn't be so hard.

He touches my face, his thumb brushing over my cheek and the permanent reminder I have from that night. "I can't hurt you. I won't."

"I'm not asking you to. I just want you... in that way. I want to see the man I know is in there. The one I know wants to *fuck me*." I used Roman's words. I've never said anything this crass to him before. Ever.

Shock hits his face, his brow furrowing, but his movements don't stop. He stalls, yeah, for a fraction of a second. I see the emotions working over his face. The confusion. The need. The love. All of it. He'd give anything to make me whole again. Even... this.

Giving me intoxicating kisses, he's searching for an answer, one I can't give. But then his movements change and become more forceful. His grip tightens and his mouth moves to my neck, his lips at my ear as he breathes. "I love you. Never forget that." And then he slams into me harder than before, my breath expelling in a gasp.

"I love you," I tell him.

A shudder runs through him, his movements quick, and harder than before and it's everything I need and want in this moment. I claw at Asa's shoulders, his back, anywhere I can get a grip on him and it only seems to drive him forward. It's almost too much and I sense the emotion working its way through me. It starts with the breathing, my heart thumping, the flashes in my head, but I can't make sense of any of them. It's just images, ones I've never seen before. Dark hair matted to a face I don't recognize. A purple Rams football hat. It's from North Thurston High School, where I graduated from.

I stare at the ceiling and squeeze my eyes shut. I don't want these memories. I shake my head and push against Asa's shoulders.

A moment later, a rumble leaves his heaving chest, and he throws his head back as his second orgasm rocks through him. I hold on, refusing to let my mind ruin this, but I'm counting the seconds before I know it's happening. Before it's too late and I burst into tears.

Asa must sense the change because he lifts up and pushes away from me. He's not looking at me. His hands move to his knees and he pants. His lashes flutter, a quick peek at me and then he pulls away completely.

And then it happens. I push away from him toward the wall and burst into tears. I curl into myself, holding my pillow. My chest feels like there's someone on top of me, but he's not. He's not even touching me.

Asa moves and swings his legs around the side of the bed, my shirt crumbled around his waist. *"Christ,* I knew we shouldn't have," he says through gritted teeth. His head twists and he looks out the corner of his eyes at my body. He's shaking with anger and annoyance. "We shouldn't even be having sex, Barrette. You and I both know it's not what you need."

"It's not you...." I shake my head, tears rolling down my cheeks. "It's me. It's *always* me." I want to tell him it's not all me. It's Roman. It's Eva. It's all the reminders that he deserves so much better and I can't give him that.

Asa turns his head and stares at me, tears in his eyes. His chin shakes when he breathes out the words, "We're destroying each other."

I nod, knowing it's the truth. It hurts. It burns. It festers inside us and we'd be stupid not to admit the truth. There's no way around it. I push, he gives in, and it's not what he needs. "You should let go."

Twisting toward me, his fingertips find my lips. "I can't," he whispers, his eyes heavy on mine. "I won't. Not ever."

He moves closer to hold me and I let him. We might be destroying each other, but the need to be with him is too consuming.

An hour later, when I watch him leave this time, my heart pounds furiously against my ribcage. He thinks I'm sleeping. Normally I can't bear to see him leave, but this time, I torture myself with seeing him disappear.

I get in the shower after he leaves, letting the warm water wash over my skin. I feel my ribs and the bones in my hip protrude. It's gross, but food doesn't hold any appeal to me anymore. I'm lucky if I can get in one meal a day.

I think back to an hour ago and the way those memories hit me while we were having sex. Somehow the nightmares I've been having turned into a flashback montage and fragments of a scene from that night.

How though? Why when I was having sex? I remember in my neuro class where the professor talked about traumatic events in your brain being encoded and you store significant details about them. Whether they get retrieved that's unknown. We sometimes chose to block them out until a memory triggers it and your brain uses its code to look it up, so to speak.

My brain looked up one detail I had never seen until now. My attacker, at least one of them, had been on the football team with North Thurston.

"WHAT'S THE NAME OF THIS CLASS AGAIN?" ROMAN ASKS, NUDGING my shoulder. "I've been looking for my book for a like a fucking week."

I snap out of my trance and realize I don't remember coming to class or sitting here. I don't remember getting the coffee in my hand or putting on the clothes I'm wearing. Time fades with each day and I simply, *don't* remember.

I point to the board where the name is written in black dry erase marker.

Roman laughs. "Oh... right."

I look down because I'm no better. Roman glances at my textbook for my photography class. "Clearly you didn't remember either."

"At least I brought a book. I can pretend I know what I'm doing." I turn in my chair so he can't see my book. "You're gonna look like you forgot."

He studies my face. He sees the dark circles and the weight loss. He sees the way I only ever wear hoodies or long sleeve shirts and jeans to hide how much my body isn't my own any longer.

"Are you okay?"

I roll my eyes and fight through the need to move away from him. "I'm fine."

He shifts in his chair and leans toward me, our shoulders touching as he slouches. "You don't look fine."

I'm not, but there's no way I'm telling Roman that. There are two girls in front of us who are giggling, and they have the laughter that makes me scream inside. High pitched and rich.

"Who is that?" I ask Roman, pointing to the one who keeps saying Asa loud enough for me to hear. I know who it is, but today, I'm not sure. She looks different from the last time I saw her. Lighter hair maybe. She freaking dyed it blonde like mine.

We may not make public appearances, but it's known around this school that Asa and I are together. Most girls know that he's taken, though he doesn't clarify what this is that we have. I don't think we need to. What business is it of theirs?

Roman looks confused for a half a second, like he can't remember and then says, "Eva?"

He's not positive either.

I'm not quiet when I speak, but I'm not exactly loud when I say, "If she doesn't shut up about Asa, I'm going to rip out her hair."

"Go ahead," Roman snorts, seeming bored as he twirls a pencil around in his hand. "It's fake."

Eva turns around, her red flush could have been endearing if she wasn't so fake. "I can hear you, *Barrette*."

I'm surprised she knows my name. "Well, good." I lean forward over the table so she can hear me a little better. "I wanted you to."

"Why are you such a bitch? You're just jealous that Asa confides in me?"

Confides in her? Doubtful. "Are you jealous that he fucks me and not you?" Oh my God, did I really just say that out loud? I want to slap my hand over my mouth. Who have I become?

Look at her. The wide eyes and the parted lips. I caught her off guard. "I'm surprised he does." She turns. "Do you even remember it? Or do you block it out in fear you'll have a breakdown."

There's a brief moment when I'm caught off guard by her words, unable to reply. It's not a secret around here that I was raped. I wish it was, but word gets out. And I'm sure someone has been there to witness the bad days when I hide under a hoodie with dark circles under sleepy eyes. With her words, I want to break down and cry. I could. I might, but I won't let her have that kind of satisfaction over me. Not this girl. She doesn't deserve it.

"Fuck *you*," I snap, the anger rising inside me to the point I'm shaking.

I will not cry.

I will not cry over *her*.

I will not cry over *this*.

I leave. I don't go to any of my classes the rest of the day, but I don't cry. Not this time.

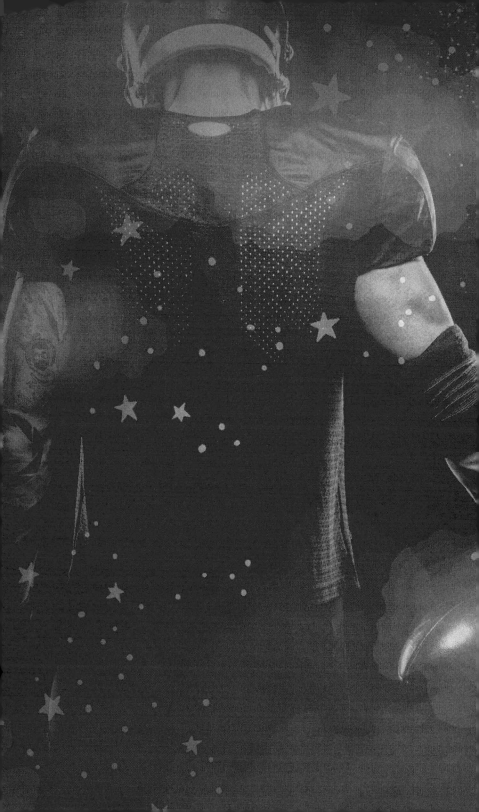

CHAPTER 16

My defensive line

ASA

Do you know the definition of insanity?

It's doing the same thing over and over again and expecting a different result.

I guess if you look at it that way, I would be considered insane.

My head pounds as I stare up at the stadium lights and chew on the corner of my mouthpiece. I contemplate and go over what she said the other night even when I should be concentrating on the game. *You should let go.*

Doesn't she know I can't? Ever. It's not an option for me.

Terrell bumps me. "All or nothing, A. Bring it."

I nod, knowing that's his nudge to get me out of my own head and in the game.

Go hard. You never know which play will be your last.

There's something about the crowd here at Husky Stadium. It's loud to the point you can't even hear at times. It makes it hard to call plays on the line, but the fact that these fans showed up here is all that matters to me. We open our scoring in the game against Stanford when I find an opening through to the end zone and run the ball for a 57-yard touchdown. It kicks the game off and leaves us all hungry for more.

All game long, number forty-eight on the defense keeps cheap shotting Roman, and I'm sick of it. Roman might be an asshole, but he's on our team, and being the captain of the team, I stand up for our players. It's loyalty and something a lot of young player's lack. Something Roman lacks most days too, but it's part of who I am, and no one is going to change that.

We fight for every yard and score again right before the half. I walk over to number forty-eight and lay my helmet into his. "Next time you take a bullshit shot on my team"—I fist his jersey in my hands—"I'll lay your motherfucking ass out *myself*."

"Screw you, asshole." He shoves me back. Terrell's there as well as Roman to catch me.

Terrell smiles, winking at me. "Pick on players your own size, A."

I shove him off me as we head into the locker room. I'm called on taunting and a penalty, but it doesn't matter. It was worth it. Nothing gets me more fired up than guys never getting called on penalties when it was clear he has clotheslined Roman more than once after a play.

Inside the locker room, Coach is going over the first half when Roman looks up at me and nods. It's his thank you.

I do the same.

In the locker room, Codey stands beside me.

I glance in the mirror, the man staring back at me isn't someone I know.

"Who fucked you up?" Codey asks, amused with himself.

I turn my head toward him, raising an eyebrow. As I grind my jaw, I can barely keep myself from knocking his fucking teeth. I don't know why, but when I look at him, I see the face of her attackers and it makes me sick. Probably because he seems like the kind of sick bastard who is capable of that type of disregard for another person.

Codey finally gets the message I'm not going to answer him and turns around and looks back at his locker.

I throw my pads around and reach for my Gatorade. After finishing the last of it, I toss the container in the garbage and sit down on the bench, staring at my hands with my elbows resting on my knees. Roman stops before me. I see the question dancing in his eyes. He wants to ask me something, but he doesn't have the fucking balls to do it.

Instead, he walks away.

I FINISH GETTING MY UNIFORM BACK ON AND HEAD INTO THE DARK tunnel with the music blaring around us for the second half. I slap my hand against the Win The Day sign as we exit the tunnel, and I'm greeted by nearly seventy-thousand screaming fans awaiting the toughest match-up they'll see all season long. Finally, my mind fades a little. The one place I can get her out of my mind even if it is just for one play at a time is on the field.

The game is too fucking close, and it isn't until almost halfway through the second half when we finally get our heads out of our asses. Our turnovers are ridiculous, so I make the call to run the ball. I get 21 yards and the safety comes up on me, hesitating, knowing who I am and then goes for my feet. He makes a good solid tackle, and I can't fault him for that.

Fourth quarter with two minutes left on the clock, Roman is held up off the line of scrimmage, so I lob it in the air where I think he'll be. He catches it in his lap for the touchdown. He stands and tosses the ball to the ref, no reaction at all as the guys pat his back.

With twenty-nine seconds to play, we make one final drive with a final 12-yard pass to Roman in the end zone to win 36-35.

It was a bad throw and Roman deserves credit for that one. Even I have to admit that. If it had been any other player on the team, I doubt they would have snagged it. He scores every touchdown that game for us other than the one I ran in. Best performance I've seen out of him all year. After the game, the team and fans rush the field.

I walk off.

Everyone is celebrating as we change, as they should be. Standing at my locker, I want to be happy. I *should* be. That win got us a possible chance at the bowl game.

Only I'm not happy. I'm anything but that. I text Barrette and make sure she's doing all right tonight. I wonder if she watched the game, and then my thoughts shift back to the other night with her and the breakdown.

The guys are talking about the game, living it up on the high on the win, and I'm annoyed. At everything. Not only at the game but how everything around me seems to be spiraling out of control. We won, but there was a point when I didn't think we would, and my mind isn't in this room. It's with the one I can't seem to shake.

Beside me, Roman's mood shifts the moment the NCAA enters the locker room.

He must sense my stare on him because he looks over at me but doesn't smile. "Good game. Best throw you made all year."

What the fuck is that supposed to mean?

"Winslow? You're up," a rep from the NCAA says, looking at Roman.

I smile because I know where this is going. They test all of us after the last game and after a bowl game as well. Random testing can happen at any time through the season. Roman knew that heading into the game. It isn't like this shit is a surprise. "Looks like you won't be playing."

Roman glares, his eyes on the cup. "She's fucked up, you know. And you're not doing anything to help her."

I rip gear away, slamming shit in my locker. We just won. I *should* be happy. I keep telling myself that. Over and over again. I *should* be fucking stoked, but I'm *none* of that right now. I'm fucking *none* of that when he mentions her. "Barrette is none of your business." I'm not in the mood for this shit. I put my pads in my locker and hang up my knee pads on the cooler and push the shelve up out of my way before I knock my head on it like I do every other time when I reach for my shoes.

"You're fucking her, aren't you?" Roman laughs.

I drop my shoes on the floor and turn around to face him. "Listen to me, motherfucker!" I slam him up against the wall. "Barrette is none of your fucking business. Keep your fucking mouth shut!"

"She is my business. I was her friend when you weren't. Just because you were there that night, doesn't mean you're good for her. You were just in the right place at the right time to pick up the pieces."

Pick up the pieces? I hang on those words. You mean save her life? I can't take it. It feels like my chest just broke wide open. I pummel his ass right then and there with as much force as I can muster. Our bodies slam against the lockers. Guys start breaking us apart and I'm so pissed that I can't even think straight. I want to kill him for saying that. I don't like the implication. The meaning. The tone... none of it.

"It's not even about you just being an all-around dick anymore," I say, watching his reaction to my every word. "It's about you having a *fucking* drug problem and acting like nothing can touch you. You're cocky and you have no right to be." I shove him back into Coach Benning. "You and I both know you're going to fail that drug test and you not only let me down, you're let the whole fucking team down, you piece of shit!"

"That's enough!" Coach shouts, standing in between us.

"Oh yeah? You're so fucking perfect, Asa? You don't think you let her down?" Roman smiles vindictively. "Not even a little bit?"

Of course he brings her back into it. I lean into Coach and glare. I don't even see him. I look straight through him to Roman. "You sure you want to do this right now, Roman?" I ask, despite us being pulled apart by teammates. "You sure you want to have this conversation, here, right now?"

"Yes."

And I can't believe it. He laughs like I'm joking with him, but I'm not and he knows that too. He knows I'm about to say shit to him he's not going to want to hear. It's like he's playing chicken with me, so I'll be the first to say it.

Fuck that. I won't. I push past Coach and I shove Roman roughly against the wall.

His arms catch himself against the lockers, metal rattling as he eyes me carefully. Coach Benning breaks it up quickly and threatens suspension, so I walk away. I walk away because I know myself and given the chance, I can destroy my future with one punch.

BACK IN MY DORM, I FIND THE BOTTLE OF RED LABEL I KNOW Terrell keeps under his bed for special occasions. It's a special occasion. It's a "fuck you" day.

I drink the entire bottle, or what's left of it, knowing damn well I shouldn't. I put my phone on vibrate because I know seeing Barrette in this condition will only lead to trouble. At some point, I pass out.

I sleep all of Sunday. I don't remember anything from that day other than my face against the bathroom floor a few times.

When I wake up Monday morning, Terrell is hovering over me shaking his head. "Dude...." He kicks me in the stomach. Not hard, but enough that I'm sitting up. "You puked on my bed last night."

I steady myself against the wall when I sit up, my hands in my hair as I try to regain some sort of composure. "Sorry, man."

Terrell looks at my face. I bet I don't look like a star football player or someone who maintains a solid GPA all year long. I look like a goddamn train wreck. He glances at me, sighs, and then walks out the door. After the other night, I can honestly say I gotta give props to Terrell for still talking to me. I remember bits and pieces of it, and I did puke on his bed. While he was in it.

What the fuck is wrong with me? What am I doing to myself?

I'm running late to class this morning and word on campus is my fight with Roman in the locker room. I should have known it would be all over the place. No punches were even thrown, but that's college for you. Everyone talks.

I sit in class, unfortunately next to Eva, who finds me and slides into the seat next to me. I'm drinking coffee and chasing that with water, Gatorade, and painkillers, trying to rid the pounding in my head.

"Rough night?" Eva asks, smiling at me.

I grunt and slouch in my chair, flipping my phone around in my hand. I haven't talked to Barrette since before the game on Saturday, and I'm getting anxious. I almost didn't even come to class, but I needed to hand in my paper.

Eva touches my hand. "I could make it better for you."

"Doubt that," I mumble, shifting away from her and scanning the room for any other open seat. There are none.

"Does she make it better?"

I look at Eva out of the corner of my eyes. "What?" My words are pushed out in annoyance that she keeps trying to get with me. Why is she so into me? Sure, I can play football, but when have I ever given any of these cheerleaders an indication I'm into any of them? I haven't. I'm nice, but apparently, maybe I need to cool it with the niceness too.

She tucks a strand of her newly blonde hair behind her ear. I fight off an eye roll that she dyed her damn hair a lighter color. "Barrette... she's your girlfriend, am I right?"

"Yeah, she is." I've never said it out loud, but even though we haven't put a label on it, Barrette is so much more than a girlfriend. There isn't even a word for what she means to me. I gesture between us. "You and I are never happening. I don't mean to sound like a dick, but you're not getting the hints. We're never gonna happen."

At first, I don't look at her. And then she laughs and I glance over. She covers her mouth. "Sorry, I just... no one has ever turned me down over someone like Barrette Blake. I honestly thought she was seeing Roman. They seemed pretty cozy in class the other day."

Someone like Barrette Blake? Like she's suddenly not good enough? And Roman? Fucking Roman? I knew they talked and had a couple classes but *together*? I don't fucking think so. And that's where I've had enough. "Why don't you just mind your own business and stick to what you're good at, cheerleading and fucking anybody but me."

I'm about to walk out of class but noise beside me draws my attention. It's Terrell. He frowns, annoyed with me, probably for puking on his bed, and then leans forward eyeing Eva. She looks like she's about to cry and I don't even feel bad about it. I played nice guy for too long. Done with it.

Terrell sits back, his eyes wide. "*Daaaamn,* Gina, why ya pissin' off the ladies?"

I roll my eyes. I don't say anything. I'm not sure I can.

Eva leaves, moving toward the rest of her friends in this class. Terrell nudges my shoulder and makes me spill my Gatorade down the front of my shirt. "Listen, A. You know you're buying me new *Star Wars* sheets, right?"

I brush the blue liquid from my shirt and glare at him. "Why you have *Star Wars* sheets should be the bigger question here."

He winks at me and pops the lid to his coffee to dump four sugars in it, then three creamers. "Because the force is with me, brother."

Once class starts, finally everyone stops talking to me. Outside the classroom, that's a different story. Coach texts and asks me to come early to the training center and ruins my plans of trying to catch Barrette before practice. I know what he wants to talk to me about. Roman. The fight. My attitude. Could be a number of things these days.

Inside his office, he stares at me with his thick, brooding eyebrows drawn together. "What's going on with you lately?"

I shrug, trying to play it off.

"No, that's not an answer. You're my starting quarterback, and if your head isn't in it, it shows on the field. Yeah, we won the last game but you and I both know we got lucky. We're sloppy. You're here to play football, Asa, not fight. You made an obligation and a commitment to this team. You understand me?"

I nod, avoiding eye contact. "Yes, sir."

He raises an eyebrow and leans forward, his elbows on his desk. "Do you? I thought you did. Shit, you're the most levelheaded player on this team, but lately, lately something's up. You need to be able to put your personal life aside if you're wanting to make a career of this."

He's right, I do, but then again, I can't. I can't put her aside.

I leave his office, head to the weights room, and it's more of the same shit as before. Roman smarting off like a tool, Codey following in his footsteps and me, trying like hell to ignore their shit. I honestly feel myself slipping. There's only so long a man can be expected to sit back and take shit day after day.

Roman, Codey, they fuck with me because they can. They know I can only do so much before I risk being suspended or worse yet, kicked off the team and ruining any chance I have of playing in the NFL. So they take their jabs and talk their crap and I've got to try and ignore it like the good little football soldier I'm expected to be. It's too much. And to tell the truth, I don't know how much longer I can take it.

My life feels like it's not even mine. My body belongs to football, my mind belongs to classes, and my heart, my soul, my very being belongs to Barrette. I have no control and it feels like every day I'm losing a little bit more of myself.

Terrell spots me while I lift and notices my mood. "C'mon, boy. Get your head in it."

He means into lifting, but I think he's probably implying so much more.

Beside us, Roman and Codey are ragging on Dem and a couple others from the defensive line. And then their conversation shifts to the cheerleaders. I ignore it for the most part, but it's fucking ridiculous the shit they talk about them. I'm the first to admit a lot of them are easy and spread their legs faster than we can blink, but they're not all like that. Some are respectable and here to learn, not fuck. You wouldn't think it by the way these fools talk though. What really fucks with my head is when they start throwing Barrette's name in the mix.

I glance over at them. Roman smirks. Codey winks.

Terrell focuses in on me lying on the bench, my arms extended on the bar. "Ignore 'em. Give me five more."

I nod and push through my frustrations.

"That's it, bud. Get it!"

I push myself because giving up isn't what I'm good at. I'm good at pushing through it. I know sacrifice and selflessness more than most. Maybe too much.

CHAPTER 17

A mood I can't shake

Cool air whips around my face, shocking, freezing. I curl into myself, wishing I'd brought a warmer jacket. I hate the cold, but I also relate to it. I crave overcast days, rain, and the stormy weather fall brings with it.

Breathing in deeply, it's shocking, the way it hits my lungs and leaves me searching for another. I stare at my shoes as I walk, wishing my mind would stop creating situations and thoughts I don't understand. I hate being in these moods where nothing's wrong, but nothing's right. I wish... I wish I could wake up in the morning and delete all the bad thoughts and be happy. It doesn't work that way. My heart wrenches in pain, lingering in despair and melancholy, only nothing makes that feeling go away. Usually I can get it to ease. Find a way to pull myself from it.

Not anymore. Not lately.

Joey walks me home from our support group Tuesday evening. She makes me laugh and though it's nice to have a distraction, I still can't stop thinking about the other night with Roman and studying, and I have yet to see Asa. He texted me last night and said he couldn't come by my dorm because he was exhausted, and I keep thinking since my breakdown, our relationship—whatever it is— might be breaking apart.

"So I went on a date and you're never going to guess with who," Joey says, her cheeks pink. Never would I think Joey's cheeks would turn pink. She's so strong and independent, and I wish in so many ways I had that.

I look ahead of us noticing the diamond-like sheen to the path. It's frosty out. "If you tell me it's Roman, we're not friends anymore."

She makes a face. A disgusted one. "What's his deal?"

"*His* deal? He's... Roman." I scuff my feet against the concrete as we walk to see if it's icy out. "He used to date Cadence, but not anymore."

"Your roommate?"

"Yeah."

"Oh." She flips her hand around. "It's not Roman."

I smile. "Thank God." And then she doesn't say anything, like I'm supposed to guess. "You know I'm never going to guess. I'm so stuck in my own head I barely know what day it is."

Joey laughs. "Well, it's not Roman... and it's not Asa."

I snort. "He can barely handle me," I mumble.

"He can, and he does, girl. Don't do that. We've talked about this."

"I know, it's just—" And then I stop myself because this conversation didn't start about me, and it doesn't need to continue that way. "Who is it? I'm dying to know."

Joey giggles and watches two guys pass by us on the sidewalk. They stare at me, one winks. I look at the ground and pull my hood up. "T-Bone."

My eyes widen and I shout, "Terrell? You went on a freaking date with Terrell Wilson?"

Playfully and barely able to contain her laughter, Joey slaps her hand over my mouth. "Not everyone on campus needs to know that, Barrette."

It takes me a minute, but when I catch my breath, I'm finally able to formulate a response. "When? Does Asa know?"

"I don't know if he knows, but yesterday after practice, he took me to get burgers. He paid, so I think it's a date." She shrugs, and for a half a second, I think about Asa saying he was too tired to hang out with me last night. "But I don't know, it's been a while. Is that not considered a date?"

"You're asking the wrong girl. I'm having sex with my best friend and I barely talk to him. Pretty sure that's not dating." And then I watch the nervousness on her face, and for the first time, I realize she's not as confident as I thought she was. She's scared that it's undefined and also, if I had to guess, uncomfortable with dating given what happened to her. "How did it come about? I didn't even know you guys knew each other."

"We take global health together and he asked if I wanted to get burgers with him. I said yes."

I can't help the smile on my face because she looks so damn happy. "Was he nice? I don't know much about him other than him being Asa's roommate."

Joey looks over at me, blinking slowly, and I know the pink in her face isn't from the cold. "He was so sweet. But he's only ever been sweet to me. He told me about his mom and how she's single and lives in Louisiana. I guess he almost didn't come to UW because he didn't want to leave her, but he was offered a full-ride so...."

"I wish I was good at something," I tease. "I need a full ride."

"I hear ya, sister. My parents can barely offer anything, and I'm going to be in debt the rest of my life over trying to get an education."

"My parents paid for most of mine, but I think it was to get me out of their hair."

Joey looks over at me. "Still don't hear from them much?"

"Nope. Last time I talked to my mom was in August. They were in Japan on some kind of mission. Next thing you know they're going to be bringing home a little adorable Japanese baby to replace the damaged one."

"She still avoids talking about it with you?"

I nod. My parents didn't take the rape well. I knew they wouldn't, but my mom looked at me like I was damaged goods and my dad, I can't even tell you the look of disappointment he had when he said, "I can't believe you put yourself in that position."

I know what you're thinking. What the fuck, right? Pretty much my thoughts too.

I've never liked my parents. I pray someday I find out I'm adopted, and my parents are cool people, like Will Smith and Jada Pinkett Smith. I think they'd be great parents for me. I read somewhere that babies choose their parents. I think I must have been confused the day I picked mine. Needless to say, it's the topic of conversation with me and my therapist, and if I even mention it around Asa, he goes crazy with rage. For a month following the rape, I stayed with Asa instead of my house. I have a better relationship with his stepmom than I do my own.

We're almost at our dorm. Joey's going into detail about the date and that Terrell kissed her on the cheek. "On. The. Cheek. Like a perfect gentleman," she gushes. "Who knew he could be so sweet."

We laugh and swoon over it because looking at Terrell, you would never ever think he was capable of being sweet. He's a 6'5" football player who pounds guys into the turf protecting Asa. And then I notice Asa is outside, sitting on a concrete bench. He doesn't notice us yet, his attention on his phone.

"Look who's there," Joey whispers, smiling at me.

My heart drops and then pulses in my chest. I gasp at the cold, or maybe the idea of seeing him. Look at him. He's beautiful wearing jeans and a purple and gold Husky hoodie. His cheeks are flushed, nose pink, eyes bright. He's just come from practice and I want to run to him and wrap my arms around his neck. I want to kiss him and publicly display the love I have for him.

A group of girls approach Asa, their laughter barely contained when he stands and takes a picture with them. They cling to him, grabbing at his hoodie and desperately seeking a connection he's incapable of. Much like myself, Asa would rather go unnoticed than revered. He hates the prying eyes watching his every move, but it comes with having the abilities he has.

He smiles, makes small talk with them and then they leave, huddled up in a group, whispering and wishing they had him. I'm jealous of the small glimpse they get of him smiling. I want those smiles for myself. As selfish as that sounds, it's true.

He looks up, scanning the courtyard and then they land on me. I'm given a different smile than they received, and if I look closer, I can see his breathing change. He swallows, his brow pinches together, an emotion passing over his features and then he fidgets, shoving his hands in his pockets. I haven't seen him in three days, and I think it's done a number on both of us. Our last conversation didn't go very well, and I'm curious to see what happens now. Will he tell me it's over?

I wasn't expecting him, but my heart thuds louder knowing he's here, for me. "Hey," I say, approaching him.

"Hey." He exhales, slowly and reaching for my hand. Our fingers brush, a jolt coursing through me. "Sorry I haven't been around."

"You're busy," I add. "You don't need to explain." Over his shoulders, I notice those same girls who were taking pictures with him watching us.

Reaching inside his hoodie, he pulls out a bag of Sour Patch Kids and holds them out. "I brought you a treat."

I rip the package from his hand. "You know the way to my heart." I hold them to my chest, but my eyes drift over his shoulder again.

He turns, glances at them and then turns back to me. Wrapping his arm around me, he buries his face in my neck, breathing in. His cold nose hits my already chilled skin, and I shy away from the cold but laugh. "I missed you," he whispers with a rough edge, his words rocking through me when his hand around me tightens. I can't explain it, but a rush hits me. An emotion only he gives and I crave.

Joey walks ahead of us by a step, laughing. "Night, B. See ya tomorrow."

"What about me?" Asa teases, smiling at her.

She turns and winks at him. "Bye, Asa."

His gaze moves to mine, a boyish smirk plastered on his face. "She likes me."

I roll my eyes. "*Everyone* does."

At my dorm, I unlock the door. The moment we're inside, I turn to face him, thinking maybe I might share my candy, but his arms wrap around my waist, his mouth seeking mine. With his foot, he kicks my door shut behind us and never breaks the kiss. His breathing catches, his lips on mine.

Okay, no candy. Only kisses. I can work with that for sure.

I sigh into his mouth, the taste of him so much better than sweet and sour. His tongue slips in my mouth, his head twisting and deepening the kiss. I reach up on my tippy toes trying to match his six-foot frame but fail miserably.

His hands slip from my waist, down the swell of my bottom and then the backs of my thighs. Before I know it, he hauls me up flush against his body. Instinctively, I wrap my legs around his waist, melting into him.

Asa moves to my bed where we fall together, him on top of me. His heat warms me, our breathing heavy, his kisses heavier. It's hot, hard, and years of want poured into each one.

With a groan, he pushes his hips into mine, needing friction. His mouth is everywhere and so are his hands. With a grunt, he pushes my hoodie up, his warm hands finding the bare skin of my stomach. Without breaking his kiss, he lifts slightly, holding himself up by his elbow. Traveling his hand lower, he reaches inside the front of my jeans. His mouth pulls away, panting against my lips when he finds the wetness. My eyes close, squirming at his touch. It feels so good.

His fingers work faster, and I grip his wrist, my body arching at the amazing friction he's creating. Every moan I give, he groans or grunts, letting me know he's getting just as much out of it.

My back arches off the bed and takes everything he's giving me as my orgasm rushes through me. He kisses me, swallowing my whimpers and pleas for him to never, ever, ever stop.

"I won't," he growls against my lips, kissing me so possessively and desperately it makes me feel whole.

His mouth is still on mine, and we're both breathing ridiculously hard now. He's practically busting through his jeans. Moving his hand to the mattress, he pushes his hips into mine, the roughness of our jeans sending a shiver through me when his hardness meets my sensitive center.

I sigh in his ear, kissing the spot below his ear. "You're so good at this."

He chuckles, the sound breathless, his mouth finding the hollow spot above my collarbone. Before I know it, he's pulling his sweatshirt and the T-shirt beneath it off. Roughly, he works my hoodie off as well. Drawing back, he gets his jeans down past his hips and then begins working on mine. I help him out and shimmy them off and toss them on the floor beside my bed with my panties.

There's no "do you want to" or hesitation. I reach for his shoulders, needing his heat back. Asa reaches between us and eases himself inside me. "Oh, God." He groans, his breath hot and heavy, crashing against my lips.

He holds still. He gives me a minute to adjust, his eyes on mine. I squeeze mine shut. He fills me completely, stealing my breath with each thrust. If only he could make me whole with this alone, but it's enough, for now, to have him like this.

Behind my closed lids, I push the flurry of feelings building and hold onto him anywhere I can.

"Look at me," he begs, and I didn't realize I broke eye contact with him.

I open my eyes, drinking in his body, the way his shoulder

muscles flex as he moves above me. I flatten my palms against his chest, sighing, my eyes fluttering closed again.

"I said look at me," he whispers, lowering his chest to mine. My hands fall away, and one of his moves to my cheek. "Don't be afraid."

"I'm not," I assure him. I try to tell myself I'm not, but he's Asa, and he can see through me even when I can't.

"I love you," he pants, and the way he says the words, they come out like an apology, an "I love you, so you have to be whole." An "I love you, so please, love me back."

And I do, so much, but I don't say it. Instead, emotion creeps in, and I wish I was different. I wish I could be anyone else but myself. I wish... for the giddiness those girls had for myself. Instead I have this, his body on mine, his heart begging for mine and I give it, but I'm not sure if it's enough.

His thrusts quicken, pushing into me two more times before he comes, his head buried into the pillow beside me, his grunt muffled by the fabric.

I cling to him, my body trembling, unwilling to let him go. He lets me, stays, covering my body with his. He breathes in, turns his head, and kisses my cheek, neck, collarbone... anywhere my skin is touching his. His kisses are tender and loving, everything I need, softly moving over my body that's broken.

I sigh. I breathe in and out, and for a moment, I'm at ease.

He pulls out and moves to the side, facing the wall. After a moment, he props himself up on his elbow and runs his fingers over my ribcage. I smile and watch his face, curling into him. He pulls his jeans up over his waist but doesn't button them. He leaves them open and it's sexy.

I smile again, because he's so damn adorable with his messy hair, flushed cheeks, and eyes full of excitement. Sex looks good on him.

With a sigh, Asa's eyes lift to my room. "Where'd you put the candy?"

I raise my head off the pillow. "I dropped it over there." I turn back to him. "I'll get it."

Prying myself from the bed, I reach for them on the floor and bend over in front of him giving him a clear view of my naked body. Turning, I toss them at him. He catches them midair and then groans, his head hitting the wall with a thump. "That wasn't fair."

"How so?"

He motions to the bulge barely concealed in his boxers. "I'm nineteen. Clearly I can go two or three times in a night."

I laugh at his expression. It's between need and annoyance. "Well, give me a minute and I'll be right back."

He winks. "Hurry."

I go to the bathroom, and when I return to the room, Asa's eyes are strangely focused on my desk next to my bed.

His eyes are colder. Something's up. He looks... mad. My heart thuds in my ears, the light next to my bed creating a disturbing shadow over his face.

Reaching for his jersey on the floor next to the bathroom door, I swallow over the dryness in my throat. "What's wrong?" I slip the jersey over my shoulders, sensing the mood in the room has changed.

Asa sits up and runs his hands over his face. He looks... broken. His eyes shift to mine, and then my desk. I follow his stare. It's Roman's sweatshirt draped over my chair.

He thinks.... No, he couldn't think that, could he?

His jaw flexes, his lips pressing together and narrow on mine. "Whose is that?"

My words come out shaking. "Roman's." I don't lie to him. "We were studying the other night."

"He was here *alone* with you?" There's a sharpness to his words I don't understand.

"Yes."

He nods slowly and then I notice he's breathing heavily. "I don't want him here, ever again. You're not to be alone with him."

I'm caught off guard by his demand, and it is a demand. By the way each word is carefully intricate, it's definitely a demand. "Asa..." I sigh. "We were just studying."

He moves from my bed, standing before me, his body taut and on edge. I watch as he zips and buttons his jeans, the way his muscles flex, the way his stomach ripples. But then I think, crap, what a mood killer. There's a good part of me that realizes the reasons for Asa's annoyance with having another guy in my room, alone, but the other part wonders why. I've been friends with Roman just as long as Asa. Clearly he wouldn't do anything to hurt me. Finally, he confirms my thoughts and growls, "I do *not* trust him."

I look at the sweatshirt, and then Asa. "So I can't have any other guy friends but you?"

He snorts, shaking his head, and a vindictive smirk pulls at his lips. I've never ever seen that look before. He reaches for his sweatshirt on my bed and holds it in his clenched fist. "I'd like to say no, you can't, but you and I both know you never listen to a goddamn word I say."

I blink, shocked, and nod. My throat tightens. My eyes water. It builds and builds, and I feel as though I'm suffocating. "Because I won't file a police report," I deduce.

He stares at me, our breathing harsh and uncontrolled. His eyes water, his jaw clenches, and his brows pinch. He's struggling and wanting to say so much more, but settles on, "Please, for me, fucking report it." He's begging. "Do it so we can have closure."

We've been over this for the last year and a half. He wants me to file the report. I want to forget it even happened. "For you, or me?"

"Us," he snaps. "*Us.* I was there, Barrette. Yeah, I didn't experience what you went through, but I've been there every step of the way for you, and you can't say that I wasn't. I saw firsthand what they did to you. Wouldn't you want them to pay for what they did?"

I can't stop from crying now and whisper, "If you want to break this off so you can see other girls, you can. I won't be mad." It's not what he was implying, but I don't know what else to say.

"Goddamn it. That's not at all what I'm saying. I don't want anyone but you."

I'm not hearing anything he says. In my head, I'm on the after and trying to push away the pain. "If I'm too much for you, here's your out."

"I can't," he says, reaching for me. His head dips, catching my eyes. "I can't leave you alone. It's impossible for me. I love you and I'm here. Like it or not, I'm fuckin' here."

My tears wet my face and I think I'm shaking, but I don't know. I don't know anything anymore other than this room feels a thousand times smaller than it did ten minutes ago. I try to pull away, but he doesn't let me. "You can let go, Asa. And you should."

He holds me against his chest securely and I can feel the tension rolling off him. "It doesn't work that way. I love you. Don't you see that? I can't just walk away."

The truth is, he's dying too, and I feel it. It's radiating from him. I've shattered the innocence in his heart. It's in his violent posture when I see him and the way his hands shake when he reaches for me. "You can, and I won't hold it against you."

And then he gives me his truth, for once. "I wish... that I could."

I pull back, afraid of what I'm going to say next, but I say the words I've been thinking for seventeen months. His eyes are on mine, a storm of emotions on his face, but anger the most prominent. "I wish you would have left me to die."

His eyes narrow, his breaths coming hard and fast. He drops his hold, his eyes roaming over my face. His hand rises to my cheek, his thumb brushing over the scar. His hands are protective and good, and everything he is inside, and I hate that it's not enough. His eyes are frantic, and I know I've scared him. For several seconds he waits before speaking. "And I would have died, too." He closes his eyes and exhales a shaky breath.

He's hurting, too, and I don't know what to do about it. I don't know how to make it better because the one thing he wants from me —I can't give him.

"Barrette," he says in a pained whisper. "Damn it."

I squeeze my eyes shut and pull away. "I can't give you closure, Asa."

He exhales slowly, his voice is pleading when he whispers, "I know."

Reaching for Roman's sweatshirt, he kisses me once and then he leaves, the door closing softly behind him. Tears of shame hit me. Why can't I just be better for him... for me?

Part Three

CHAPTER 18

A devastating discovery

ASA

I beat my hand against Roman's dorm room door. I tell myself, don't kill him. Your chance at going pro is over if you do, but it's tempting. It's so fucking tempting I imagine it in my head. It sits there and stirs. I find pleasure in it. Look, I'm mad. Not at her, okay, maybe a little, but Roman, I'm fucking furious with him.

He opens the door and immediately groans. "What?"

I slam his sweatshirt into his chest with my fist. "If I ever hear about you alone with her again, I'll break your fucking face."

His jaw snaps closed. "I'd like to see you try, *golden boy*." And then he smirks, a bitterness to the end of his words. "What, are you afraid she'll be on my dick soon? What makes you think she hasn't already?"

Don't react. Don't!

I know Barrette hasn't been with him. She wouldn't. That's not what I'm upset about. I'm mad he had the nerve to say something so derogatory about her knowing damn well what she went through. How could he? Why would he?

Because he's fucking Roman, and pussy is the only thing that matters to his pathetic ass.

Anger hits me so hard I can barely stand. His words, they're off. They hold meaning and power. They're vindictive and push venom into my veins. It courses through me, stirs to life and takes every single ounce of self-control I have not to snap his neck. I doubt I could, snapping someone's neck certainly doesn't sound easy, but God, I want to. I shove him back against his door, my fists gathering up the front of his shirt. "What the fuck are you talking about?"

He laughs again, and Codey surfaces from the room, a beer in his hand, along with two more of our running backs on the team. They try to break it up, as does campus security who suddenly surfaces out of nowhere.

They pull me away from him, threaten to call the coach, but I raise my hands and back up, shaking with pent-up frustration. Behind them in their room, I notice a girl on the floor, naked, sleeping. Something about the way there are four men in that room, alone with her bothers me. I look at security, and then Roman. I eye the security guard holding me back and point inside the room. "Do your goddamn job and make sure she's actually coherent."

His eyes shift to the girl, then the guys. "Is she awake?"

Roman smirks. "She's sleepin', dude. Nothing's wrong with her."

"Yeah, right." And then I do something really idiotic. I send my fist through the wall outside their door and think, after the fact, what a horrible idea that was. I swing my dead eyes to the guard. "Do your fucking job!" I scream at them, basically losing my shit over the girl lying on the floor. "Go in there and make sure."

He does and kneels down after covering the girl up with a sheet on the floor. "Ms.? Wake up."

"She's fine," Roman repeats, following the officer. He reaches down and shakes her shoulder.

At first, she doesn't move, but I can tell she's breathing. It's instant when it happens, and just like I can't help the nightmares about that night, I can't help the memories that flood through me in flashes. Barrette. Her face. The black and blue. Me carrying her from the woods. It's all too much and I can't take it. I shake. I scream at them to do something. I lose my shit over a girl I've never met before because I can't get out of my own head long enough to know this girl, she's not Barrette.

After five minutes, the girl wakes up, smiling. I don't know whether I'm relieved or disgusted. She sees me by the door, swaying and slurring her words as she asks, "Holy moly guacamole. Did I fuck Asa Lawson?"

Jesus Christ. Bile rises in my throat. "No," I snap, backing away from her. Besides the sheet on her now and campus security flanking her sides, she's still completely naked and no way I want her near me.

Roman and Codey laugh. "He wishes," I hear Codey mumble.

I don't even look at them, or her. Fuck this shit.

I hold my throbbing hand and walk away.

I fight the urge to return to Barrette's dorm. I want to see her. No, I think I need to see her, and for that reason, I shut my phone off so I don't text her. I can't always be the one who saves her. At some point, she has to want to save herself, and I need to let her.

And she can't give me closure like she said.

I CAN'T GIVE YOU CLOSURE.

Those words stick with me. I can't shake them just like I can't shake the idea that for a week, I haven't seen Barrette. I don't have time between studying for finals, practice, game reviews, and my hand is a problem, but I text her every single day so she knows I'm thinking of her. Wednesday, Coach Benning pulls me aside in the weight room. He's worried about my hand.

"What'd you do?"

I shrug. "It's fine."

"I didn't ask that."

"I know." I chew on my lip and contemplate a lie, but resist. "I punched a wall."

"And our upcoming bowl game never crossed your mind in the process?"

He's not mad, but he's not happy with me either. Two weeks ago, I told him I wouldn't make mistakes like this, and now here I am trying to deny it. I make eye contact and push myself away from the treadmill I had been on. I reach for my towel and scrub it over my face. He's still waiting on an answer. "No, sir, it really didn't at the time."

He nods, unpleased. "I get that you boys have lives and girlfriends and all that, but the next time you get wrapped up in it, remember that you came to this school to play football and get an education. There's plenty of time for all that other crap later."

All that other crap? Like saving your girlfriend from going down a really dark path? He has no idea what goes on in my personal life and I get it; it's not his job. His job is to make sure his starting quarterback doesn't break his throwing hand a week before their biggest matchup of the year.

"I hear ya," I say, walking past him. Usually I wouldn't be so abrupt with him, but I'm just not in the mood.

I decide to call Barrette when I'm leaving the gym.

She answers eventually, sighing. "Hey." I wait and try to make sense of her words, the mood she's in. Her voice is lighter. "How was practice?"

I walk slower, my phone pressed to my ear. "Rough. I'm dragging ass this week." A group of girls walk toward me, all of them staring at me and waiting. I smile at them, and when they try to stop me, I shrug, point to my phone and continue walking. I hate being rude, but this girl on the phone, she deserves my attention for at least a few minutes. I feel bad that I can't spend more time with her when she's all I think about.

Another sigh and I can hear her moving around her room. "I bet. I can barely make it to class and back without being tired." She laughs, the sound sparking my own. "But today was okay."

I swallow over the lump forming in my throat when I think about our last conversation. "I...." I breathe out slowly and stop walking. I look up at the sky, wishing the hazy black sky held answers. "I'm sorry about the other night."

"Don't be."

"No, I should be. It was wrong of me to assume. I just don't want you around Roman."

"I know, and I won't. I get why you were mad. I do. He's not... he's Roman, and you're right, I shouldn't trust him as much as I do."

Something in her tone, or maybe just the words she uses that sends a shot of adrenaline through me. I wonder if he said anything to her about the other night when I returned his shirt. But I don't get the chance to ask before she sighs into the phone again. "I get why it's hard, Asa," she says, her tone soft and gentle. "You're just looking out for me, and I'm just that girl... one mental break down from being Britany Spears in 2007 and shaving my head."

I laugh.

"What?"

"I'm trying to picture you with a shaved head." I let out a low whistle. "It's pretty hot."

"You're the worst." She laughs and I hear a zipper sound in the background.

"What are you doing?"

"Well, I'm sucking on those Sour Patch Kids you got me, and packing."

I stop walking. "Are you going home for Thanksgiving?" I'd been nervous to hear what her plans were.

"No, I'm going to Bellingham with Joey. I guess her mom makes a mean smoked turkey. She's picking me up in a few minutes."

"That sounds like fun." I sigh in relief. That makes me feel so much better. She hasn't been home to Boston Harbor since she left last August, and I don't think she ever plans to return. I can't say I blame her on that one. I certainly didn't want her on campus without me here, and then part of me wishes she would come with me to my dad's.

Barrette's gentle breathing brings me back to the moment when she asks, "You could come with us."

"I'd love to, I really would, but I promised my dad I'd come home this year." I hate that I made that stupid promise. What the fuck was I thinking? Dinner with him, or dinner and possibly sex with Barrette someplace other than her fucking dorm room. I'm definitely not just thinking about sex. I'm not, but... it's unfortunately at the forefront of my mind a lot of the times. It's irritating.

I'm at my dorm room when she makes a humph sound. "That sucks."

"Yeah, it does."

"Can I see you when you get back?"

I smile and breathe in. At least she doesn't hate me after my temper tantrum the other night. "I'd like that."

"It's a date then...." And then she gasps. "Well, I just mean, a date as in a plan. Not like a boyfriend-slash-girlfriend way."

I laugh again and flop down on my bed. "Barrette?"

"Yeah."

"It's okay to call me your boyfriend." I wish we were saying this in person, but I guess I might as well just say it now.

"I didn't, I mean...." Her words trail off in a jumbled mess before she growls.

"What's wrong?"

She doesn't answer for a moment, and I can just imagine her chewing on her lip and worrying about what to say next. "You make me crazy."

I pinch my eyebrows together and sit up. "Uh, okay. What's that mean?"

"I just mean you make my heart go crazy and I lose my words." She sniffs and I think she's crying. Panic hits my chest and I flip the phone over to FaceTime. She growls again but accepts it. "Damn you!"

"Sorry, but I had to see your face for this next part."

Barrette scrunches her nose up and rolls her eyes like she knows what's coming, but asks, "What part?" anyway.

"The part where I tell you that you're more than a girlfriend and you know that. You're, in the cheesiest way I can explain it, everything to me."

And she's crying, her attention on her door when there's a knock at it. "I have to go. Joey's here."

"Barrette?" I ask again, grinning.

She looks down at the phone and tucks her hair behind her ears. "What?"

"I love you."

She wipes tears from her eyes. "I love you."

Opening the door, I hear her invite Joey in. I'm quick and strip my shirt off. "Barrette?"

"Jesus." She looks down at the phone. "What now?"

I smile and tilt the phone lower so she can see my chest and stomach. "If you decide you need a break, call me tomorrow and we can you know, make use of FaceTime again."

"Oh, I...." She swallows visibly, her eyes on my chest, and her mouth opens in a tiny gasp.

Joey takes the phone. "So that's what Lawson looks like without a shirt." She hands the phone back to Barrette. "Does he have a twin brother?"

Barrette starts giggling. "No." And then she looks at me, narrowing her eyes and pointing her finger at the screen. "I have to go make Joey's parents love me and adopt me. Stop teasing me."

She finally hangs up on me because I won't stop talking and then I smile because fuck, it felt good to flirt with her. I can't remember the last time we had a conversation like that.

I THINK ABOUT DRIVING HOME THAT NIGHT, BUT IT'S LATE WHEN I get done with practice. The room is quiet, Terrell having flown home on a red-eye flight to see his mom in Baton Rouge for Thanksgiving. He'll spend most of his time on a plane, but he says it's worth it to spend time with his mom even if it's just for a meal.

I have to agree with him. I'd love to spend even just an hour with my mom. I think about flying back to Ohio soon, but I know given my extreme moodiness these days, it's probably not a great idea given how I left that state.

Speaking of my mood, as I'm sure you can guess, I don't talk to Roman. Hell, I don't even acknowledge him, on or off the field. I control the plays, and for him, that's bad news when he's looking for yards. Fuck that guy.

Early Thursday morning, I head home.

The moment I'm out of my car, my thoughts drift back, as if they never left, to Barrette. I think about calling her but decide against it.

I get back home in under two hours, which is pretty good considering the holiday traffic. I head up to my room and set my bag on my bed. It looks the same as it did when I left it in late July. I open my bag and pull out a couple hoodies and jeans. I throw my Husky hoodie on and then find my hat. As I stand there in my room and watch the sky turn lighter knowing the snow is on the way, I hear heavy breathing and the patter of little feet. It's my favorite little monster. I smile when I feel the tug on my jeans and reach down to pick her up.

I hold her close to my chest. "How's my girl doing?"

Livia smiles at me, reaching for my hat. She says something, but who knows what that might be. It's more of the toddler noise I can't understand just yet.

"How are you, pretty girl? Keeping out of trouble?"

I don't expect her to talk, but she starts saying something and acting like I should know. I hear a knock and Carlin appears at my door. She smiles, taking in the sight of us. "She misses you when you're gone."

I set Livia down on my bed and sit beside her. She goes through my entire bag digging out clothes and the football I have in there. With a smile, I watch her eyes light up as she rolls the ball around on the bed. "I thought she would forget me."

"She'll never forget you, Asa." Carlin sits down beside Livia and runs her hand through her blonde curls. "Every Saturday afternoon she's glued to our television with your dad."

I snort. "He watches my games?"

"He never misses one."

I don't know why, but it surprises me that my dad watches my games. He wanted me to play for Oregon or even Ohio State where he went. Never for the Huskies. Wasn't even on his radar. He didn't think I'd get the attention I needed to go pro playing for UW. It wasn't about going pro for me; it was about being with Barrette. I almost let the scholarship go after the accident, but I was committed at that point, and I never back out of a promise. I went because Barrette needed to get away from this town and I knew there I could protect her.

I think Carlin can see how tired I am and what the last month has done to me. "Are you okay? School and football getting to you?"

Looking down at Livia, she's handing me a hat, so I take off the one I have on and put the one she gives me on top of my head, all the while she's giggling like we are sharing a secret between just the two of us. She does this twice more before I answer Carlin; it's my way of stalling. I'm not okay.

"No... it's just been a rough month."

"I can tell. How's Barrette doing? I've been meaning to call her and check-in. I put together a care package for her. Just girly stuff to make her feel better. I'll give it to you before you leave."

I run my hand through my hair and exhale a heavy breath. "It's day by day with her. I just... I try to be there as much as I can for her, but sometimes, I don't think I'm enough."

"Unfortunately, Asa, it might always be that way for her for the rest of her life."

I nod, thankful she said that to me. From the day I held
Barrette in the shower, I knew her life, and mine would never be
the same. I understood that at any moment, even if she was
happy, darkness could creep back in and she'd be back to square
one. She couldn't, even when she tried, just snap out of it. I had
to give her time. Her time frame, not mine, and I needed to let
go of the fact that if she didn't want to report it, I couldn't
make her.

Carlin reaches for my hand. "You're exactly the kind of friend she
needs."

I've never given Carlin the credit she deserves. I'm curious to
know how she even puts up with my dad, but she's a good woman
and I know I've never given her a chance to be a mother to me,
though she's been a better parental figure than my dad has been over
the years.

I DON'T DO MUCH THANKSGIVING DAY, BUT I DO OFFER TO HEAD
into town to help Carlin pick up some last-minute things at the store.
Needing to clear my head, I look up the one grocery store in
Olympia that happens to be open. But I don't go there just yet. I
make a stop. The moment I round the inlet and set sight on the
towering pine trees, Barrette's words come to mind.

I can't give you closure.

I still can't shake it, and then I think, maybe, if I return to the
woods, maybe I might find closure there. When my mom died, I
went home to our house and lay in her garden. In the middle of the
backyard with bugs and birds attacking me, I'd lain down and looked
up at the sky. I'd felt at ease knowing she wasn't in any pain any
longer.

So I make the incredibly bad decision to head out to the water by

Roman's parents' house. Guess who came home for Thanksgiving? Yeah, that motherfucker.

Lucky for me, most of the woods on the inlet are public land so I won't get caught for trespassing. You know damn well he'd call the police on me at this point.

The walk through the woods is eerily familiar, only it's different. It's cold, wet, and muddy. Moss covers the tree trunks in every corner, and I think about turning back because I can barely breathe let alone not shake to death with how cold it is today. A layer of frost clings to the breaks in trees, giving the ones that have fallen to the ground a slippery grip.

I know the exact spot it happened. I'll never forget it. With a sigh, I lay down on the ground where I found her and think to myself, this a new level of fucked-up. What the fuck is wrong with me? "You've lost your mind," I tell myself, sitting up.

I feel something sharp under my hand and lift it immediately, looking down. Nothing cut me but when I look at the ground, that's when my heart stops beating. Hell, the entire fucking world stops in that moment. Nothing. No air. No sounds... it could have ended, and I wouldn't have known.

It's a hat. A familiar one. And though I know this could be just a coincidence, it's not. I rip it up out of the ground from under the leaves it'd been buried in. A purple North Thurston Rams hat.

Do you know where this is going? No? Pay close attention to this next part.

I don't want to be right. I don't, but something tells me my discovery is spot. Fucking. On.

With hatred in my steps, I make my way through the woods and to Roman's door. I pound my fist into the door. His dad answers, tries to make small talk and invite me in. Remy hugs me, as does his mom, but they can tell by the way I'm shaking, something's up.

"Where's Roman?" I bark, barely able to get the words out as I grip the hat in my hands. I take a breath and look down, noticing my clenched hand is trembling.

Roman walks into the room. He sees me, rolls his eyes, and then steps onto the front deck closing the door behind me. His body is tense, his face pale as he looks at the hat, then me. "You bring back my shirt, now my hat... what's next, my used condoms?"

"I want you to tell me why."

He groans and flops his head to the side. "What are you talking about?"

I toss his hat on the ground at his feet. *Calm down, fucker. Calm down before you lose it.* We're silent for a long moment. I step toward him, inches from his face. Silence falls between us. It's heavy and loud, or maybe it's just in my head. My body sizzles with adrenaline, my voice shaking when I say, "You have one option. You turn yourself in."

"Or what?" Roman asks, a bitter edge to his words, his face blank and masking his emotions. "A fucking hat doesn't prove shit, Asa." His eyes slide over my face contemplating his next move. "I live here, or did you forget? Just because you found my hat in the woods doesn't mean I had anything to do with it."

Did you catch the slip?

CHAPTER 19

Shock and awe

BARRETTE

Snow hits my face and makes me regret the words, *"Let's go to Bellingham."*

In the winter, it's so cold and usually covered under a thick layer of snow. I love snow, though. It's peaceful and everything I needed. "Your parents are the best!"

"They are." Joey smiles as her dad, who has two little boys attached to his legs and a squirt gun in his hand spraying down the basketball court so they can slide on the ice.

"Do they know?" I don't have to expand on my vagueness for her to understand. She knows.

"Yeah, they unfortunately had to take me in for a while when I went through my 'shock and awe' phase."

"The what?"

Joey adjusts her black scarf around her neck and shivers, wrapping her arms around her waist when the wind picks up. "You'd think with my layer of beauty I'd be warmer, but I'm not." And then she looks over at me, a sadness in her eyes. "I went through every motion you did. I was sixteen and didn't know any better. So afterward, I basically shut down for months. The only reason I'm not a crackhead or in a mental hospital is because of my parents."

"The only reason I'm not your roommate there is because of Asa." We laugh, even though it's not funny, but it is when you know what we've been through. I've never asked her this, and I can't help the way my voice shakes when I ask, "Did you get the test done?" She shakes her head. "I didn't know at the time that it was a possibility. It was a small hospital and I simply went in for a cut on my neck and left. It was days later when I finally told my parents. I didn't know the guy, and by the time I could do something about it, the test would have been inconclusive."

I nod.

"Barrette, you're never going to heal completely unless you step up and say to yourself, I'm ready to put this behind me."

"Do you think I should report it?"

"I think you should do what makes you comfortable."

I snort, blowing warm air into my hands. I breathe in, the smells of Thanksgiving all around me, and I'm really glad I'm here because at least this isn't a tofu turkey like my parents' cook. This turkey her parents are smoking is thirty pounds and all meat. I can't remember the last time I was this excited. "My parents made a tofu turkey once."

Joey stares at me like I just told her Santa Clause was fake. "You poor, deprived tiny person."

I think back to Joey's comment about her "shock and awe" phase. "So what do you mean shock and awe?" A shiver works its way through me and Joey laughs. We go inside because she says I might die of hypothermia given my lack of body weight. Her twelve-year-old brother weighs more than me. "I understand the shock," I go on to say, taking a seat on the couch with her. She hands me a cup of hot chocolate. "But what's your awe?"

Joey doesn't answer me right away, but eventually she sighs. "It's when I accepted it wasn't going to control me. I was angry, I hated, I had shame... but I also had love and joy, and a family who was there every step of the way. So my awe moment came when I chose to feed the side I felt more comfortable with. I got help. I saw a therapist and went to support groups. I made friends and connections, and I gave them everything I had to give because that was the side of myself I loved. I didn't want to wake up sad, and though I still have days where the ugly wins out, I'm damn good at saying 'fuck you, I win this time.' Regardless of him not having a face or a name, he will not ever take anything else from me, and that includes my future."

Her words sink in. Every single one of them. Slowly. I let them. I don't say a word. I breathe in and smile. I think... no, I know, Asa and Joey are my awe. I hug her and tell her, "You're my soul mate."

"You're my other half... quite literally. You're like, half of me." She looks at my too-bony legs, and then her curvy ones. "Okay, maybe I'm like three of you."

And then we laugh and eat the best turkey in the world that's real fucking meat.

CHAPTER 20

A storm he prepared for

ASA

Roman isn't stupid. And I never knew him to be. Do you know what his major is?

Criminal justice.

His face twists, his expression guarded, and he shrugs. "I don't know what you're looking for, Asa."

I step toward him, but I don't touch him. "You know goddamn well what I'm looking for." Every part of my being aches to hit him. I want to so bad my hands are shaking, my entire fucking body is shaking, resisting reaction. My muscles are coiled, ready to react.

I don't.

I don't because there's one advantage Roman has over me, and it goes back to his major. If I so much as lay a hand on him, he can and will press charges against me. And while my mind is certainly on Barrette and finding justice for her, it's on me as well. I have a bowl game coming up. I have a future. I've done my research on this for the last seventeen months. If he's found guilty, he will go to jail. He'll lose his scholarship. His football career? It will be over. And my personal favorite, he will have to register as a sex offender for the rest of his life.

In my heart, I know without a shred of doubt he had a part in this. I don't need this fucking evidence of his hat.

"I was in my room that night. I have three girls who will gladly testify to that."

"Guess you better gather your witness list, huh?"

He leans in, his tone haughty and provoking. "I don't have to gather shit because I didn't rape her." He snorts. "If I wanted Barrette, which we both know I could have, she'd gladly let me." He straightens up and shoves his hands in his pockets. He watches the stages of emotions across my face. The anger, the desperate need to react, and the way I'm barely holding it together. "Oh, I see what this is. You're just pissed off because when you came home, that virgin pussy wasn't waiting for you."

I squeeze my eyes shut. *Don't hit him. Don't do it!*

Swallowing over the bile rising in my throat, I force a smile when his dad comes to the door, and then Remy. My smile isn't one of happiness. It's one of "I caught you in your fucking lie and you're going to pay."

"Are you sure you don't want something to eat?" his dad asks, wiping his hands on a napkin. "We have plenty of food here."

"No, I was just leaving." I pick up the hat on the ground. "I think I'll go ahead and give this to the police. They can add it to the mound of evidence already inside that sexual assault forensic evidence."

Roman's dad looks to him, and then me. "What are you talking about?"

Remy gasps. "That's why you were searching the woods the next day?" Her hand slaps over her mouth and Roman's face pales in the process. She swallows and backs away from him. "You said it wasn't you."

"It wasn't," he growls, flexing his jaw, his sister screaming at him, demanding to know what's going on.

I wink at him. "I guess you have nothing to worry about then, do you?"

If you look at his face, he knows he does. He fucking knows it and I hope it eats him alive to know. Regardless, I have my answer. I step back, my control slipping. I have to distance myself from him. If I don't, I'll kill him. I know it.

I throw his hat at him. I don't need it. "You'd better put your criminal justice knowledge to use." I turn around and walk away, but then I stop before I walk down the steps. I glance over my shoulder at him. "I never told you where I found your hat."

His chest rises and falls, and his eyes widen, but I can see his struggle not to go after me. He knows too, if he has any chance—which he doesn't—he can't lay a hand on me.

And then I leave. I can barely keep the car on the road as I drive back to my dad's house. My hands are shaking so badly I nearly drive the car in the ditch twice. I can't breathe. I can barely catch a breath. I roll down the windows thinking I need fresh air, but that only makes it worse.

Nausea hits me about the time I pull into my dad's driveway. I stop the car, open the door and vomit in the grass. Standing up, I run both my hands over my face. I want to call Barrette, but I also don't want to ruin the rest of her day with Joey. I pray Remy doesn't and she hears this from me, and not her.

A door opens and closes. I look up to see Carlin outside who notices my appearance. "Oh my God, are you okay?"

I shake my head just as my knees hit the ground.

I PACE MY DAD'S HOUSE. HE'S ON THE PHONE WITH HIS FRIEND. He's a police officer and is giving us advice. I want a plan before I say anything to Barrette.

He tells us she needs to file a police report. She's still within the statute of limitations.

I don't want to ruin Thanksgiving for her. I don't. But if I don't get to her first, this could destroy her completely. Despite my better judgment, I call Remy first. With a shaky grip on reality, I press her contact in my phone.

"Don't tell her," I bark when she gasps my name, and then realize Remy probably didn't have anything to do with it. I shouldn't be so mean to her.

"I would never," she cries, sobbing into the phone. "Oh God, Asa. I can't believe this. I don't think it was just him. It couldn't have been."

My heart races. Anxiety hits my stomach. Do you notice the way my shoulders square up? "There had to be." My dad motions for me, the last few hours wearing on his face. I nod. "I'm heading up to see her now. Where's Roman?"

"He's with our dad and Leonard, his attorney."

I picture Roman sitting there in their den, his leg bouncing, his nerves shot. And then I have these gruesome images of him and Barrette and what my mind imagines what happened that night. Only now, all these violent situations that have played out have a face. "Whatever you do, don't tell anyone about this," I growl, unable to keep the venom from my voice.

"I won't," she adds without question. "I swear, Asa. Anything you need, just let me know."

I hesitate to add a thank you, but I do because she didn't do this. Her vile brother did.

I hang up and tuck my phone in my pocket. Turning to my dad, I reach for my keys, my eyes on the already set table and the dinner I can't stomach to eat. I feel awful for Carlin. Her words are nothing but tender and assuring but her face, it screams, I wanted you to enjoy today.

I reach for a roll on the table and then some turkey. "It looks good."

Her hand touches my shoulder and then to my back. "You're too sweet, honey."

Dad clears his throat. "Are you going to drive up there tonight?"

I nod, emotion bubbling, and I think I can handle this, but I have no idea if I'm full of shit. So much has been building up to this over the last year and a half. I knew at some point Barrette and I would both be at our breaking point and it seemed that we were there, and if the wind blew just right, we'd be over the edge, unable to find our way back. Would this be it?

"I can't tell her this over the phone," I admit, tears flooding my eyes. I just... I can't believe it. I can't even begin to wrap my mind around the fact that all along he's been around her, and alone with her in her room. I start shaking again and set down the roll and turkey in my hand.

Carlin begins to rub my back.

Dad reaches for his keys. "You're not going alone. I'll drive you. You have a game Saturday."

I nod. Damn it. I'd forgotten about that in the haze of everything unraveling around me. How could I tell her the worst news of her life, and then leave her again? And then I think of Cadence. I know they aren't that great of friends anymore, but how is she going to handle it? Roman and her dated, if you can call it that. How would she feel to know her boyfriend raped her best friend? How would she feel not knowing?

Thousands of scenarios play out in my head, but I can't make any one stick to decide what, or even how to do this. I flash back to when my mom was sick and the doctor told her, "There's nothing more we can do. It's just... too advanced."

They told me, "It's time to take her home and let her be at peace."

The fighter in me wouldn't accept it. I researched and pleaded with doctors. I begged them to try a different approach and natural therapies. They had to find a cure as far as I was concerned. In the end, nothing worked, and my mom finally said, "Baby, everything happened the way it was supposed to." I had no idea what she meant until the day she died and she whispered to me, "You were my cure."

I'm still not sure what she meant by that, or if I ever will, but my point being, I'm at that stage. The fighting. The unable to accept this as the end. I refuse to.

"I think—"

My dad knows where my headspace is at. Crazy. And he shakes his head. "Asa, you're not going alone. It's a two-and-a-half-hour drive, and you just collapsed in the driveway not more than an hour ago. I'm going."

I can't argue with him. At this point, I'll be lucky to get on the main road, let alone down I-5 without wrecking. "What did Les say?"

Dad grabs his coat from beside the couch and leans in to kiss Carlin. "He said Barrette needs to file a police report. A hat at the scene isn't evidence because there's no way to say that he was there at the time. We don't know that. It's a possibility, but you don't know."

"It was him. I know it," I seethe.

"But you don't have proof, Asa. The first step is her reporting it. She then needs to decide to press charges. They'll request a DNA test from him. If he refuses, it'll go before a judge to ask for a warrant. If the judge feels like there's enough evidence, then they'll issue a warrant."

Like it or not, this wasn't going to happen as quickly as I want because I know Roman isn't going to willingly take a DNA test. "Then what?"

"Then it'll be assigned to a detective and the process will start with collecting evidence, interviewing suspects, and then they'll decide what charges will be filed."

Adrenaline and anger pulses inside me. I want justice, and I want it right now.

"How do I tell her?" I've never once asked my dad for advice. Ever. We've always been complete opposites. But now, on the edge of everything I don't understand, I ask him.

My dad peers over at me, but then looks back at the road, his grip on the steering wheel of his truck tighter than normal. "I wouldn't just blurt it out," he says, his voice low and hushed. "You need to sit her down and maybe tell her about the hat and ask her what she remembers from the night."

I look at him, and then the road. The windshield wipers are working overtime, desperately trying to clear the blanket of snow pummeling down on the roads. It looks like something out of a *Star Wars* movie when they're traveling at light speed.

My phone lights up with a message, the shocking brightness burning my eyes. I squint, trying to make out who it is. It's Barrette.

My heart drops to my stomach as I slide my finger over the screen to read it. It's a picture of her eating a giant turkey leg that's bigger than her face and the words, *It's not tofu!* Underneath it.

Holding the phone up, I stare at her smile, and it's one I haven't seen in years. My chest aches at the sight, and then I think, what the fuck am I doing? Do I need to tell her? Can't I just pretend I don't know and tip the police off? Maybe.... No, I stop myself. I can't do that because if she ever found out that I knew and didn't tell her, it'd be worse than ruining a smile.

CHAPTER 21

What she didn't tell me

ASA

I had no expectations on what to expect telling Barrette. I didn't. I had fears, but no idea what she'd think, or feel, or how she'd react.

With the snow, it takes my dad and I three hours to get to Bellingham. In that time, I text Joey and test the waters. I tell her I'm coming to see Barrette and I need to talk to her. She calls me lovesick and laughs. And then, then I hit her with it.

Me: I think I know who raped her.

Joey: Asa, if you're not completely sure, don't tell her.

It's then, ten minutes from Joey's house, that the panic truly sets in. My words, my accusation could possibly send her back over the edge. Am I wrong? Do I think it's Roman?

Yes, I do. Without a doubt, I feel that shit in my fucking bones down to my soul. He either did it, or he had a vital part in it. But the fact remains, I did not have proof aside from a goddamn hat. In the world of evi̶d̶ence, it's nothing.

My hands shake and I stare at my phone. I question my sanity and my need for this to be true. It's accurate to say, in a lot of ways, I want my theory to be correct. I want it to be Roman because finally it would, or could, mean closure for both of us. I want a face to the monster.

I look at my dad and drop my phone in my lap. "Joey thinks I shouldn't say anything."

He frowns. "You have to. She needs to file a police report right away, Asa. It's imperative she does this now, regardless if you think it's him or not."

"But..." I choke on my words, swallowing back emotion. *Suck it up, ya fucking pussy.* I clear my throat and square my shoulders. "What if it's not him?"

"Do you really believe that?"

"No."

"Then you tell her because if she finds out you know something, and you don't tell her, your friendship will never be the same." Kind of like ignoring her for four years because you're afraid of telling her you love her. You're afraid of her waiting for you and missing out on life.

When we pull up to the house, my dad looks over at me. We sit for several minutes without talking. Darkness has taken over. The glow reflecting off the snow is orange and glistening.

We get out of the car and I follow my dad through the walkway, where he stops, cursing under his breath. He inhales as if he's setting himself up for something. He turns, faces me, and pulls me into a hug. "I love you," he says, choking out the words. "And I'm sorry you're being put in this position, to tell her this."

I nod, unsure of what to say, but settle on "I love you too," and it's then, as that term of endearment leaves my frozen lips, I realize that just might have been the first time I've said it to him.

He nods thoughtfully and reaches for the doorbell. Joey answers, her face blank and emotionless. I hate she's mad at me for doing this.

I bury my hands in my pockets. "Where's Barrette?"

Joey opens the door wider. Barrette's sitting on the couch with two younger boys. Her eyes drift to mine, smiling. I watch Barrette's face, the excitement to see me, and then I look at her. Really look at her. This isn't the same girl I once knew. Her eyes are clear, no trace of makeup, her hair pulled back in a ponytail braided over her shoulder. For a moment, I see a fourteen-year-old Barrette, laughing, stealing my baseball hat and telling me I can have it back if I can catch her. I try to make myself think of every happy memory I have of her because I know the possibility of never seeing that side again is real.

No matter how hard this will be, I have to tell her. I face her, and I don't know what my expression is. It could be one of a thousand different ones coursing through me, destroying my composure.

I hug her, kiss her cheek, and then ask her if I can talk to her outside. She nods, swallows slowly, her eyes drifting to my dad, and then me. "Is everything okay?" Her arms drop from around my neck and I hate how the missing heat hits my chest. I take her hand and lead her through the door to the porch that hugs the house.

"I uh..." I struggle to find the words. I reach for her hand again, holding it in mine. "I went to the woods today when I was back home and I...." My words die off and I realize I don't have the guts to say it.

"I found Roman's hat," I tell her finally before I lose my nerve, "right next to where I found you that night," I spit the words, like they taste bad in my mouth.

Do you see the look in her eyes? The sadness rolling through her as she moves back a step? Do you hear her heart breaking?

I do. I can hear it. I caused it. I destroyed it. Do you see my face? Do you notice the tears rolling down my cheeks? I'm a fucking mess.

Her face contorts, her hand covers her mouth, and pain finds residence in her features. It morphs and shifts and wrenches, just like her heart.

"I'm sorry." I hate those words. They're easy and empty, but I say them because I don't know what else to say to her.

Barrette gasps and then stumbles into me. I grab her arms, steadying her right before she collapses against me in sobs.

I SPEND THE NIGHT AT JOEY'S PARENTS' HOUSE. MY DAD FINDS A hotel to stay at and says he'll drive me back to campus in the morning. I play football with Joey's brothers in the basement and end up giving Joey's mom fifty bucks because I broke a light. Those are the lighter moments of the rest of Thanksgiving. The ones where thousands of families around the country are counting their blessings and saying what they're thankful of.

But there are darker ones. The moments when I hold Barrette in my arms and pray she finds comfort with me there. I crawl into bed with her, which happens to be a pullout couch in the basement. She won't stop shaking, but here, I hold her. All of her weight is on me. Her body, her thoughts, her burdens, I'll take them all and see her through them regardless.

I'm here for her, and I can't let go. I think that if I'm here, if I can save her thoughts from going completely dark, I can save us. Not forever, but right now, in this moment because where we go from here says a lot about our relationship and its meaning.

"Did you always think it was him?" she finally asks after an hour of awkward silence where I debate on asking if she's okay, and realize what a braindead question that is.

I tighten my grip on her to see if her shaking gets any better. It's after three in the morning and my entire body is worn out. Two-a-day practices have nothing on this feeling. "I think a part of me wanted it to be."

Gradually she begins to calm down, the shaking subsides and the tears slow. "I think I knew," she says, the regret of so much more etched in her sad eyes. "But I'm afraid of what it means."

"What it means?" I repeat, not following what she's implying. She shifts beside me, propping up on her elbow. She chews on her lip, contemplates, and then finally whispers, "He's a college football player with a future. I'm a nobody, and I was drunk at the time. I know how this works. I'll be painted to be a slut and targeting him."

I don't want to believe her, I don't, but her words are sadly justifiable. They are, unfortunately, true. They shouldn't be, no is no, unconscious or not, drunk or not, drugging someone and raping them has no place in this world.

I'm afraid to answer, scared if I say anything, she'll fall apart again. I know she's still struggling to understand, to make this newfound discovery fit into what this means for her, but at least she didn't push me away.

"I remember the hat," she whispers, like it's a confession. "I remember a tattoo on the guy's hand." I struggle. I watch her face through the light filtering in from the hallway. She sighs, in maybe relief, I don't know, and then presses her face on my chest. "I don't remember what the tattoo looked like, just that it was on his hand and up his arm."

"You remember the hat?"

Her breathing catches, holds, then she sighs and lifts her head to look at me. I tuck my arm under my head and watch the emotions on her face. "I didn't until Roman was in my room that night. He asked me something really weird, about our sophomore year of high school and if I remembered us kissing."

I can barely breathe, let alone swallow thinking of his lips on her, much less inside her. "You kissed him?"

"Sophomore year. Just once."

I nod, waiting for her to continue and I know she can tell I'm bothered by it.

"But he asked what I would have done if Remy hadn't interrupted us."

"Remind me to thank Remy," I growl, trying not to interrupt her, but failing.

She continues, a small downturn to her lips. "He said he would have tried to fuck me, and something clicked in my head. The hat. I remembered seeing a purple hat."

Rage rolls through me in waves, drowning my self-control I breathe in and out again, desperately grasping for some sort of composure for her sake. "You need to file the police report tomorrow," I growl.

Her voice is timid, like a child admitting their fears when she whispers into my chest, "I'm scared."

I cup her cheek hoping she senses the sincerity behind my words. "It's going to be hard, but I know you can do it," I say, kissing her forehead. "I will be by your side through all of it. I won't leave."

She sighs, her head against my chest now. My arms wrap around her, pulling her tighter. "Thank you."

I hold out hope that we may have suffered and the road still won't be easy, but we're at least holding our own as the play clock winds down.

CHAPTER 22

The night I said no

In downtown Olympia, there's a police station. It's in the middle of the city, tucked away next to restaurants and a falling economy. Inside it, I sit at a table next to a woman who calls herself a sexual assault advocate. It took me a year and a half, but I'm here, ready to take back the control. I won't let them take anything else from me.

The officer, a male one, hands me a box of tissues and asks me to tell him what happened. As if I remember, as if I *want* to remember.

They ask questions and expect answers.

What I remember? A hat. A tattoo. Swabs in my vagina and needles for shots. The feeling of everything inside me being silent, because my words meant nothing. I remember looking at a form and seeing the words *Rape Victim* in bold black letters and my control over everything I was going through was an illusion. My struggle was internal, an unseen battle I couldn't put words on, until, *until* I walked into the doors of that police station.

It didn't matter that the cop asked me questions like, what I was wearing and if I had been drinking, if I was flirting and maybe led him on, to finally, did I ever verbally say no?

I sigh and state the facts. The only one that matters as far as I was concerned. "My denial, my no, my fucking voice went unheard, and that's all that matters."

He nods, takes notes, but it's his demeanor that upsets me. I shouldn't be made out to be the villain here. I did nothing wrong.

I stare at the cop and think, why would he and how could he assume I'd asked to have my face smashed with a rock or raped in a forest? I shake and cry, and then eventually yell, "I may have been drunk, but that fucking report, the blood they took from me in the hospital had been tainted."

An official police report is filed that afternoon, and Asa's dad helps me hire an attorney. He requests for a DNA sample from Roman. His attorney immediately responds back, why'd I wait so long to file the police report. Is it because the accused has an upcoming bowl game? Did I want revenge because he broke up with me in my dorm room two weeks ago ending our two-year relationship?

I gasp and stare at my attorney who I barely know. "We've never dated. *Ever*."

He nods and gives me a look of understanding. "He's probably panicking. From here, we'll present our case to the judge and ask for an arrest warrant to be issued."

Are you laughing? I am, because that's the defense Roman gives when asked to give a DNA sample.

Because Roman refuses the test, denies any involvement, no arrest is made, and he's cleared to play in the game Saturday afternoon.

It could take weeks, if not longer. For now, he's free to—all joking aside—roam about the country.

It's hours later, on Friday morning and I'm standing in the police station with Asa's dad. I look up at the gray sky. With knots in my stomach and barely able to walk, I never thought I'd be strong enough to report it. But I do, and I did it because justice, even if it's only internal, is the right thing to do.

I reach in my pocket to the note Asa gave me before he left this morning.

I can't be there with you, but I'm with you, always.

I go where you go.

Love, Asa

A rush of serenity hits me. If it hadn't been for him, I'm not sure I would have done this and I have him to thank.

FRIDAY EVENING I MAKE AN APPOINTMENT WITH MY THERAPIST. Asa is at his mandatory dinner with his team, and though I want to see him, it's not an option tonight.

So I go to my therapist. I haven't talked much about Lexi, but that doesn't mean she hasn't been an important part of the last year and a half. She has been.

It's been a month since I've last seen her, so I start with the new developments with Roman. She encourages me and assures me it's the right thing to do.

Then I tell her about Asa. Out of everything I've told her, it's my relationship with Asa she's concerned about. He's always a topic of conversation with us. I understand why, I do, but I also think without him, I wouldn't have even gone to therapy in the first place.

"Tell me about you and Asa," she says, twirling a lock of her hair around her finger as if she's bored. She's not. I think she just plays with her hair when she's concentrating.

"Like what?" I shift in the chair, aware of the fact that this is a concern for her.

"You're sexually active with him now, right?"

I laugh nervously. "Sexually active sounds so clinical."

"Okay." Lexi quirks a half smile. "Are you two having sex?"

I can't stop the smile when I say, "We are."

"And?"

"It's good."

Her eyes narrow. "You know my feelings on this, right?"

"Yes, I do. It can create an unhealthy attachment for us." Too late. We're there.

"And are you two considering that?"

Nervously, I run my fingers through my hair. "I haven't talked to him about it."

Lexi nods and sets her notebook down on the table in front of her. Look at the set frown and the wrinkles on her forehead. Disappointment is written all over her face. "You need to have the conversation with him about it. Victims of sexual assault crimes will often form unhealthy relationships with alcohol, drugs, and sometimes sex because they use it as a coping mechanism. You might feel better when you're having sex with him, am I right?"

"Well, yeah. It feels good."

"And that's great, Barrette, but it's important to remember your boundaries and recognize what makes you uncomfortable."

I listen. I nod, but I'm not entirely sure she believes me.

I'm not entirely sure I believe me or what to make of what she's saying. I know I don't want to end things with Asa, nor do I want any part of our relationship to change.

JOEY PLACES HER HANDS ON MY SHOULDERS, HUNCHING TO MAKE eye contact with me. "You're like, so short. I feel like I should kneel to be at your eye level." I roll my eyes at her humor, then comes the "you're cute, *but*" part. "You've been through a lot. Maybe we shouldn't go."

I've been through a lot? Have I? Hasn't she, too?

I breathe in deeply and tie my hair back. I stare at myself in the mirror wearing everything I hate. Like makeup. Like gold and purple paint on my cheeks like those little glitter Ws all the cheerleaders wear on their faces. It looks like a pep rally threw up on me.

"I'm going," I tell Joey. "*We're* going, and we're gonna be normal people, *regardless.*" I had it in my head that today I was going to be normal. I wasn't going to think about the police report I filed yesterday or the fact that they made me feel like shit about waiting for so long. I was going to be a nineteen-year-old girl for a night and experience college the way I was supposed to. Without cares. Without worries of not coping in crowds, or not wanting a beer, or worse, will he listen if I say no? Sure, I know I still need to be aware of my surroundings, but I can and will have a good time.

Joey laughs, wiping gold-dusted glitter from her black jeans. "Regardless of what?"

"Regardless of the fact that he will be playing, and I have to see his face."

Her expression changes. "I think I saw my attacker once in line at Starbucks."

My eyes widen. "What did you do?"

She inhales, preparing herself, and then offers a soft smile. She tucks her makeup into her bag on her bed and then faces me. "I bought his coffee."

"What?" I gasp. "Why?"

"I don't know why. It was morbid of me, but something snapped when he looked at me and his face paled. He knew I knew who he was. He had tattoos and piercings, and I wouldn't forget that. But I looked back at him, smiled, paid for his coffee. He told me 'No, that's okay. I got it.' I smiled and said, 'No. What a powerful word that holds so little meaning to most.' And then I left, burst into tears and spent the next four days in therapy." With tears in her eyes, she exhales, ridding her body of the anger, and grabs my face between her hands. "You look like a tiny cute plum."

I laugh, rolling my eyes. She drops her hands from my face and pats my leg. "Now, let's go cheer on these dogs."

"It's pronounced, dawg."

"Gotcha."

I REALLY HAVE NO IDEA WHAT TO EXPECT AT THE FOOTBALL GAME. It's been a whole year since I've been to a live game. We sit in the student section. It's rambunctious and not at all what I should be around, but something happens while I'm suffocating between sweaty gold and purple bodies. It happens when I see Asa play the game of his life, despite the one person he'd like to kill being on the field with him. His confidence doesn't waver, at least not on the outside. Here, with seventy thousand people watching him, he gives them what they come to see. A true leader.

The calmness he has on the field is unheard of. He's always like that too. Sometimes I think the world could crumble around him and he'd still be able to throw a football. He plays with more passion, more commitment than I've ever seen, but then again, I don't know that much about football players. I know about one, the guy who saved my life in more ways than I can tell you.

It's not all easy watching the game. Not only am I so short I could pass for a child—which means I can't see shit—Asa takes a couple of rough hits that leave me a little on edge.

I slouch uncomfortably in the hard plastic chair when he's slow to get up. Watching him get injured is never easy. It always sends a jolt to my heart and sickness in my belly. I can guess why, but it seems every play he's left wide-open by Codey. Codey is Roman's roommate. He'll defend that guy no matter what because Codey worships him. Unfortunately for Codey, he'd be a nobody on campus had he not been roomed with Roman—the campus manwhore—freshman year. "I hope he's okay."

"He's fine," Joey replies, leaning forward. "He's tough and look"—she points to the fifty-yard line—"T-Bone helped him up."

"Aw, cute." I grin and waggle my eyebrows. "So when's your next date?"

"He asked me to go to Baton Rouge for spring break."

"Really?" The excitement I have for her date is crazy. "Are you going?"

Joey rolls her eyes. "I'm a broke college student who can barely afford lunch most days—which let's face it—probably isn't a bad idea for me, but I don't think I can go."

"Why not?" I watch her face, the pink flushed cheeks from the cold and her pretty dark eyes. "I mean if you can't, that's one thing, and I get it, but is there something else?"

"Does Asa know him very well? "

"I think so. They've been roommates for two years and last spring break they went to Mexico together. Between football and classes, they spend a lot of time together. I'd like to think he knows him."

"And what does he say about him?" she asks, her eyes on the field. "Is he a good guy? I've heard he's kind of a player."

"Oh, well, yeah. He's been around, but he's always been very nice to me. Asa's never said a bad thing about him."

She snorts. "Has Asa ever said anything mean to anyone before?"

"Uh, yeah. Ask him his thoughts on Roman these days."

Joey laughs, her eyes darting to mine, then the field. "True."

Speaking of Roman, he sits on the bench most of the game, and when he does play, he's wide-open and Asa throws anywhere but him. I can't say I blame him. If I had the ball, I'd probably nail him in the dick with it.

I think, right then, what if it's really him. I think back to every conversation I've had with him, shifting through hundreds of different memories, but I can't pinpoint any one that screams, yes, it was him. I still don't know, but I have my suspicions. Especially after the way he acted in my room that night.

The game is a blowout with the Huskies winning 41-14. Asa dominates the game in both passing yards and running the ball himself for two touchdowns. With their spot in the Fiesta Bowl secured, there's a whirl of students rushing the field. I'm not comfortable enough to go down there, and Joey tells me she'd rather jab her eyeballs out than rush the field like a lunatic. So we wait. I wait.

As selfish as it sounds, I want Asa's attention to myself. When I talk to him now, congratulate him, thank him for what he's done for me, I want it to be just us where he isn't being pulled in every direction.

He knows I'm here. He looks over at me, smiling. I wink, but I'm sure he won't see me this far away.

It's another hour of press and autographs before I see him again. He's showered now and smells so good, a herd of press surrounding him. He's struggling to get away from them when I catch his heated gaze on mine. I stand with my back pressed into the concrete wall and smile.

Watching him from a distance brings back all the memories of yesterday at the police station. The filing, the questions, all of it. For the most part, I've pushed the thoughts aside and I'm able to look past it, but they're still there, still on the surface, waiting to come forward. The moment his blond hair comes into view, I'm no longer uneasy. Quite the opposite, actually. I'm relieved that through all that, through eighteen months of me being undecided and living day by day, of me needing days where I couldn't handle myself let alone my thoughts, Asa remained the one consistent part of my life. Because of him, I've pushed forward and made the next step to healing.

In many ways, there are unhealthy aspects to our relationship. Parts we're probably going to have to discuss sooner rather than later, but for now, I have Asa. My messy-haired boy who always puts his girl first.

Terrell walks up to Asa and throws him over his shoulder. I know Asa is nearly two hundred pounds so that couldn't have been easy, but Terrell does this with little effort.

He carries him over to me. "This boy *needs* to talk to you. He's been talking about you all day, and frankly, I'm tired of it."

"T-Bone, put me down," Asa orders, his breath expelling in a gasp.

Terrell sets him on his feet, runs his hand over Asa's head like he's some kind of caring mother, pats his back and then his head again.

Asa rolls his eyes, his posture stiffening. "That's not true."

"I'd argue that, but I have a lady to impress," Terrell pats Asa's head again and then steps toward Joey, who hasn't left my side all night. "Lady." He holds out his elbow for her like she's supposed to take it.

Rolling her eyes, she sighs and tucks her arm inside of his. "You're so weird, but strangely adorable. If you can call a six-foot-five man-child adorable."

"Oh, you can. I'm very adorable. Just wait. I'm like a real-life teddy bear."

We both laugh as Terrell walks with Joey, both of them smiling. I sigh. "He's not going to break her heart, is he?"

Asa laughs. "No. He's a good guy."

"Good. Because I'd have to kick his ass if he wasn't."

He raises an eyebrow at me. "Is that so? Don't you think you're a little small to go around making promises like that?"

I stand on my tippy-toes. "Small but mighty."

"That you are," Asa says, winking at me and tugging at the front of my hoodie. "Good game, huh?"

"I forgot how exhilarating it was to see you play in person. Those were some hard hits, but you played so well."

He smiles, and then his expression shifts, morphs into something else as he glances over my shoulder. And then his eyes dart in the other direction. A group of students approach—all girls—and push their chests out as they come face-to-face with Asa. "Asa! Can you sign our shirts?"

I see they're all wearing hoodies with his name on them. Cute.

He surprises me and leans into me, his left arm wrapping around me. "Yeah, sure." The whole time he keeps that one arm around me. I'd like to think it's his silent gesture to them, to anyone, he's taken. They all talk about the game with him, offer their support and congratulations. He smiles politely, thanks them, and then asks me to follow him.

We're down the hall in the other direction near the bathrooms. He takes me down another hallway to a dark area of the stadium where there are no crowds.

"Thank you for coming," he says with a grin, knowing this is the first game I've been to in a long time. "I didn't think you'd be ready to come here after everything."

"It was nice seeing you play again," I admit, because it was. I motion around the stadium. "I forgot how much I missed this. But I needed to experience this. For nearly two years, I've foregone everything I loved because I couldn't handle it, but something happened when I left that police station with your dad." Asa's brow furrows in concentration, hanging on my every word. "I saw it for what it was. A start in the right direction for me."

We stare at one another, lost in the moment. I fidget, wishing I knew what he was thinking. He surprises me when he grins.

"Kiss me." He's not wasting any time, and I think maybe we

should slow down, but to hell with that. Live for today, right? Then he adds, "I really need you to kiss me because *you* want to."

I do, and his lips are cool against the heat of my mouth, no doubt because I've been thinking of this kiss for hours. It's not a tentative kiss, but it's also not gentle by any means. It's exactly the way Asa is. Full of passion.

He sighs into my mouth, pulling back, and then takes my hand before he winks. But then, as with anything in life, the night changes. What I thought I had a handle on, takes a turn.

Asa sees him first, and tension rolls from him in waves, his posture stiff and unpredictable. I twist in his arms, but he shields me, a protective stance as he backs me up against the wall behind me.

Do you notice the way my heart plummets and my breathing goes from heavy to stopping altogether? What about the way Asa's eyes turn cold and violent? It's all an indication of the one person I never care to see again, regardless of what the police report leads to.

He walks toward us, not a care in the world, smiles at me but turns his cool gaze to Asa. "Next time I'm open, *share*."

Share? He certainly doesn't mean it in that context, I assure you.

I can't see Asa's face to judge his reaction, but he answers rather calmly with, "Didn't see you."

Roman halts his steps as if he intended to walk by us, but then decided not to. "Oh, and Barrette?"

I don't say anything, but our eyes meet, and there's something incredibly different about his expression. Scary? No... that's not it. Intimidating? Nope. Have you ever looked up Ted Bundy? Remember how he drew his victims in with his handsome looks and charming personality? Then he turned into a monster, disturbed by an insurmountable evil that resided inside him? In that moment, that second my gaze locks on Roman's, I think to myself, he played his part well. Normal, well-liked star athlete who could have any girl he wanted, and did. But that's what makes him dangerous. With that look, I see right through the charm, the blue eyes and the dark hair and all that resides is that insurmountable evil I talked about.

He whispers the words "Lawyer up, honey" in passing, a cunning smirk playing on his face.

I grip Asa's jacket, and I think in that fraction of a second when Roman and I caught a glimpse of one another, he knew I saw through him. Asa turns and faces me, his expression somewhere between livid and worried. It's half and half. He looks down at my hands in his, then slides his eyes back to mine. "I'm sorry. I pulled you away when I saw him. I didn't think he'd have the nerve to follow us."

"Yeah," I expel another heavy breath, my shaking and trembling starting up again. "Well, I didn't think he'd have the nerve to start the case off with lies."

His jaw snaps closed. "What?"

"He told his attorney that we had been dating and he broke it off last week. Apparently, me choosing now to file the report meant I was trying to get revenge over him."

Can you take a guess as to what Asa's reaction to that one is?

Complete and utter hysterics. Ha. He freaking busts up laughing. "He fuckin' wishes," he says with a chuckle, though there's a hard edge to his words as he shifts his cold eyes down the hall where Roman is gathered with a group of women.

There's a part of me that wants to run to them and tell them not to go anywhere with him, but then again, my thoughts went back to that cop that questioned me yesterday. "What evidence do you have that it was him other than finding a hat that may or may not have been his?"

My answer? My vagina test.

Yes, I said that, because I panicked and forgot the name.

I pray I haven't let justice slip through my hands.

Asa pulls me into him, his hands on my hips. "Let's go. If I'm here any longer, I'm going to go after him."

Nodding, I twist and begin walking with him, his arm slung around my shoulder as we pass by groups of girls staring at us. I don't look at them; instead, my eyes are on the ground. My thoughts unintentionally drift back to Roman. I try to recall any memory of that night again, but still, nothing more comes to mind.

Asa must sense my mood and tightens his grip. "You okay?"

We're outside the stadium now, the night so different from the noise of the last few hours. I stop, my eyes drifting to his, and then up at the sky. "I hate that I can't remember any details, but I think maybe that's a good thing because the idea of remembering something so brutal might be too much."

Asa pulls me into his arms, holding me close. "You were drugged. There are always going to be parts of it you're never going to remember."

He's right, there will be, but it doesn't stop me from wishing I could.

We start walking again, slower, heading toward my dorm when he laughs lightly. "You're handling it better than I thought you would though."

I look up at him, reaching for his hand that's slung over my shoulder. "Handling what?"

"Everything since I told you about the hat and going to the police."

"I'm relieved."

He pulls away slightly, just enough to see my face. "You are? Why?"

I curl in closer to him, refusing to allow any space between us with the cool night air whipping around. Letting go of his hand, I brush my hair from my face. "Because. I don't know that my fear would have ever allowed me to make the decision on my own to go to the police and file the report. This gave me the push I needed. You did."

He breathes out what I can only assume is the breath he'd been holding waiting on my words. "I was just in the right place at the right time."

"Like the night you saved me."

A smile lifts his lips, blinking slowly. "You're worth it." His head dips forward and I think he's going to kiss me, but then some students in the distance scream his name and I jump. His hold tightens when they approach, wanting his autograph and pictures with him. And though he keeps me tucked to his side the entire time —aside from pictures as I'm sure they don't want me in—Asa never gives any of the women pawing at him an indication he's not totally devoted to the girl purple and gold threw up on.

CHAPTER 23

Boundaries

We're back at my dorm, standing at the door when I unlock it. "It's crazy how they worship you," I tease when another group passes by, giggling and fawning over his every move.

Asa leans his shoulder into the wall, rolling his eyes. "They're clearly misinformed."

I bite my lip, remembering just how bad I want to be alone with him. "Oh, I think I understand it." His heated stare locks on mine, and suddenly it feels like a thousand degrees in the hallway. There are students passing by, all of them wearing dawg gear, celebrating the win, but I don't see any of them. I don't think Asa does either. We're trapped in a moment only we share. Out of the corner of my eye, I notice some of his teammates trying to coax him away. "Lawson!" they scream, waving and jumping around.

He laughs and flicks his hand at them, as if to say, go away.

I grip the front of his jacket in my fists and sigh. There's no other place I'd rather be than in his arms. "Did you want to go party with your team?"

Asa's smiling, and though I know all his smiles, this one feels unfamiliar. He shakes his head and backs me up against the door, his hands on my hips. "You're where I want to be."

Taking a shuddering breath, I smile, too, and his lips find my neck and trail up my jaw, his body crowding mine. "Do you want me to leave?"

I shake my head frantically, violently. No way I want him to leave. "No," I gasp, my hands sliding from his chest to his shoulders. I rise up on my tippy-toes to bring his lips to mine. "I want you here with me. Always." And when his warm lips find mine, I know he's exactly what I need, our pulses sharing the same rhythm.

There's a beat of silence before Asa clears his throat. I push the door open.

"We don't have to do anything besides hang out," he reminds me when we're inside my dorm, and I'm looking at my bed, and then him. He shakes his head like he's trying to rid himself from naughty thoughts.

I laugh nervously, remembering what Lexi told me about sex. "My therapist says having sex is unhealthy."

Peeling his jacket off, he smirks. His scent hits me: male, sweat, hotness. "She must be doing it wrong."

My laughter comes easy that he makes light of it. "Probably. We can watch a movie." Before I get my iPad off my desk, Asa grabs my hand, halting me. His expression is conflicted. "I mean it. We don't have to do anything. I didn't come here expecting us to have sex."

I grin. "Not even a little bit?"

He tucks a strand of my hair behind my ear. "Well, yeah. A lot of me wants it, but I didn't come here for that. I want to be with you."

His calmness, his warmth, it's everything I need tonight. "Let's just see where it goes from here." My hand slides into his and I lead him over to my bed setting the iPad on the nightstand.

Asa follows, kicking off his shoes and his sweatshirt next. I do the same, but I take my jeans off too. It's more comfortable that way. Naturally, Asa groans and falls face-first on the bed dramatically.

"You're making it difficult," he mumbles into my pillow and then grips it in his fists.

I don't know what it is about seeing him take his frustration out on my poor undeserving pillow, but it sends a jolt of desire between my legs. I want to crawl on top of him and show him how much I want him.

Asa twists his head at my laughter ringing through the room. He's still flat on his stomach, glaring. "Put something on. I can't lay here with you if you don't have something on."

My eyes flicker from his to the movie now playing on my iPad, the colors reflecting off the jar on my nightstand and Asa's tense features. I look back to his face. He's still glaring at me. Rolling my eyes, I move toward my dresser, pull on a pair of cotton shorts and throw my arms up in the air. "Better?"

He rolls over and scrubs his hands over his face. "No."

"Too bad." I take a few steps toward the bed.

"Fine." Suddenly he sits up. With a smirk, he peels his shirt off and tosses it at my head.

The scent of him hits me. I breathe in slowly. Damn him. "Ugh" is my response. "You're not playing fair."

"Homefield advantage."

"For who?"

"You." He winks, lying back down on the bed and tucking his hands behind his head. "But I won the coin toss."

With him stretched out on my very small twin bed, I make a slow pass over his body. From his long legs, his hips and the way his jeans hang low, I fight the urge to jump on him. The top of his boxers peek out just a little bit. A fraction of an inch higher, the cut lines of his V is where my eyes fixate. I take another step closer, as if he has a gravitational pull over me.

His breathing quickens, his stomach flexing when he moves his hands from behind his head and sits up. Swinging his legs around the side of the bed, he reaches for me, his hands circling around the backs of my bare thighs. Higher, higher... tentatively, as if he's dealing with a bomb that's about to detonate, his hands find the swell of my bottom.

I concentrate on breathing in and out, trying not to hyperventilate. His head leans against my stomach. I thread my hands through his hair, my body trembling with want. And then he squeezes my backside at the same time a rumble leaves his chest. Desire, need, love, it's all written in his eyes when they lift to mine and he tips his head back, lids heavy.

I move, lifting one leg on the edge of my bed, then the other so I'm straddling him. I don't sit, though. I keep about an inch of frustrating space between our hips. We're both panting when Asa's strong hands return to my butt. This time he slips them underneath my shorts to my bare skin.

His mouth finds the space between my neck and shoulder, his scruffy jaw gliding over my sensitive skin. The way his quick pants hit my already heated skin, it's too much. I need more.

I need all of him.

His hungry lips search mine in an almost frantic manner and when they finally weld to mine, I bring my hips in line with his and rock against him. It's everything, and so much more. Tingles shoot through me. I gasp, I moan, heck, I'm not even sure what my reaction is because I pretty much lose the ability to comprehend anything, let alone remember to breathe at that point. It's a blur and Asa's reaction is similar. His kisses turn frantic, as if his next breath depends on mine. His hands working in sync, with determination as he removes my shirt and then my bra.

"Asa," I gasp, pulling my mouth from his while driving my hips back and forth over him. We stay like that for what seems like forever, me rocking against him and his mouth moving lower, toward my breasts. Just before his mouth reaches their destination, he pauses, his hands trailing up my sides. With a gentle touch, he waits, his hands closing around them, his eyes on mine. He waits.

We haven't been here before, believe it or not.

His eyes search mine, cheeks flushed, breathing barely controlled.

Here's an athlete in pristine condition and I make him breathless. Me!

Asa pauses, his mouth an inch from my right breast he's holding in his hand. He's asking, silently waiting for me to tell him it's all right.

I blink slowly and coax his head forward with the slightest pressure on the back of his head, my unspoken consent. Tentatively, his lips brush the puckered hardness of my breast. It's everything, and so much more. My hips halt, my entire body bursting into flames. If he wasn't holding onto me, I would swear I'm floating. As cheesy as that sounds. And then he parts his lips, his tongue darting out. The wetness, the heat... I moan at the intense rush that floods through me, my eyes rolling back, my spine arching and my fingers digging into his hair. His tongue flicks across the hard nipple. My panties are drenched, a slickness suddenly allowing me to grind against him with ease.

He closes his mouth around the pebbled skin and then he sucks, and I can't look. I squeeze my eyes shut, throw my head back, and hump him. His hands drop from my breasts to my hips, coaxing me along and driving my movements. Sliding me against his length, he lifts his hips to meet mine while never parting his mouth from my chest. It's unlike anything I've experienced before, yet familiar because everything he gives me, the friction between my legs, his hot tongue swirling and sucking, it rushes up on me and before I know it, my orgasm explodes out of nowhere.

I cling to him, gripping his hair between my fingers and forget all about any boundaries, where we are, everything. I scream out, louder than ever before, and if someone had been listening outside my door, they would have known exactly what was happening in here.

Suddenly, Asa grips my hips, his mouth moving from my chest and halts my movements. "Fuck," he groans, his words shaking. "I'm gonna come. Stop." And then he lifts my hips up, breaking our connection.

I pant against his ear, unable to control my breathing. Part of me wants to see him come. So on the edge he can't stop from coming in his jeans. Yes, please. I'd like to see that. I don't say that, but I do let out a little giggle and then slap my hand over my tomato-red face. He doesn't find much humor in it, his eyes heavy-lidded as he flops himself back on my bed, his chest rising and falling quickly.

I watch him, the flickering of the movie reflected in his eyes. I slide my stare lower to the barely concealed strain against the denim. Reaching out, I touch him there. His eyes flutter closed. I trace the button of his jeans, slowly, then unbutton them. I unzip and push them open. Carefully I begin to lower his jeans and boxers, but Asa stops me and sits up. He takes my hands in his. "We need to slow down."

I stare at him in disbelief. "Why?"

"Because," he sighs, "your therapist was right. We should talk about what makes you uncomfortable."

I move to sit in front of him. "Nothing you've done so far makes me uncomfortable."

He nods, his breathing slow, but then his hands find his hair. "I don't think that's entirely true."

I shake my head even though I know what he's talking about. The night I told him harder, and he reluctantly gave me what I wanted. I don't answer, and he groans, reading the emotions on my face. "That's what I'm talking about. I see it on your face. You have to tell me because we can't do anything until I know everything that bothers you."

He waits for me to respond, his eyes anxious when I don't say anything.

"Tell me," he begs.

It hits me then. Since I told him what the therapist said, I bet he just spent the last fifteen minutes obsessing over it and finding a way to let me down that we weren't having sex tonight. I chew on my lip and try to recall that night and what set me off. "It's not what you did... I think it just sort of surfaced out of nowhere if that makes sense."

He stares at me. "No, not really."

"Okay." I draw in a careful breath, seeing he's frustrated with me. "How about this? If anything you do makes me uncomfortable, I'll tell you right away and we stop."

He nods, unconvinced but nodding nonetheless.

I can see his mood has changed and tears surface. "Asa, come on. Believe me."

"I do." His words come out strangled. My eyes dart to his, and I see his are glassy, wavering. "I will never be rough with you. I just can't. Ever."

Feeling like I've won, I nod and crawl on his lap. I nibble on his jaw and straddle him again. He gave me an out and I'm not taking it. I know what I want.

He sighs, his head tipping back to reveal his neck. I take full advantage and reach between us, my hand slipping inside his boxers to see he's still hard and ready. "You're not helping," he growls, bringing his mouth to mine.

"That's my plan. I'm looking to sack the quarterback, and I think I just broke through his offensive line."

That gets him. "Fuck it," he mumbles, and I'm on my back in one quick movement and he's hovering above me. My panties come off first, then his jeans pushed down just enough for him to enter me. I stretch around him, spreading my legs wider to drive him deeper inside. He lifts up, watching my reaction. "I love you," he pants, his brows drawn together in concentration. "I love you *so fucking much*."

"I love you," I tell him, over and over again, clutching him to my body. He brings his chest to mine, pushing into me a little harder, but still, careful. He slows his pace and kisses me. The weight of his athletic body pressing to mine, the dewy warmth of his skin, it sends my heart kicking wildly against my breastbone.

Digging my heels into the mattress, I shift my hips, feeling the euphoric shift between us, two lovers tangled together. Threading my fingers through his hair, I yank. The harder I yank, the harder his thrusts come. Okay, so no rough for me but I can basically pull his hair, and he digs it. Weird. Sinking my nails into his back, his pace quickens, his hand gripping my waist, my butt, the sheets, anywhere he can grasp something. Pride swells in my chest. We're making progress.

He breaks our kiss long enough to whisper another "I love you," and then he buries his face in my neck, wrapping his arms around my torso. I grasp his face with both my hands, wanting him to look at me when he comes. With two more thrusts, he stills, pouring himself into me.

I sigh in relief, the weight of him heavy, but exactly what I want. While our breathing slows, I run my fingers up and down his back, giggling.

He rolls off me. "If I didn't know any better, I'd have a complex that you're laughing."

"But you do know better." I look over at him. "I'm just laughing that we start a conversation with boundaries and now look at us."

He moves to his side, propping his head up by stealing my pillow from me. "I've never been able to tell you no."

"Ha." I snort. "You told me no when I asked you to take my virginity."

This one earns me an eye roll. "Only because I knew if I did, I wouldn't leave." His hand reaches out to touch my cheek. "There was no way I could take that from you and still disappear from your life."

When he talks like that, it all makes sense. Everything he's ever said to me, did for me, all of it. He really is here for me. No matter what. And then I think, what did I do to deserve this? How'd I get so lucky?

The realization flashes over my face, like a revelation of sorts.

He touches my cheek and then reaches for my hand. He brings our hands to his mouth, slowly kissing my knuckles. "Now do you see that you're everything to me?"

I nod. "I do." And then I think about when he left and how badly it hurt me to know he gave his virginity to Heather Randal. Why though? "But I have one more question."

"Anything you want to know, I'll tell you."

"Why Heather Randal?"

At first he stares at me, his expression one of confusion. "Huh?"

"Heather. Randal. Why did you have sex with her two days before you left?"

The anger hits him in an instant, like a flash of lightning through the sky. Quick. And honestly, beautiful. Every emotion he has is incredible with the way they play on his expressions before I feel it hit me. "What the fuck are you talking about?" He narrows his gaze at me, a frown puckering his brow. "I *never* slept with her."

My eyebrows furrow. "What? But Roman said—"

Asa's runs a hand through his hair, his breathing kicking up. "That motherfucker." Pain smears over his face, quickly replaced by a look of disgust.

I open my mouth, but nothing comes out. I drag my lower lip through my teeth and stare at him.

"Of course he had to fucking take that too," he sneers, his tone dark and low, his breathing fanning my face gently when he turns me to look at him. "I've *never* been with anyone but you. Never even kissed another girl."

Tears push their way down my cheeks. I blink, fast, surprised, confused at his admission. "You... didn't?"

He shakes his head without saying anything. My entire world shifts. It's crazy to think, but it does. The room feels like it's closing in on me and I'm trapped in a corner, unable to escape. Tears blind me now. Roman. He took it from me so I couldn't give it to Asa. I know that now. When my eyes meet Asa's, my heart flips in my chest. His expression is one of devastation.

I don't ever want to see this expression on his face again. I twist in his arms, holding his face in my hands. "Nobody can take from you what you didn't give them. I don't care what they took, what he took, I gave it to you."

His face is unreadable, the muscles unmoving. He doesn't even blink.

I take in a breath, leaning forward, and press my lips to his. "The past doesn't matter. It's what we make of the future."

His warm breath tickles my lips as he whispers, "I love you even at our darkest moments." He presses his lips to mine, once. The idea, the clarity that he'd waited for me, it pierces my skin like a papercut. Sharp. Precise. Burning. The gravity of it weighs on me. He'd had so many opportunities, yet he remained true to me. Drawing back, we stare at one another, tears in our eyes. His hand moves from my cheek to my jaw, slanting my head up. "You've been my only."

My heart swells in my chest to the point I think it might burst into flames for him. His love, it's a sensation. There's no need for him to reach out and touch me. I feel him without being touched, and finally, finally I understand it, despite his assurance it had been there all along. You can't make yourself believe someone loves you when you think you're unlovable because of what happened to you. You can't get there until your mind is ready. And mine happens right before his eyes.

If I could rewrite the past, I would, but maybe it wouldn't look like this if I did. What happened to me, to us, it sucks. It's dirty and vindictive, but it brought Asa to me, and I don't know if it would have happened otherwise.

Am I okay now? Did I magically become fixed?

No. Not even close.

And though I honestly feel like I may never be, *this*, having him and knowing our future is together, I'm slowly putting that puzzle together again, one broken piece at a time.

CHAPTER 24

Where we go from here

ASA

"I don't want to leave this room."

"Me either." I sigh and pick through the last of Barrette's Sour Patch Kids. "But I'm starving and you've worn me out."

Barrette gasps. "I have not." I look over at her. She's blushing. I raise an eyebrow, smirking. "Okay, maybe a little," she agrees." Do you have plans today?"

With a grunt, I swing my legs over the side of her bed and stand, still completely naked. She blushes again as her eyes roam over my body, lingering on my dick. "Food first," I remind her, "but I do have a position meeting at three and then some conditioning." Reaching for my jeans, I pull them on and glance around her room in search of where my shirt went last night. "What do you say I take you to breakfast."

Barrette stretches out on the bed, my jersey she's wearing rising up and revealing her tight stomach. How someone so tiny can actually have muscle definition is beyond me, but she does. "I think I can eat," she says, her head resting on her hand. She's staring at the new mason jar I gave her this morning. "But I have a question for you."

"And?"

Her eyes move from the jar to mine. "Are we like, *dating?*"

I look over at her again and she's gazing at me with a perfect combination of playfulness, tenderness, and heat. "I think...." I pause and step toward her, my hands on either side of her hips. I kiss her hipbone, then the other. She threads her hands in my hair as I whisper, "We were dating long before last night."

"Good." She yanks my head up. "Because I'd like to start calling you honey. Or babe. Or maybe Bear."

"Bear?" Laughing, I sit up. It's nice seeing this side of her again. I almost forgot it existed in the first place.

I find my shirt on the floor next to my shoes. I smile because it smells like her.

With a grin on her face, she reads the quote I taped to the inside of the jar.

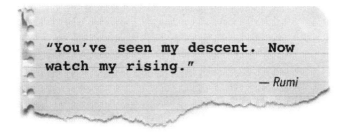

"You've seen my descent. Now watch my rising."
— *Rumi*

She sits up and reaches for my hand, urging me forward. "This one might be my favorite." I don't know why, or how, but it's the first time she's noticed the busted knuckles. How they went unnoticed this long by her is beyond me because it looks fucking brutal. "Oh my God, what happened? Is that from the game?"

I shake my head. "No." A ball of emotion works its way into my throat and I struggle to maintain a neutral expression. She waits and runs her fingers gently over my knuckles, waiting for an explanation.

"I returned Roman's shirt before Thanksgiving," I tell her, my words slow. I don't want to tell her about the girl.

Her worried ocean eyes find mine. "You hit him?"

"No. I hit the wall beside him." My chest tightens at the admission.

"Oh." Her eyes are on mine, so many unspoken questions playing them.

I draw in a breath, hoping it gives me courage. It doesn't. "When I went to his dorm, there was a girl on the floor and all I saw was you."

Her brows collapse, her hand on her mouth concealing her gasp. "Was she...?" Her words pause, her chin shaking with emotions she can't contain. "Did he...?" Again, she can't continue.

"I don't know. She was clearly drunk, but I think okay. Campus security took her." I move closer and sit next to her on the bed. She rests her head on my shoulder, her breathing heavy. Guilt rushes through me. For not telling her sooner, and for no reason at all other than if I hadn't left Barrette the night of the party, none of this would have happened. But then again, I can't think like that. Just because I hadn't been at that party, didn't mean it couldn't have happened in the four years I was gone. I think about Roman. Every good memory I have of my childhood friend is now tarnished by his betrayal.

I stop myself from the thoughts flooding through me. I'm tired of feeling this way. I won't let myself any longer and I won't let *her*. She deserves better.

I cup her cheek with my hand and twist to face her. "This is just another reminder that going to the police was the right thing to do." Gently, I grab her by the hips and place her on my lap. She rests her forehead against mine. "Please don't worry. I'm going to protect you."

She has that look on her face. The one that screams you've lost your damn mind. Actually, it's shock. It's similar to the one she gave me last night when she found out I was a virgin until her. "Asa, I'm scared of what this means for you."

I lean back, searching her eyes and trying to understand where she's coming from. "What do you mean?"

"You're on the team with him. He's well-known and I just, I don't know...." Panic rushes through her, a tremble working its way to her hands. "You saw him last night. He doesn't care. I'm worried about his reaction."

"Hey." I cup her face in my hands and make her look at me. "We're gonna be fine," I assure her. "We'll figure it out."

Blinking slowly, she sighs, her shoulders sinking. Wrapping her arms around my neck, she kisses me and then draws back. "Should we see if Joey and Terrell want to get some breakfast?" Though her words are light, there's an underlying worry to them.

"Sure."

Life and happiness, it's fragile. It can all go away in a matter of seconds. Never take that for granted. I would never take Barrette and her love for granted. Not ever. And there is no way in hell I'm going to give Roman the chance to destroy that.

"Asa, oh my God, you were amazing last night!"

Believe it or not, that's not coming from Barrette. That's from the group of girls and their parents next to us at Portage Bay Café. Perks of being a UW football player, we got to skip the lines and they got us a table right away. Only problem is that you'd think we were royalty because every girl around twenty seems to know who I am.

Seated beside me picking at a plate of french toast, Barrette says very little to the conversation around us. The one where Terrell is telling Joey about the Bahamas and swimming with the pigs. Last year the team went to the Bahamas for spring break as a bonding experience. I hear none of that. What I hear is the unsettling nervousness of Barrette and the way she's not eating. I know her, and I know where her mind is going. She's scared of what all this means now that it's out in the open.

I smile at the girls, give them an autograph, a picture, and then I wrap my arm around Barrette. My touch is welcomed, at least I think it is when she melts against my frame.

Terrell looks at the two of us and winks. "So, B... spring break? Whatta say ya come to Baton Rouge with us?"

She looks at Terrell, then me. "You're going?"

I swallow. Shit. "I uh." I glare at Terrell. "I hadn't committed to it yet." Picking up my napkin, I toss it at his head. "Dick."

He laughs. "He's telling you the truth. He didn't." And then leans in with his hand on Joey's. "It'd be fun if we all went."

Conversation fills around the table of Baton Rouge, but I can't tell how Barrette feels about anything, let alone Baton Rouge. Anxiety gnaws at me. Needing to know if she's okay, I lean in and place my hand on her thigh. She jumps, her body tensing. All of her. It's like she doesn't even recognize my touch, let alone me. Her head turns, her expression cloudy. She's elsewhere.

I remove my hand, my posture rigid.

"I'm sorry," she whispers, shaking her head and curling into my side. "I don't know what that was."

"It's all right." I'm hesitant, but I kiss her forehead. I press my lips to her warm skin and I keep them there, hoping it's a reassurance she needs that I'm nothing like the guys who took advantage of her. I'd never harm her in any way.

Joey notices the change in Barrette's behavior and smiles at her. "Hey, B. Wanna get pedicures while they're at their position meetings?"

Barrette nods, smiling. "I'd like that."

I pay for breakfast while Barrette and Joey use the restroom.

"What the fuck?" I slap my hand against Terrell's chest. "Why'd you do that?"

He stares at me, blank-faced but smiling. "I'm sorry, but yous need to buck the fuck up and take that girl out. Not this shit where you take her to fuckin' brunch."

In theory, he's right. I should take her out on a real date, but that's not what's bothering me. Barrette's reaction is. "I know that, but she spent all of spring break last year in the hospital from an anxiety attack while we were living it up." It's just another example of all the times I haven't been there for her when I wished I had been.

Terrell leans his massive shoulder into the wall outside the restaurant and squints into the sun. Blowing on a breath, he shrugs. "I didn't mean anything by it, but you can't always protect her, nor should you feel guilty about when you're not with her."

I'm not convinced. Barrette and Joey exit the restaurant and onto the street. I watch her walk toward me, picking apart her every mannerism. She smiles, and it's genuine. It's not forced.

"We're gonna go get pedicures," Joey says.

Terrell wraps both his burly arms around her. "My favorite color is red."

"Boy, I'm not painting my nails your favorite color." She flips her dark hair over her shoulder. "I'm my own person."

I take a moment to look around. The streets are crowded, people bumping into us as they pass by, while the smells of salt and sea invades my senses. I watch Barrette beside me, my body blocking hers from the people passing by us. Her eyes are on mine.

"I'm okay," she whispers, her hands gripping the front of my jacket. I believe her. I have no reason not to. "I think an afternoon with Joey is what I need."

I nod, winking at her. "You do. Try to relax."

A smile finds its way to her lips. "You too."

"I think that can be arranged." My hands make their way to her hips and I yank her against my chest. She breathes in, pressing her cheek to my heart. "Can I see you after practice?"

"I would love that. You can help me study."

Chuckling, I draw back. "We never actually get any studying done."

"Who says I want to actually study?"

Ah, yes. There's my girl. I kiss her once more before she disappears up the street with Joey. Terrell grins watching Joey. "She's a cool chick."

I level him a serious look. "Don't hurt her."

"Bitch, please." He gives me that "you're crazy" expression he's so good at. "I'm a fuckin' gentleman."

I raise an eyebrow and pull out my phone to check the time. "*Can* be."

"Listen, man." He motions me forward toward the pier. "I know what she's been through," he adds. "I won't hurt her like that."

"I know you won't. I'm just warning you that if you do, you'll have to answer to me."

After basically laughing in my fucking face, he shoves his hands into his jacket, his dark eyes on mine. "We haven't even had sex, and I can tell you without a doubt, I've got it bad."

That's surprising. Leaning into the railing on the pier, I sigh, running my hand through my hair. "I know what you mean."

He glances over at me, then the water below us. "Joey said Barrette went to the police." I nod. "You think it's him?"

"I know it is," I seethe, the anger working its way through me again.

"So what are we gonna do about it?"

"Nothing. The police will handle it."

Terrell's nostrils flare and his eyes level me. "That's not what I mean."

I stare at him, unsure. "What?"

"I'm talking about the team. That was bullshit last night."

He's right. It was bullshit. I took some hard hits all because Codey wasn't protecting me.

"I'm not about to sit back while they destroy your million-dollar arm," he adds.

"I'm not worried about me. I'm worried about Barrette. When this gets out, who knows what's going to happen."

"I've got her," he assures me. "We all do. Our team, they play for you and defend you. No matter what."

I fucking hope he's right. Like it or not, our relationship started in the aftermath of tragedy. Because of that, we're both clinging to an unhealthy hope that together we can deal with it.

My high school football coach once told me I could have all the talent in the world, but if I didn't have the ability to finish things, I'd never do anything with my life. I know exactly what he was referring to and for Barrette, I'll make sure this is finished. Roman and whoever else was involved will pay for this.

CHAPTER 25

A new kind of reality

I think I read this somewhere, but I can't remember where. When you become fearless, you become limitless. Is that true? Can someone really become fearless?

I don't remember the first month after the night I was raped. It's all a blur. I spent a good amount of time at Asa's house, in his bed, avoiding reality. I didn't talk to anyone and the only food I ate was anything Carlin forced me to eat. My point is, I didn't have to face anyone and have them ask, what are those bruises from? Is it true, were you really raped?

And if I did get those questions, I had a panic attack and had to basically run away. A month later, I moved to Seattle and into a dorm. I thought being in college I wouldn't have to deal with any of the questions because who would know, right? Big city. College. Why would anyone care?

For the most part, that's exactly how it was. No one knew anything. Until the panic attacks were a weekly occurrence and my therapist suggested I join a support group. From there, it got out that I was, in fact, a victim of sexual assault. But still, no one has ever said anything to my face.

Until....

"That's her, isn't it?"

"Yeah."

"Do you believe it?"

Until those are the whispers following me as I'm walking to class. I don't know who they are, but I imagine they're girls. Sounds like a girl. High-pitched. Maybe a cheerleader?

"I don't know. I can't see Roman needing to rape a girl. Look at him. Wouldn't you just willingly spread your legs for him?"

"I know, right?" another girl gasps. "Seriously, so hot."

Then they laugh. Like it's funny.

"I heard she's dating Asa Lawson."

Now I know who it is. The way Asa Lawson rolls off her tongue, like she'd do anything to be with him. Eva. Turning on my heel, I face them, the bitter cold wind of the morning slapping my face. "For your information," I spit, smiling at them with a sudden edge I didn't know I had and quite possibly want to bottle up and store. "I am dating Asa Lawson. He's mine, and you can stop your fucking games. He's always been mine. Not yours." I pause and point to Bethany, her sidekick. "Or yours, or anyone elses. He doesn't belong to this school as your legend of football. He's mine. All *fucking* mine." I have no idea where the words are coming from, just that they're pouring out of me like I'm speaking in tongues and have no control over what comes next. I take a breath, gasping, unsure what's coming next. They stare, wide-eyed, slack-mouthed.

Eva's the first to speak, blinking rapidly and adjusting her bag on her shoulder. "I'm sorry." That's all she says, and then walks away. I want to run after her and rip her bleached hair from her head, but I'm not going to do that because everyone is staring at me. And I do mean everyone.

I'm a good person. I am. Until I'm given a reason to show my evil side. And these girls, they're bringing out everything bitter inside me.

I knew my life would change forever when I filed that police report. A new kind of reality—other than Eva and her friends—I hadn't prepared for it to hit me Monday morning in class.

The one I had with Roman.

Part of me thought he wouldn't come to class. Why would he? He knows I'm in it.

But that wouldn't be Roman. He's a shithead and specializes in making everyone uncomfortable. The moment he enters the room, bile floods my mouth. Looking at him makes me physically sick to think of what he did. In my dreams, he has a face now, the face of a villain playing the leading role in my nightmare.

Gossip and wandering stares follow him as he pushes past the doors, entering the room and casting a lingering glance my way. He sits next to me, leaning into my shoulder. "Drop the fucking charges, Barrette," he seethes.

A shiver works its way through me, despair and anxiety battering me as I contemplate if going to the police was the right thing to do. I don't know what to say. Trembling takes root in my hands and I drop the pen I had been holding.

Panic creeps up my throat, my heart pumps wildly in my chest. My fight-or-flight instinct kicks in and I don't know if it's just my mind playing tricks on me, or if I'm remembering details about the night. I move my gaze from the teacher's to Roman's.

His jaw clenches and a malicious grin slips over his mouth. "Is that a no?"

Panic bubbles inside me, but I refuse to let this get to me. "If you're so innocent, why'd you lie?"

To my surprise, he laughs. I want him to suffer. I want him to pay for what he's done. He runs a hand through his hair, a few loose strands falling over his forehead. "I didn't lie. We've had a relationship."

I'm trapped in his gaze, completely immobilized. I can't wrap my head around his reaction, or mine, let alone tell myself to move. I'm paralyzed. "No, we didn't. We were friends until you *raped* me."

At the word, he averts his gaze to the teacher, but his words hold a menacing edge I've never ever thought I'd hear from him. "What makes you think you didn't ask for it?" And then his eyes slide to mine.

My body locks up, my hands clenching my sides. Rage hits my chest and the hatred in my eyes radiates through me.

Amusement dances in his eyes, a cocky smirk plastered on his face. "You did. You fuckin' begged me."

"To stop," I shout, causing the entire class to draw their attention to us. I want them looking. I want them to know who he really is.

"Well played." His lips pull into an arrogant smile, his voice dropping. "But I don't remember it that way. Guess it's your word against mine."

"Fuck you," I lash without thinking and slap him across the face. Nausea churns in my gut, my spine rigid with tension. I'm so sick of this shit with him. I won't let him manipulate me.

His cheek reddens, his jaw locking like he wants so badly to smash my head into the table. He smirks and gestures between us with a flick of his wrist. "You already did, or so you say."

"I'm not dropping the charges. In fact—" I stand and push away from him. "—I can't wait to face you in court and see the look on your face when your entire future is taken away from you because of what you took from me."

And then I stalk away without another glance. My hands shake as I dial Asa's number and press the phone to my ear. He answers on the first ring. "You okay?"

"I need you." I can barely get the words out I'm shaking so bad. "Right now."

"I'll be there in a minute," he rushes to say, and I can hear the noise in the background of his professor asking why he's answering his phone in class. "Send me your location."

I hang up and send him a pin drop to where I'm at. He's right, he's there in a few minutes, just enough time for Roman to walk out of the classroom with Codey and two linemen flanking his side.

Though I'm not sure calling him to defend me had been my

intention, I knew he'd protect me and get in Roman's face. It's who Asa is to his core. He fights for what he believes in.

Reality slaps me in the face. I shouldn't have called him. I should have walked away.

Any minute I know I'm going to throw up. I just know it. It's rising and rising, and the moment I see Roman approach Asa, the anger takes over. I don't want him anywhere near him. Suddenly, I understand Asa's need to protect me because I feel it then. It pulses through me like the need to breathe does. Natural and effortless.

I step toward them, my pulse ringing in my ears.

"Stay away from her," Asa warns, positioning himself between the two of us.

A crowd forms outside the building, Roman and Asa face-to-face on the stairs. "Why?" Roman asks, smirking as he runs his hand through his hair, never leading on that inside, his world is crumbling over the truth he's afraid of being revealed. He puffs his chest out. "You gonna stop me?"

The sounds of hushed conversations and the thump of my heart tickles my ears. I wet my dry lips, urging myself to step forward and stop them. Asa can't touch him. My body is screaming at my head as a violent battle starts up. *Move!* I scream at myself, but I'm rooted in place by my fear.

"You're going to pay for all your lies," Asa spits at him. He glances at me briefly and though I know I shouldn't think this, he's devastatingly beautiful when he's angry. With his heavy brow pinched together, he turns back to Roman. "And your betrayal."

Tension bleeds into the air as they face-off, two childhood friends, their bond destroyed by a lie. My heart aches that I'm the reason for it. I put myself in a compromising position, and Roman, he took what wasn't his. That's the bottom line here. I can't blame myself any longer. It's not fair to me, or anyone else who's ever said no and their denial went unheard.

Pain slams into me and I know I have to gather the strength to stand up for myself and Asa. I can't let him touch Roman. They're

yelling at one another, their harsh words inflicting pain their fists
wish to follow up on, but they both know what happens if they do. I
reach for Asa, and he jerks his head up, his eyes burning with undis-
guised rage. He steps back, forcibly trying to calm himself down.
Suddenly we're surrounded by members of the team, and I notice
Terrell first. "What'd up, A?" he asks, coolly glancing at Asa and then
Roman. "Ya cool?"

Asa shakes his head, unable to reply

Roman groans, crossing his arms over his chest. "Jesus Christ,
mind your own fucking business, man."

"*He's* my business." Terrell steps toward Roman, his thick massive
frame towering over Roman's. "And *she's* my fuckin' business. So I
suggest you get to steppin'."

Roman fixes his dark eyes on me, but he doesn't say anything. He
backs up a step, smiling. "Keep your distance, B," he taunts, his eyes
ablaze with a new kind of heat. His eyes flick to Asa and he leans in
over Codey and Waylon who are trying to pull him away. "That pussy
was mine first."

That does it. Those are the words that get Roman flat on his ass.
Not from who you think though. Believe it or not, it's Terrell who
sends his fist into Roman's face. And I have to say, it's gratifying.

Security is there in an instant, and it's broken up quickly before
anything else can happen, and the football players yank Asa away.

"I'm gonna kill him," Asa seethes, his voice void of any emotion.
He's lost it. Completely. The good... it's slowly disappearing because
of me and I can't, I won't let that happen.

"No, you're not," Waylon tells him, backing him and me up and
out of the way of the crowd. "Coach wants to talk to us. *All* of us."

Asa nods but doesn't let go of my hand. The remaining players
shuffle aside, and I'm left in the midst of all of it next to the one I
fear isn't going to let this go. Not this time.

I stand next to him, tilting my chin up defiantly and piercing him
with my stare. "Leave it alone," I remind him, knowing what he's
thinking. "He will pay for what he's done. But not by you."

Asa reels me into his arms, closing the gap between us, pressing his body against mine. "You need to file a restraining order," he tells me, his voice bordering on a growl.

"I will. Right away. I'll do it now, but you have to promise me you're going to let the police handle this."

He nods.

"No." I grab his face between my hands. "Don't, Asa. You can't ruin your future over this. Not ever."

He pins me with troubled eyes. "I won't let him hurt you again."

My eyes widen. "It's not up to you. You touch him and your career is over. He knows that."

Asa sighs, stepping back to create distance between us. He scrubs his hand over his jaw, tension filtering into the air again. When his eyes land on mine again they're full of fire. "Fuck my career."

"No." I move closer, ignoring the questioning stares around us. "Don't say that. He's already taken so much from us." His chest is heaving, his anger so embedded in his words I fear there's no stopping this turn in him, but I know I need to. I need to because he was there for me when I needed him the most and I'll be there for him through this. "I love you, Asa. And I don't think I could live with myself if you gave it all up and let him win. You wouldn't let me give up, so I'm not letting you."

It takes him a moment before he really hears the words I'm saying. When he does, it hits him like a bullet to the chest. He yanks me hard against his chest, holding me there. And though I want to believe that's his promise, I'm not so sure it is.

CHAPTER 26

2B1

ASA

The quarterback of a team has to keep them together. It's the most difficult position in sports. The number one trait of all the great ones? Competitive spirit. Without it, it can destroy your team. He has to be cool under pressure.

Me? Today? I'm none of that. I'm anything but that stereotypical quarterback. Football has always made me feel alive, but now, in my anger, I've never felt so distraught and alone.

I knew when Barrette went to the police both our lives would never be the same. What I didn't expect was for Roman to react this way. Actually, I knew he would. I just hoped he wouldn't.

Coach looks at me, then Terrell, then Roman and the rest of the fifteen members of the team who were involved in the argument outside Smith Hall. "Someone better start talking or you're all suspended from the team. I'll start fourth string if I have to just to prove my fucking point that this childish behavior will not be tolerated on this team." Coach Benning looks to me, then Roman and Terrell. "I mean it. What the fuck happened?"

Commotion takes over and everyone is talking but me. With my hands in my pockets to hide the shaking, I remain livid and uncontrolled, ready to turn into a complete maniac and slam Roman's head against the desk until he admits what he did.

Coach silences the room. "That's enough!"

Stepping forward, Roman clears his throat. "Just a misunderstanding, sir."

This is where I snap. I can't take it any longer. "Bullshit it was," I bark, refusing to let him get away with this. I don't care what the risk is.

That starts another argument before Coach grips the edge of his desk and flips it over in front of us. Playbooks, pictures, his UW mug filled with coffee crashes to the floor in front of us. "Enough! Everyone out. Lawson and Winslow, you stay."

"Can't I stay?" Terrell teases, trying to lighten the mood. "I don't wanna miss all the fun."

Coach drills him with a death glare. "Get the fuck out."

He does and Coach turns to look at me, and then Roman. "I've had enough of your shit so both of you better start talking. What's this I hear about rape?"

My eyes snap to Roman's, waiting for the lie, only he doesn't say a damn thing. He just stares at the ground like it's going to answer for him. Well, if he's not going to say anything I might as well. "Roman raped my girlfriend."

"No charges have been filed," he spits out with a venomous edge toward me.

"*Yet.*" Our eyes lock, mine betrayed, his controlled. "No charges have been filed *yet*, but they will."

"Oh my God," Coach sighs, scrubbing his hands over his face. Letting out a sigh, he points to the door. "Winslow, wait in the hall. I'll be talking to you in a minute."

He grumbles something, slams the door and then I'm left alone with Coach. It's then that I feel something like a kid in trouble, my anger is still very much present and taking over.

"Listen to me, Asa. I understand you're angry, and by the sounds of it, you have every right to be." He takes a breath before his intimidating stare moves to mine. "With that being said, you're the captain and you need to control the team," Coach yells, the veins in his neck protruding. Look at him. It looks like he's going to have a heart attack. "You're a leader whether you like it or not, and I expect you to portray yourself as one, on and off the field."

There is no arguing with him. He doesn't want to hear it. He's right, though. I haven't been acting like a leader.

"With that being said, I will be looking into what's going on with Roman. I do not tolerate this kind of behavior and neither will the NCAA. If charges are filed, he's suspended immediately pending investigation. Between you and me, he's already in a great deal of trouble and his chances at playing in the upcoming bowl game are subject to their approval, not mine."

I nod. I can tell by looking at him he doesn't want me to say anything. Bile burns my throat, threatening to spill over. Rage pounds through me in an angry beat.

Thump.

Breathe.

Thump.

Breathe.

"Send Winslow in."

I leave without another word. Closing the door behind me, I see Roman's eyes drift to mine as he's leaned against the wall. I level him with a glare, my voice dripping with venom when I say, "I will do whatever I have to do to make you fucking pay for what you did," I speak slowly, treating him like the idiot he is.

"I don't think you will. I know where your priorities are." His jaw twitches, his cheek and eye swelling, his expression revealing zero emotion.

"You have no idea where my priorities are."

"Well then, I'm looking forward to it." He pushes himself off the wall, his shoulder slamming into mine as he passes by.

Quarterbacks are usually adept at staying cool under pressure in front of thousands. But this play, I have no control over the outcome.

"I THINK WE SHOULD MOVE OFF CAMPUS," I TELL BARRETTE, pacing her dorm room. She's holding a piece of paper. A restraining order. Only it wasn't filed by her today, it was filed by Roman's attorney on his behalf. It's against me and her. Barrette counter filed one of course but the fact that Roman even had the nerve to do so just goes to show you just how fucking delusional he really is.

Barrette stares at me, my words slowly sinking in. "What? What are you saying?"

"That we should move in together. Off campus. Away from all this bullshit."

She blinks, and I think she sees the rationality in it. "But don't you have to live in student housing for your scholarship?"

"No. UW doesn't require student athletes to live on campus. I'll probably have to get some kind of clearance, but I'll talk to Coach and see what he says. My dad's friend has a house here in Seattle. It's only two miles from campus."

Barrette's expression shifts and I don't know this one. Is it shyness? Nervousness? I can't tell and it's killing me not knowing. "Asa," she says, and I know it's disappointment. "What happened today, with your team and me, us, all this crap, I can't do that to you. I refuse to let you put your career in jeopardy over me. It's not fair to you."

I can't believe what she's saying. And I refuse to let her think I wouldn't risk it all for her. I move toward her and kneel in front of her. I slide my hands up her thighs and wait for her to look at me. "Everything that's happened to you, that's not fucking fair, Barrette. Your ability to say no was taken from you. I'm fully capable of making my own decisions. And I choose you. Every goddamn time, I choose *you*."

It takes her a moment before she finally realizes what I'm saying, but when she does, emotion floods her face, her hands grasping my face to pull me to her.

I may not have any control over what happens with Roman, but I can control what happens between me and Barrette.

"Are you sure we should move in together? I mean, I can always get an apartment off campus or something but for me and you... is that what you want?"

My arms circle around her waist. "It's what I want. I want to know you're safe. This way I can control it. We can have separate rooms if you feel it's moving too fast."

She arches an eyebrow, a giggle working its way through her. "Yeah, right."

I have to laugh myself. "It wouldn't be easy, and I'd probably sleep on the floor in your room every night, but I'd do it for you."

Barrette slides to the edge of the bed and then onto my lap, her arms around my shoulders. "Today, in class, I wanted the world to stop when he sat next to me. But when I saw you, I realized it didn't matter what happened. I had to save you, just like you saved me." Her right hand slips off my shoulder and touches my cheek. I lean into her warm touch. "Together, I know we can get through this. *Off campus*. I can't be here anymore than I have to."

"So you'll move in with me?"

She smiles. "Only if we get a king-size bed. I'm so tired of trying to sleep on this twin bed with you."

I wink. "I like the way you think. More room for activities."

She pushes against my shoulder. "You're such a boy. I meant for sleeping."

My lips find hers when I whisper, "Sure you did."

This is one change I'm ready for.

CHAPTER 27

Off Campus

ASA

"No. We don't need that."

"Are you crazy? That's four dollars and thirty-eight cents an ounce." He points at the label like I should know these things. "Look at the tags."

I don't.

"You do not need brand name orange juice, Asa. If it has oranges in it, it's orange juice."

Those are the remarks you hear when you're grocery shopping with Terrell. He even makes me put back my Sour Patch Kids. It's like going with my mom again and I strangely feel like a child when he schools me on how to read labels to find the best price for toilet paper. You don't think about these things when you're living in a dorm and everything is paid for.

Now that I'm living off campus, I have to think about a food budget and things like remembering to pay the power bill. All worth it if you ask me to be away from the drama on campus. It seems everywhere we go now, Barrette is stared at and talked about. I don't know how she manages to attend class without breaking down but every day she surprises me and keeps pushing forward.

I pick up a bottle of laundry soap and put it in the cart, waiting for Terrell's permission. He frowns and then looks at the shelf. "If we get the bigger bottle, it's cheaper in the long run."

I groan. "You know what, next time I'm just giving you a list and you're going by yourself."

He smiles and continues walking down the aisles with me. "I happen to enjoy grocery shopping. You just suck at it."

"I don't suck at it. You're impossible to please." He glances down at the list in his hand the girls gave us and then stops in his tracks. "Oh, hell no. Are they serious?"

I burst out laughing when I see what's written. "I can't wait to see what they say when you try to bring them the cheap version of tampons."

His frown deepens and it's like he's being asked to rip off his toenails. "Do you think we can just tell them they were sold out?"

"Not likely."

"Then you grab them."

I cross my arms over my chest, smiling. "Nope. You're the one that said you *love* grocery shopping."

Yep. We're arguing next to the feminine products because neither one of us wants to put the tampons in the cart. Finally, it's me who reaches for the box and tosses them in the cart. "You're being ridiculous," I tell him, wondering how he was raised by a single mom and feared tampons.

"I don't fear them," he lies, pushing the cart forward into the frozen food section. He doesn't let us buy fresh fruit. We have to buy frozen because apparently it's a waste of money to buy fresh ones.

"Bullshit." While I stand next to the cold glass doors, uninterested in his rambling over the price of frozen fruit, a group of girl's stroll past us, giggling and trying to capture our attention. "Can you reach that bag of blackberries for us?" One asks, motioning toward the top shelf. I recognize them from campus but I don't know their names, or care for that matter.

I reach for the bag and hand it to them. "Here you go." They smile and flirt asking if I'm Asa Lawson. I nod. "I suppose I am," I tell them, closing the door behind me. I'd rather stick my head inside the freezer behind me than have a conversation with anyone today. Thankfully they leave after telling us good luck in the upcoming game.

Halfway through the trip, our conversation shifts from my lack of money management, thank God, to the bowl game in a week. Everything is crazy at the moment and the bowl game is the last thing on my mind. It needs to be number one and it's Terrell that reminds me of where my focus needs to be.

"No matter how much you stress out about this, it's not going to change the outcome," he tells me, checking the price of pizza rolls. His downfall. He eats them every night after practice. "It's out of your hands and hers."

He's right. I can worry myself to death about what's going to happen, but it's not changing anything. I nod and try to focus on anything but Barrette and Roman. It's useless. Like it or not, my thoughts are intent on making sure she's okay through the entire process. I pushed her to file charges and if this breaks her, it's on me.

"She's stronger than ya think, A." He tosses a bag in the cart. "And I got your back. I'm not going to let anything happen to either one of you."

I also know what he's implying. It's not just Barrette's case that's bothering me. I fear our bowl game because our team isn't the same since the rape charges became public knowledge. Not only is Barrette restricted from attending the game because of the restraining order, Roman holds a lot more clout on the team than I gave him credit for and like it or not, the dynamic changed the day of that fight on campus.

"You're the captain of the team and I guarantee you, they've got your back just the same." I try to listen to him, but it's distracting when he's now searching through his coupons in his hand as we're at the register. He hands me a stack. "Be useful. Look for the one on this shampoo. It's in there somewhere."

To piss him off, right before the cashier reads the total, I toss a bag of Sour Patch Kids on the scale and hold my hands up. "Can't take it back now. It's already scanned."

He glares at me, which, if you knew Terrell, his glare is fucking intimidating as hell. "You just threw off my entire budget by 99 cents."

Remind me never to go with him again.

The cashier smiles as she counts out the money Terrell hands her. He even gives her exact change.

BACK AT THE HOUSE, THE GIRLS ARE BAKING PIES TOGETHER. I have to admit, this part of living off campus and coming home to a house that smells like apple pie is totally worth it. Maybe not worth Terrell and his constant need to budget everything from our groceries to the exact amount of time we can spend in the shower every morning, but worth it to see Barrette's face every night before I fall asleep.

As we put away the groceries, Joey holds up the box of tampons and laughs. "You can't expect me to use these ones. Take them back. I don't want a vagina full of cotton pieces."

His eyebrows raise fractionally. "Why would there be cotton pieces in your vagina?"

Beside me, Barrette starts giggling, her cheeks tinted pink with embarrassment. "I can't even believe we're having this conversation."

"Because they're cheap and the cotton in them doesn't absorb. It just comes apart. Trust me, I'm a girl and I've tried them all."

Terrell shrugs. "They were a dollar cheaper than the Tampax brand. Just use them."

She tosses the box at his head. "Then you're getting the cheaper version of sex next time."

"What's the cheaper version of sex?" He stops what he's doing and stares at her, a bag of whole carrots in his hand. He won't let us buy baby carrots. Nope. You have to buy the whole ones and cut them down to baby sizes.

Smiling at him, Joey makes a jacking off motion.

He grabs the box and his receipt. "Fine. I'll get the Tampax brand."

I pull the Sour Patch Kids from my pocket and send them Barrette's way. "He's a nightmare."

She laughs and eats the green ones. "You're telling me. Last week he made me brush my teeth with toothpaste he made from scratch. It was awful and I still can't feel my tongue."

I wrap my arm around her shoulder. "Is that pie for me?"

She nods. "Yeah, it was to cheer you up."

"And I need cheering up because?"

"My attorney called. The DNA results will be in Monday."

Heat hits my face, my blood pressure rising. I try to remember Terrell's only advice today that made sense. Somewhere between his lecture on the price of tampons to the frozen fruit debates. What's going to happen is going to happen. No amount of worrying is going to change the outcome of this. I had to trust that it was out of our hands and in the judge's.

"I'm fine," I tell Barrette when she moves to hold my face in her hands.

She searches my eyes. "You don't look fine."

Leaning in, I press my lips to hers, the taste of sour sugar on both of ours. I swallow and try to compose my voice before I whisper, "It's going to be okay."

She nods. "It will be. And we have pie."

"I asked him for vanilla ice cream," Joey snaps, staring at the ice cream container of mint chocolate chip.

I laugh. They have no idea what I went through today. "Mint chocolate chip was on sale. Vanilla wasn't."

"That cheap bastard." She glares at the pie in front of us. "How are we going to have ice cream with our pie now?"

Barrette reaches into the back of the freezer to the ice cream she stashes in there. I only know this because it's what the three of us do when Terrell's sleeping and not policing us. "I say we make him eat pie with mint chocolate chip and we have the vanilla I bought last week."

We eat half the pie before he returns with the Tampax. Joey pushes a plate with pie and one scoop of mint chocolate chip ice cream next to it. Do you think he eats it?

Ha. He never admits defeat and despite his distaste for anything minty, he eats the pie with the ice cream.

Joey sighs and puts the plate in the sink. "We're gonna crack him someday guys."

I don't share her optimism on this one.

CHAPTER 28

What you don't hear about

BARRETTE

When you hear the word rape, what do think of? Sexual assault, right?

What do you see when you think of it? A man forcing a woman to have sex with him, am I right?

It's not always a man forcing a woman. Sometimes it's a man forcing another man. Or a woman drugging a man.

Let me tell you about the things you don't hear. You don't hear about the after. The "what happens next" part. Sure, there are stories of surviving, and some of them not. There's strength and truth, and downright heroism in what women, and men, go through, but you rarely, if ever, see the in-between. The messy details that get pushed aside when the verdict is read.

What I learn from the very beginning is that nothing happens right away. Even the warrant for arrest. It's after Asa and I move off campus and into a house with Joey and Terrell. It happens two days after Roman is suspended by the NCAA, the day before the Fiesta Bowl. He's not suspended because of the rape charges brought against him, but he's withdrawn for a year from competition after failing a drug test. Somehow it makes me feel like testing positive for cocaine trumps rape. Because in this case, it does.

My case goes to trial. It's drawn out and unnecessary.

And then came the messy parts that involve detectives and prosecuting attorneys and a male judge who just so happens to be a huge fan of college football. It's hard to stomach, and even harder to endure the favoritism and the downright fucking lies his attorney tells the jury to convince them that given his status as an athlete, I targeted him and asked for it.

"It was consensual sex," Roman's attorney explains to the jury as he attempts to solidify their case.

"If you think what I looked like after that night was consensual, I'd hate to be your wife," I tell them.

He has the nerve to push back with "What did you look like?"

"Look at the pictures taken by the sexual assault nurse. I dare you."

The jury sees the photographs taken that night in the hospital. And for the first time, I did too. Though I hadn't prepared to see myself so vulnerable and on display for the entire court room, it isn't me I'm worried about in those moments. It's Asa. The anguish, the rage, the yelling at the bailiff when he's escorted out, I hate that he had to hold me through all that and now see it again.

The sexual assault forensic exam I had, the one that humiliated me, came back with three different DNAs. One is, in fact, Roman's.

Did you think it was him? Did you want it to be? Or did you pray, please, don't be him? I think in some ways, I thought all of the above.

He says I asked for it and verbally told him yes.

Even with the overwhelming amount of evidence and injuries conclusive to me being brutally raped, his attorney insists it's consensual and that given my small frame, Roman might have been a little rough with me without meaning to.

And yeah, Asa has to be detained, again, at this point.

Honestly, I couldn't believe the injustice I experienced in those first few days of the trial. It was no wonder women didn't report sexual assault if this was the treatment they received.

Unfortunately for me, this is how Roman's attorney paints a picture of me.

I flirted so I asked for it.

I drank so obviously I was making poor judgments.

I willingly took drugs, so it's okay.

I told him I wanted it, so it was his word against mine.

As the trial moves forward, they accuse me of targeting a star athlete and Roman refuses to cooperate with who else was present and state multiple times, "I don't know who was there. It was just me. We had sex, she was fine, and I don't know what happened to her after that."

Later, his story changes. He knows who was there. He just, you know, forgot he knew the other two men. I'm horrified to know the other two other guys took turns with me, because why not? She's unconscious, she won't remember.

Three times throughout the trial, Asa is detained and eventually banned from the courtroom because of his outbursts when he finds out the other two men who raped me were in fact, the ones who helped him carry me to the car after he found me. I didn't know them up until the trial, but when I see Greg, and the tattoo on his hand, that's when I knew where the memory came from.

For a while I thought maybe it had been Xander, but it wasn't. He willingly took a DNA test. I never knew Xander to be that kind of guy. He could be a douche, but a rapist? Truth is, I don't think there is any single trait to define a rapist. I certainly never thought Roman would be one.

And then comes the verdict because that's the part that matters, right? That's the part of all this when you find out who is guilty, and who is simply a victim of circumstance.

Six months from the day I stepped foot in the Olympia Police Department, a jury finds Roman Winslow guilty of aggravated sexual assault and sentences him to three years in jail. He's required to register as a sex offender for life. He's suspended from UW and had his scholarship revoked. His football career is over.

But it's not enough.

Nothing is enough when I look the judge in the face at the sentencing where he overrules the jury and he says the words, "Low-risk to re-offend," and gives him one year in county jail and three years of probation.

Probation. That's like fucking detention. Asa loses his shit on the judge, nearly costs him his own scholarship and career, but if you ask me, it's justified for us to feel this way. Toby and Greg, they receive a maximum sentence of five years. They, in many ways, take the fall for Roman.

Even after all that, the pain, the reminders, the anxiety and the depression that follows, it's unbearable. Though I don't know how, I manage to continue on. I keep pushing forward. I go to therapy, and I go again, and the next day, and the day after that. I talk to Joey. I talk to Cadence—who testifies against Roman. I talk to Remy—who also testifies against him. I talk to two other cheerleaders who came forward that they, in fact, don't remember, but think something might have happened in Roman and Codey's dorm room. None of that matters because in this case, the justice system failed me. They failed us. They failed women all over the world because regardless of being guilty, justice doesn't always follow.

And finally, I talk to my boyfriend. I let Asa hold me at night. I confide in him and let him help me through it all. I don't turn away from him and I keep moving forward. It's not easy. There are still days when it's too much. Days when I think I can't take this any longer. I also have days when the nightmares are so bad I can't sleep. Before they had no face, and now that they do, it's terrifying.

I keep going because if I don't, me, Waylon, Joey... our voices mean nothing. I keep going because they might have broken a piece of me, but my attackers, they don't get to decide how I live my life regardless of the decision. I'm taking back my power. I'm rewriting my own story.

There comes a day when you have to decide. Are you going to turn the page or close the book?

I'm going to the next chapter.

THE NIGHT AFTER THE TRIAL ENDS WITH THE VERDICT SHOCKS US all, Asa and I lay together in bed, in our home we've been sharing for the last six months. We try to make sense of what it means.

"What happens now?" I ask him, my head on his chest as I listen to his breathing, my eyes on the mason jars lining our headboard. Each one displays a quote he's put inside to remind me that I can and will get past this. My favorite one?

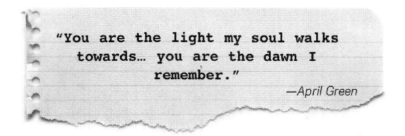

"You are the light my soul walks towards… you are the dawn I remember."

—April Green

Asa turns his head, his breathing light, his words whispered like a feather touching my skin. "We move forward."

In the last six months, I didn't think we could ever get past this, especially with the rage and aggression Asa showed through the entire process. "How?"

"I don't know." He sighs, his chest expanding with his breath. His hand moves to my cheek. I twist my head slightly and look up at him. "I love you."

"I don't know how you do." It hurts to say that, but it's the truth. I've put him through hell. Asa would have been better off to let me go that night and went on with his life without me. I'm thankful he didn't, but it will never stop those feelings.

"I do," he tells me, pressings his lips to my forehead. "I made a promise to you that night I would always be there for you and I'm keeping it. Always. I go where you go."

"I'm afraid," I admit. It's a natural reaction.

"Don't be. You've changed. *We've* changed. Be proud of that. Just because we had this one setback doesn't mean we've lost the play clock. It just means we have to work harder for that first down, but we still have possession of the ball."

I lift my eyes to the glitter-glowing mason jar and smile. He's right. We have control over our next play.

CHAPTER 29

An unexpected visitor

I'd love to go as far to say that I'm healed. I'm all better and it's like it never happened. Trauma doesn't work like that. It's a process. A sentence never served until it's ready to release the hold on you. Where's my field of roses and happy ever after? Unfortunately, it's forever tied to the ones who took it from me.

In the months following the trial, when I knew it was over, when I knew Roman and the others were finally behind bars, that's when reality hit me. What *we* went through. What we'd overcome. I had Asa to thank for that. He saved me. Not because he needed to, but because he wanted to.

It didn't mean the road was easy for either of us. It came in waves, each one of us struggling to tread water at different times and leaning on one another to stay afloat.

After practice one night, he finds me on our bed, lights off, the mason jars he'd made for me over the years now filled with twinkle lights to keep them bright. I stare at them. Every single one of them a reminder of what he gave me over the years.

Hope.

Encouragement.

He begged me with quotes not to give up. Not tonight. Not ever.

Asa closes our bedroom door behind him, a soft click followed by his footsteps. I look up, tears in my eyes. "Why'd you do it?"

He gives me an apologetic look. "I know. I forgot to put the clothes in the washer again, but Terrell yelled at me for running the washing machine during 'peak' hours." He flops down on the bed beside me, his hair still damp from his shower. "And then he gave me a lecture about wasting laundry soap."

Though I want to laugh, I don't. I do smile and curl up next to him, my hand on his chest. "That's not what I meant."

His eyebrows rise fractionally. "What then?" His hand runs up my back, his lips pressing to my forehead.

"Why'd you stay with me through all this? I mean, I know you love me and all that, but I gave you nothing in return." I twist in his arms and rest my chin on his chest. He lifts his head, peering down at me. His expression is one I've seen countless times over the years. Love. Compassion. Devotion. It's all there. He holds my stare, waiting, the glow from the twinkle lights casting shadows on his face.

He blinks, a soft smile pulling at his lips. He sits up and holds my face in his hands when he whispers, "Honey, love is supposed to be selfless, not selfish."

Emotion floods through me, my eyes stinging with tears, my heart beating faster than before. His words sprinkle down on me like glittery confetti. "How'd I get so lucky to have found you in this life?"

His eyes dip to my mouth, his damp hair falling in his face. He kisses me, once, twice, a smile plastered to his lips. "I like to think we found each other."

I fight the urge to cry. I don't need to. Not anymore. This is our beginning.

Asa is so much more than I've ever given him credit for. He's rare. He keeps his word. He doesn't care that he doesn't receive the same devotion in return, he just does it. And I'm going to love him as fiercely and with the same passion he's shown me through my worst.

He pulls back and winks at me. "I'm starving."

"There's a pizza in the freezer we can cook." I wink. "Then we can watch movies naked since Terrell and Joey went out for dinner."

"I like the way you think."

THERE'S NOTHING MORE ADORABLE THAN ASA WHEN HE'S confused. His brow pulls together and he strangely resembles a pouting toddler. I just want to pinch his cheeks.

He stares at the cardboard box on the counter, and then the smoky oven. "Clearly 450 was not the right temperature. What were they thinking?"

Laughing, I wave smoke from my view and rip the batteries from the smoke detector that won't stop. "Or you left it in too long."

He frowns. "Well, then, that's your fault. You distracted me when you took your shirt off."

"I did not." I motion to his bare chest. "You started it."

We're just about to start an argument, the playful kind that ends up in bed when the doorbell rings.

Asa stares at me, the burnt pizza smoking between us. "Expecting anyone?"

"No. Maybe Joey and Terrell forgot their keys?"

Reaching for my shirt, he throws it at me and then grabs his own. "Maybe it's the pizza delivery guy to rescue us."

"Not likely." I chuckle, slipping my shirt over my head, watching him walk toward the door.

He opens the door and leans against the wall casually. "Hey." And then he opens the door wider and in walks Cadence. She's been crying.

We don't talk like we used to back in high school, and I think we've grown into entirely different people. Regardless, she was there when I needed her during the trial.

I step toward her. She glances at me, then Asa. "I'm sorry. I should have called first."

"It's okay. We were just not eating pizza," I tell her, only to have Asa roll his eyes. I wave her inside and gesture toward the couch. "Come in."

Asa clears his throat and then coughs from the smoke in the house. He opens a window, but it doesn't help. "I'm gonna go get pizza."

"Pepperoni and pineapple," I tell him, smiling as I sit next to Cadence on the couch.

"Pineapple doesn't belong on a pizza," he tells me just before kissing my temple.

I argue that it does, but he waves his hand in my face and tells me I'm crazy. When he leaves, I reach out and touch Cadence's knee.

"You guys are adorable together," she says, and then bursts into tears.

I hand her a box of tissues. "Are you okay?"

She nods but continues to cry. "I just... I can't believe I didn't see it. The warning signs were there with Roman all along and I never saw it."

I hesitate to ask, "What do you mean?"

"I ignored the fact that he never gave a shit about what anyone else said. Even with me. I'd tell him I didn't want to do something and he'd make me do it anyway. I had a fucking threesome with some girl I never met before because he forced me to. He's just... awful and for so long I let it go because I loved him." Taking the sleeve of her sweatshirt, she wipes her tears away. "After you were raped, he said some things that, looking back on it, should have been warning signs that he had something to do with it."

My throat tightens, my heart skipping a beat. That same panicked feeling I always get when the word rape is mentioned consumes me. I fidget and ask, even though I don't want to know, "What do you mean?"

For a minute, I don't think she wants to tell me. "I asked him where he was that night because for an hour, his story didn't add up. He wasn't with Monika like he said he was and when I caught him in the lie, he blew it off. Then when I asked if he knew anything or saw you, he said he saw you with Tony and Greg by the water, but that was it. Before that, he said he never saw you the rest of the night."

I sigh and hold her hand tighter. "Cadence, you have nothing to feel guilty about."

"But I do," she cries. "I left you when I knew I shouldn't have. I knew better than to leave you with them in your condition. And then I thought to myself after everything happened if I'd trust Roman, drunk, alone with you, or any of my friends and the answer was always no. That's when I should have known and spoke up sooner. But... like everyone else he manipulated, I was scared of what he'd do if I came forward and said something."

I think about that night a lot more than I want to, even three years later. I wonder if Asa hadn't found Roman's hat if he would have ever slipped and caught himself in a lie he couldn't talk his way out of. Or would the guilt have gotten to him and he confessed? What about Tony and Greg, would they have ever admitted if Roman hadn't ratted them out? They were minors and their lives were over before they even began. I had no doubt in my mind Roman played a way bigger role in that night than he claims to.

"I don't know why I'm telling you this now, after everything you went through and bringing it up again, but I just wanted you to know that I'm sorry. I should have been a better friend. I'm sorry the judge was a prick."

I reach for her and wrap my arms around her. "I shouldn't have shut you out like I did. I guess I just clung to Asa and I'm not even sure why."

Cadence smiles, her bloodshot eyes focusing on mine. "I'm glad you did. He's a great guy and you deserve each other."

I hadn't realized how long we'd been talking when Asa comes through the front door, Terrell and Joey following him.

"Oh my God, I'm starving," Joey notes, taking a deep breath with her face next to the pizza boxes.

Asa laughs and holds the pizza box up higher. "Didn't you go out to dinner?"

Joey snorts. "Yes, but I went to dinner with Terrell. He made us share a meal because it was cheaper than two meals and he ate most of it."

Terrell tosses his keys on the counter. "It's ridiculous that a steak dinner would cost forty-five dollars. I can make that at home for cheaper."

Beside me, Cadence stands with a cautious smile on her face, her cheeks still red from crying. "I'll get going."

"No, stay." I reach for her hand, refusing to let her leave. "Have some pizza with us."

"I shouldn't. You guys have your own thing going." Her eyes drift to Terrell and Joey. "I don't want to impose."

"You're not," Asa says, winking at her as he sets the two boxes on the counter.

"What's that smell?" Terrell asks, squinting his eyes at Asa. "Did you burn something again?"

"No," he lies, smiling. He still can't lie without smiling.

Terrell lectures him on oven safety and fire statistics for removing the batteries on a fire alarm. All of which Asa blows off. "I'll put the batteries back in." Terrell gives him a look that screams "do it now." So he does. "You're being ridiculous."

Terrell snorts and looks at the receipt from the pizza Asa picked up. "No, what's ridiculous is that you spent forty dollars on two pizzas when this one was ten dollars. If you wouldn't have burned it, you would have saved yourself thirty."

"Oh my God, leave him alone." Joey knocks her hand against Terrell's burly chest. "It's his money."

Ignoring Terrell's speech on our money spending, which happens daily, Asa makes his way over to me, his arms around my shoulder. He watches me for a moment and then asks, "You okay?"

I smile. "That depends."

"On?"

"If you got me a pepperoni and pineapple pizza."

He rolls his eyes. "I know better." He does. And then he watches me, waiting for my real answer.

"Cadence is just struggling with the reality of it all," I tell him, knowing any mention of Roman will only set him off.

My eyes drift to Cadence, who's now sitting with Terrell and Joey in the kitchen, a glass of wine in her hand. I hadn't thought about our situation in terms of a new reality for anyone but myself. Asa, Joey, Terrell, Cadence, Remy, Roman's parents, the football team, every single person involved in that trial or who had been there for us through it, they were all affected. Now here we were, months later, still trying to adjust and it's not going to be easy.

I'm a firm believer now that everyone in your life plays a role. Even the villains. They might be the one testing you, and in the same sense, using you. They might love you, but then turn around and teach you a lesson in heartache. The ones who are truly important, they bring out the best in you, keep you fighting and in turn, remind you that it's worth it to keep them in your life.

Love is supposed to be selfless, not selfish.

CHAPTER 30

Moving on

BARRETTE

THE EXUMA CAYS
BAHAMAS

"This much skin should be illegal." I think there should be certain times in your life where you wear a bikini, and times when you shouldn't. For me, it's the shouldn't. Always. It's not that I have anything against them, it's just for me personally, I don't like to show that much skin anymore. It's a fear, really, one I haven't outgrown and at this point, I'm beginning to think I never will. But here I am, wearing a bikini and staring at myself in the full-length mirror, sweat beading on my forehead with the insane humidity suffocating me. "I don't know about this." I curl my hands around my waist, hiding myself. "It's too much."

Joey sighs and gives me a look that says "You're kidding." When I don't budge, she lays it on thick. "The trial's over and scumbag is at least in jail still. Your boy won the Heisman Trophy this year... we're celebrating." She fans herself. "Holy shit, it's fuckin' hot here."

Joey's right. We have a lot to celebrate. I just wasn't so sure I wanted to do it half-dressed. "We can still celebrate fully clothed."

She puts her hand on her hip and twirls. "Girl, I'm a size fourteen... and I'm wearing a fucking bikini next to a girl who's the size of my leg." She stares at me with confidence. "And I'm going to rock it like I own it. Because I do, but you need to let go. You need to embrace the fact that you control your environment. They don't."

I know exactly what she's referring to. And even though I've gone to therapy and I've talked endlessly in support groups about my fears, they don't just go away. I wish they did, but I know enough about trauma to understand it doesn't work that way.

But I can make an effort. I keep the bikini on and slip my dress over it. Joey does the same and reaches for her bag on the bed. I watch her, the confidence that exudes from her and I think about what it's like to have that kind of self-worth. She doesn't question anything, and then that gets me thinking about something that's been bothering me for a while.

Sex.

Asa and I haven't had much trouble in that department, but it's... how do I say this right... vanilla sex? Maybe that's the right word. Given my history, he's always very careful and gentle with me. Which, I appreciate, but there's more to an intimate relationship, isn't there? I shouldn't be afraid to try new things.

"Joey, can I ask you something personal?"

She smiles. "Yeah, anything."

Fear pricks my skin, and suddenly it's even hotter in this room than it was before. I have no idea how to word it, so I just blurt, "How do I give a blow job?" And then I quickly flop back on the bed and cover my face with my hands.

Just as I suspected, Joey giggles. "Gurl, you haven't given that poor guy a blow job yet?"

I shake my head.

Joey lays beside me and reaches for my hand to uncover my face. "Are you scared?"

I twist my head to face her. "It's the one thing I fear. I don't know why, but I do. I even think about it and I want to throw up. Maybe it's because of how vulnerable it leaves me. I have no idea."

"Honey, that's normal. For a long time, I didn't either. I still struggle with doggie style."

I giggle. Like a child.

That gets her laughing too. And then I ask, "Why do you struggle with that position?"

"Because that's the position I was in. With a knife pressed to my neck and my head against a dirty toilet seat in a bar."

Pain hits my chest, hard. My breath expels in a gasp. "Oh my God, I'm so sorry. I shouldn't have asked that."

Joey squeezes my hand. "Yes, you should have. If we're going to be best friends, we talk about this. Everything and anything, okay?"

I gather up the nerve to ask, "Do you do that position now?"

She nods. "Yeah, but it wasn't until Terrell that I was comfortable enough to do it. Now it doesn't bother me anymore. We talked about my boundaries and he was nothing but gentle and sweet."

When you look at Terrell, you wouldn't think there was a gentle bone in his body, but he's a big teddy bear. I sit up, my lips trembling when I admit, "I don't know why it bothers me because I don't think it has anything to do with my attack. I think it's a fear."

"And that's normal."

I draw in a careful breath. "But I want to try. I'm tired of living in fear, so, how do I do it?"

Joey bites back laughter. "Well, I think this might be something you're gonna have to talk about with Asa."

"But I want to know what I'm doing."

"Okay, well, have you ever had a popsicle?"

I nod.

"It's a lot like that. You wrap your lips around it and suck on it, right?"

"No, I bite it."

She bursts out laughing. "Guaranteed to be your last blow job if you do that."

I flop back against the bed again. "Ugh."

"B, it's fine. Just do what comes naturally to you and ask him what he likes."

"Will he tell me?"

"Pretty sure he will."

Before I can ask more details, there's a knock on the door. Joey turns toward the door and smiles. "Ready?"

Though I'm not, and my face is the color of a tomato, I nod. Truth is, I haven't been ready for anything that's happened the last year, but I keep going and push through it all.

Asa enters the room and my world shifts. Everything I've been fearing melts away at the sight of him. It always does. I think I've said it before, but my physical and emotional reactions shift completely when he's around. He smiles, and I forget where I am. Don't worry, you're not stuck in some kind of cheesy romantic comedy where the woman's sense of self-worth depends on the man. It's deeper for me and Asa. Together we got through the worst parts of our lives, and it made us stronger.

I don't notice Terrell behind him, though it's pretty freaking hard not to because of Terrell's size and dark skin. I don't notice anything besides Asa when he's smiling at me and giving me that look. The one that says if I could, I'd strip you down completely and ravish you. And I'd let him because hello, look at him. He's six feet of pure sex.

Okay, enough, right? I'll stop.

Asa moves toward me, winking, and places his hands on my hips. "You look beautiful," he whispers, pressing a kiss to my temple.

"So do you." I brush my hand against the stubble on his cheek. I love that he has a beard at the moment. Usually during the season, he shaves it off, but I'm digging the ruggedness it gives him.

And then he groans and grips my hips a little tighter. "It's hard to believe we've been living together for over a year and I still can't get enough of you."

I hoist myself up to wrap my legs around his waist. "I agree." We fall back on the bed with a giggle from me. "Let's not go out today.

This place is beautiful. We could take a walk on the beach, make love...."

Terrell clears his throat, his arm hanging around Joey. "I don't think so. Knock that off. I hate being late and we have a date with pigs that we've already paid for. I have bets with JoJo on who gets bit first."

"You're the one who's going to get bit." Joey squishes Terrell's cheeks playfully. "They're gonna think you're a big cupcake."

Asa lifts up, winking, his hands low on my bottom. "We got time for this later." I take his hand and let him peel me off the bed. I pout because I'm still not very social and hate going out, but I'm trying new things. Like social events. And the Bahamas, swimming pigs, and apparently, bikinis.

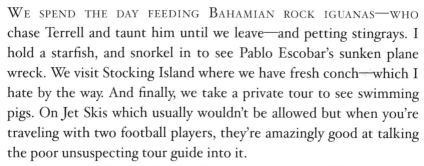

We spend the day feeding Bahamian rock iguanas—who chase Terrell and taunt him until we leave—and petting stingrays. I hold a starfish, and snorkel in to see Pablo Escobar's sunken plane wreck. We visit Stocking Island where we have fresh conch—which I hate by the way. And finally, we take a private tour to see swimming pigs. On Jet Skis which usually wouldn't be allowed but when you're traveling with two football players, they're amazingly good at talking the poor unsuspecting tour guide into it.

Everywhere I look there's blue skies, white sand beaches, and amazing turquoise water. It's the most beautiful place in the world, but then again, I've never been anywhere but Washington.

With my body pressed against Asa's back, I can't believe less than a year ago, nothing in my life made sense, aside from this guy in front of me. My rock.

I hold onto him as tight as I can. I cling to him, much like I have in the past, only now it's for a different reason. It's because I fear for my life and I'm certain he is a good football player, but not so much at operating a Jet Ski.

"Slow down!" I screech, feeling as though I might bounce right off this thing and be eaten by a shark.

Asa laughs as if my screaming in his ear is funny. And then he pins the throttle. "Hold on, honey."

Hold on? Ha. Since he thinks this is funny, I slide my hands lower down his chest, lower, and lower, until I find the spot I'm looking for and grip him. "How about I hold on here?"

His speed slows, his hand easing off the throttle, but he doesn't stop. He draws in a quick breath and then turns his head. "You could but you probably shouldn't."

"Why's that?"

It's difficult to hear him over the wind and the slapping of the water against the Jet Ski. "Because if you do, I might see how you feel about public nudity and sand."

I think about it for a half second. I move my hand. "No way."

Laughter shakes through him. "Worth a shot." He lets off the gas completely and nods in the distance. "Ever seen a swimming pig?"

I've never swum with pigs. Have you? I'm a nervous wreck the entire Jet Ski ride to what I learn is an uninhabited island where pigs live. They're not native to the islands, but they sure look comfortable roaming the white sandy beaches.

Asa laughs in front of me when he kills the engine. He touches my leg and I jump. "I'm so nervous," I tell him, barely able to control my laughter. "Do they bite?"

"No, but I do," he mumbles, smiling wickedly at me as he nibbles on my shoulder.

I notice a smaller one swimming over to us. "Oh my God, it's a baby piggy."

Terrell jumps off the Jet Ski and into the sapphire-blue water. "Ah, this one loves me," he says, petting a big black one that looks like it could be his pet.

Joey shakes her head as she pets a smaller brown and white one.

He's not as small as the piglet at my feet. I smile at him, reaching down with a shaking hand to touch the pig's ears. "I'm going to take you with me!"

"B, we can't even keep plants alive let alone a pig," Joey adds, giving me the same look she gave me when I brought a stray kitten home and he ran away the next day.

It's true though. Between Joey, Terrell, Asa, and me living under the same roof, none of us have remembered to water the plants. We even tried succulents. Can't even keep desert plants alive. Probably because if we use too much water, Terrell lectures us on how much it costs per month to water plants.

The moment we're off the Jet Skis, the pigs invade us. I can't get enough of how adorable they are. We wade into knee-deep water and I'm still holding the baby one in my arms.

Asa looks over at me, the sun beating down on his golden skin. He tips his sunglasses up and eyes me and the piglet. There's another one that's been at my feet for a while. He's a big black and brown one that might be the mom or the dad of the piglet I'm holding but I'm not sure. Fearing I might get bit for taking their baby, I set the piglet in the water. "I didn't mean to take your baby. Here, have him back."

The bigger pig doesn't leave. He stays at my feet, leaned against my leg. I kneel down to pet him and before I know it, he's crawling all over me.

Asa rolls his eyes. "Should I be concerned about your relationship with this one?"

I don't say anything because Terrell's booming laughter draws our attention. "Oh my God," Joey yells. "It's pooping! Take it!"

She's holding one of the babies and it's pooping on her, which Terrell thinks is the funniest thing in the world.

"Take it!" she screams, holding the piglet out. "Or I'm gonna drop him!"

Terrell takes it, or tries to. It's still pooping all over him. "It's shitting, ya'll."

I don't think I've ever laughed so hard in my life than I do at the scene before me. Chuckling himself, Asa slings his arm around my shoulder, the baby pig swimming at his feet now. "We can't take them anywhere."

I laugh and pick my adorable piglet up. "I'm gonna keep him. He can be our baby."

"Or I can put a real baby in you," Asa whispers, his lips on my shoulder.

"Yeah, right." I laugh it off, but there's something about the way he's looking at me. Like it wouldn't be the worst idea yet.

AT THE BAR, IT'S UNLIKE ANYTHING I'VE BEEN TO BEFORE. NOT only am I constantly thinking about Asa's baby comment, it's hard to keep up with the amount of attention the guys receive. It seems people know exactly who Asa is. We're nowhere close to home so it seems unreal he'd have a following here. Apparently, college football is a thing though.

Have you heard of Exuma Cays? It's a playground for the rich and famous. We end up at Chat 'n' Chill. There's live music, amazing food, and tons of women. Not once does Asa look at any of them, despite them gawking at him and Terrell both. One in particular hands me a drink. "Here, sweetie." I'm gathering she's probably a waitress, maybe, but her eyes are on Asa as she slides the drink toward me. "It's on the house."

Panic floods through me, but I don't let it take over. "No, thank you. I don't drink." I haven't since that night, and I doubt I ever will again. I never want to feel that vulnerable again.

Asa leans into me, his nose brushing my jaw. "If you want a drink, have one. I wouldn't let you overdo it."

I know he wouldn't, but it's a trigger for me. "I even smell alcohol and it brings me back to that night," I tell him. "I don't want any."

His expression shifts and I can't tell what he's thinking. "It's fine. If you're not comfortable with drinking, I respect that."

Why is he always so sweet to me? I touch his warm cheek. He got a little sun today. It makes his eyes look more golden. Like rich honey with spots of chocolate. I sink against his side. "Thank you."

Conversation flows around the table, Terrell and Asa talking about the upcoming draft and who they think will get picked up from UW. It's then I realize, watching them relax at the table, this is the first time in a while I've seen them this laid-back. Our lives since the trial ended haven't been easy. Asa's career is exploding since winning the Heisman Trophy and I know it's just going to get worse. Pretty soon he's going to be starting his senior year of college football. He'll graduate in May, and then his plan is to enter the draft the following year. Terrell has the same plan.

Asa leans in, his shoulder pressing to mine. "Dance with me?"

I drift my stare to the dance floor where he leads me. Before I know it, we're dancing, our bodies pulled tightly together. To our left, I notice Joey and Terrell are doing shots with an elderly man who keeps yelling, "It's my birthday!"

"He's like a hundred," Asa says, laughing. "I'd be doing shots if I lived that long too."

I stare at him. "What makes you think you won't live long?"

The corner of his mouth dips down, carefully watching my reaction when he says, "Concussions."

I hate that injuries like this are a reality now. I pick at the ruffles on my dress. "Are you worried?"

"No," he tells me, and I know it's a lie. "I'm not worried." And then suddenly his lips are on mine.

His mouth devours my mouth, kissing me like he's never kissed me before. I think maybe it's because he's trying to change the subject away from injuries, but I'll take it. It's dominating, but not forceful. He's giving me no room to question his intentions.

It's aggressive and controlling, like he can't get enough. I'm entirely lost in the kiss, forgetting everything around me. His tongue sweeps my lips, a warm, coconut-flavor from the rum he'd been drinking earlier. I open my mouth all the way and allow him access again. He tilts his head, deepening the connection. It's everything I need it to be, and then some. Soon my thoughts drift back to what Joey and I talked about. My breathing picks up and Asa notices, chuckling against my lips.

Before I'm ready, he breaks the kiss, sighing against my lips and holding me tight against his body. "This isn't easy."

"What? Dancing? Or how awkward of a dancer I am when you make me weak in the knees?" Not that I was thinking about putting your penis in my mouth. Nope. That's not why.

Resting his forehead to mine, Asa rolls his eyes. "No, seeing you half naked and other guys gawking at you." His eyes shift to behind me. "I want to yank their fucking eyes out for even looking at you, let alone thinking they have a chance."

I look at him like he's lost his mind. "They don't."

"Oh, I know," he says, a haughty edge to his tone. There's one thing about Asa that hasn't changed. His confidence. "How about I show them exactly who you belong to."

"I think you did with that kiss." I fan myself playfully. "I'm still recovering."

He snorts and grabs my hand. "Come on. Let's go wish the old guy happy birthday."

I follow him, because he's dragging me through the crowd, and we find our way over to Joey and Terrell at the bar.

"Here!" Joey hands me some fruity-looking drink. "It's fucking delicious!"

"It's thirty dollars, it better be," Terrell notes, always careful of his spending. Terrell literally came from nothing. If it hadn't been for his incredible football talent, there would have been no way for him to go to college. Because of that, he learned early on how to pinch pennies. He budgets out every single expense down to how much we use in electricity every month. Don't ever go grocery shopping with him. It's depressing. He says no to everything good.

Reaching for a shot on the bar, Asa slaps his hand on Terrell's shoulder. "Lighten up." And then his eyes are on mine as he downs the shot. I look at the drink in my hand. I can do this. I can. I'm with my friends. I'm safe with my friends and they're not going to leave me. More importantly, I can have one drink and stop there, right?

So, I take a drink. And it's freaking delicious. Before I know it, it's gone and I'm giggling. My cheeks are flushed and newfound heat courses through my body. One I'm familiar with, but it's more than that. I'm... horny? I don't know if that's the right word but all I can think about is having sex with Asa.

He watches me closely, his hands never far from my body and it only makes it worse. "You're adorable," he tells me when I try to convince him I will, in fact, skinny dip in the ocean if he wants. He searches my face, then my lips. "What do you say we find our way back to our room?"

I sigh with relief. "Yes."

Joey notices we're leaving and smiles. "Be good, kids."

I wink. I have a plan. Maybe not a good one, but it's a plan.

LIQUID COURAGE IS A THING. IT TOTALLY IS. SOMETHING ABOUT that fruity drink relaxed me enough that I'm going to get outside my own head for a night. And I'm going to go down on my boyfriend.

In our room, Asa stumbles around, he too feeling the effects of the sun and drinks he had at the bar. I laugh when he falls back against the bed, his shirt off, board shorts hanging low on his hips. He looks delicious.

After stripping out of my bikini, I step toward him completely naked. I kneel at the end of the bed and slide my hands up his thighs under his shorts. He lifts up on his elbows, smiling down at me.

Thick strands of his hair fall against his forehead and he winks at me.

I bite my lips, trying to find that little boost of courage I know I'm going to need to make this next part happen. I can do it. I know I can. I will not fear it. With a deep breath in, I move my hands to the band of his shorts and tug. He lifts his hips and allows me to slide them off along with his boxers.

Believe it or not, I haven't spent a lot of time staring at his penis, and never this close that I can remember. My head is level with him. He sits up and tries to pull me onto the bed.

I shake my head. "I want to try something," I whisper, my hands returning to his thighs. I'm not sure he knows where I'm going with this because I've never initiated this kind of thing. A couple of months back, he went down on me, which I thoroughly enjoyed, but I couldn't return the favor.

Until now.

I take him in my hand, my mouth inches from him and suddenly he's hard as a rock, his eyes wide. His hands fly to mine. He sits up. "You don't have to do that."

I smile and lick my lips. "Something tells me you want me to."

He swallows hard, blinking slowly. His eyes are heavy with desire. "I uh...."

It's nice to see him at a loss for words. I look up at him. "Just relax."

His chest rises and falls quickly, but his hands fall away and flatten on the bed as he leans back slightly, giving me room. "Okay."

My heart pumps wildly in my chest, heat coursing through me. I lean forward, my lips pressing to the head of his penis. Asa gasps, his hands gripping the sheets. And then it's his reaction that pushes me forward and gives me the rest of the courage I need to take him in my mouth.

But then I pause and pull back an inch. "I don't know how to do this," I admit, my hands shaking. I look up at him.

His eyes find mine. He swallows again, but he doesn't say

anything. Maybe he's stunned speechless by seeing me with my mouth on him.

I lean forward again, one hand at the base of his penis and then lower my mouth on him, sliding my tongue against him in the process. It's awkward and makes me want to gag when I feel his hips twitch. "Jesus Christ," he pants, and he hits the back of my throat by his movement.

I gag that time, but I keep doing it because of his reaction. I had no idea I could make him feel like this, out of breath and squirming. I struggle to breathe. It's like someone is choking me, but he's not touching me. I notice the whites of his knuckles gripping the sheet.

It's a flash of a memory and hands I fear. Not his, but it's a reminder, one I hadn't been expecting and sets into motion what I didn't want to happen. It builds and builds and soon, like usual, the anxiety, the rush, the need to run away from the ever-present pressure in my chest, it surfaces out of nowhere and tears surface. Before I know it, I'm crying, but I refuse to stop. I want to push through it and find a means to an end. Maybe if I keep going, I can push through to the other side and finally give myself to him completely, with no restrictions.

Asa notices. He tries to stop me. "Hey, hey, look at me."

I don't. I cry, shake, and continue.

"Damn, Barrette, stop." His voice is soft but strained. With more pressure, he places his hands on my face and lifts. He puts his fingers under my chin, forcing me to look at him. "*Stop*. You're upset. Don't do this if it makes you uncomfortable."

"I'm so sorry," I cry, my body shaking. "I don't know what's wrong. I know you want it."

He yanks me up and holds me to his chest. "I don't fucking care about that."

"But you want it."

"Well, yeah, but not like this. Not if this is your reaction." His voice is hard, his eyes tight with anger.

I rest my head against his chest and listen to the thumping of his heartbeat. "I'm sorry."

He wraps his arms around me, rubbing my back. "Don't be."

For a moment, he holds me, and I let him. I breathe through what I'm feeling and focus on him. I refuse to let myself ruin this. I can do this.

I squirm out of his grasp. "I want to try again."

He shakes his head, his eyes narrowing on mine. "No."

"Asa." I sigh and move my hands to his thighs. "The only way I'm going to move on and find myself again is to keep trying. Let's just... go slower. Tell me what you like."

I can see the internal struggle. He obviously wants this. He doesn't say anything, but his hands fall away. I position myself between his legs. His breathing kicks up. He's into it and encourages me by saying, "Fuck, baby, that feels so good."

Maybe that's what I'd been missing before. His words. His reassurance.

I smile. Though the tears are still there, I'm no longer shaking. My stomach tickles and things are happening. I'm... turned on by it and still don't know what the hell I'm doing.

"Is this right?" I ask, pausing to stroke my hand up and down him.

He nods, his lids heavy. His head rolls back when I go all the way down on him and tighten my lips around him. I do that once, and then slide up again keeping my lips tight like I'm biting, but with my lips.

That gets him. His grunts and lifts his hips again. Then he yanks me up, off him and onto my back on the mattress.

"Why did you stop?"

"I don't want to come in your mouth," he growls and positions himself at my entrance.

I giggle, my lips swollen as his find mine. "Why not?"

His kisses hold his words captive, but eventually, he mumbles, "Because all I've thought about today is this pussy."

His vulgar words tremble through me and my legs spread wider. I move my hands to his hips, and then lower and cup his ass, driving him into me.

"Do it harder," I beg, trying to angle my hips at just the right angle to get him inside me further. "Oh my God... it feels so good with you that deep inside me."

"Fuck, I'm gonna come," he pants out against my lips.

"Me too."

Somehow, I end up on top of him and we come together. I smile down at him when our movements slow. He's still inside me, grinning, and then he chuckles. "What the fuck made you want to do that?"

I shrug. "I don't know. I've been thinking about it since you did it to me and I never repaid the favor."

He lifts me up, wrapping his arms around me. "You know I never expect that from you."

"I know." I trace his jaw with my fingertips. "But I want us to have a normal relationship. One where I don't burst into tears anytime we do something sexual that reminds me of that night."

Shock hits his face and his lips tighten. "Did you remember something?"

"Your hands." My words tremble though I don't mean for them to. "Your hands gripping the sheets.... I remember his hands when he was on top of me. His knuckles were white."

Asa sighs, his jaw clenching. He lets go of me and then lays back on the bed. But then he jerks his head to mine. "We're not doing that again."

I glare at him. "Yes, we are, Asa."

"No."

Anger shoots through me. "Yes, we will." I move away from him and stand next to the bed. "And I'm going to get really good at sucking your dick and you're going to come in my mouth. Maybe even all over my face. Something dirty. I'm going to be the best blow-job giver and you're gonna be begging me for it." Before I know it,

I'm yelling at him and he's laughing. "Why in the heck are you laughing at me? Stop it."

He doesn't. He's laughing so hard his chest is shaking, his eyes dancing with amusement. "It's just funny hearing you say shit like dick and telling me I'm gonna come on your face."

Nice. He's making fun of me.

"Ugh, you're such a jerk." I turn away from him and stalk toward the bathroom. Slamming the door shut, I use the bathroom and then when I've calmed down—not really—I open the door to find him there. "What do you want?"

He guides me back into the shower, still smiling and turns it on. "Practice makes perfect."

Water hits my body, but when he pushes down on my shoulders to bring me to my knees, he winks down at me. I've never seen this side of him, so sure of what he wants sexually with me. He's been just as reserved as me when it comes to trying new things, always afraid of what it will do to me. But this time, this time he's showing me what he wants, and once more, it gives me the courage I need. Maybe that's what had been missing before. His sureness that I can do this.

Water beads down his chest and I take him in my hand again. He smiles. "I really want to come in your mouth this time."

And he does. He talks me through it all, telling me how much he loves it and how fucking sexy I am, and then he comes in my mouth. It's... weird. I had no idea what it'd taste like, but I'm not exactly a fan of it. He laughs when I spit it out in the shower.

"I said you could come in my mouth, not that I'd swallow."

Another laugh as he moves toward the spray. "Quitter." I slap his shoulder only to have him yank me toward him. "I'm kidding."

"I know."

He cups my cheeks, his words sincere when he whispers, "I'm proud of you."

"I'm proud of you."

His fingers brush the tattoo on my chest just above my left breast. The one that reads, *"Sometimes fear does not subside and one must chose to do it afraid."* It's a quote by Elizabeth Elliot, and the quote he placed inside the mason jar he gave me the day he won the Heisman Trophy and Roman had been granted work release. On a day where we should have been celebrating Asa, he gave me the words I needed to hear to keep pushing forward because he knew I needed them.

That tattoo, it's a reminder that it's okay to have fears.

His hold reminds me of the night after I was released in the hospital, when he was holding me because I couldn't even draw in a breath without thinking I was going to fall to the floor and crumble completely. But this time, his hold means so much more because he's not supporting me any longer. I'm standing with him.

When I first started going to therapy, Lexi told me, you tell your story when you're ready. I loved that she said that to me because it was as if she was giving me the okay to move at my own pace. She gave me control. I didn't have it completely, fear has a way of holding it hostage, but tonight, Asa gave me back that control I thought I'd lost.

"COME WITH ME."

I sit up and rub my eyes. I look around and notice quickly that it's not even light outside. I thought we were on vacation and sleeping in. I make eye contact with Asa. He's smiling. "Where?"

He motions to the windows. "To watch the sunrise."

I sigh and reach for my dress next to the bed. "Is there pancakes?"

Asa chuckles and tugs on my hand. "Yeah, they serve them on the beach."

"Really?"

He sighs. I'm annoying him. "No, but come on."

I groan, and complain, but I follow him outside our room to

where Terrell and Joey are waiting for us. Joey's holding three coffees. She hands me one, then Asa. "Do you know why we're up so early?"

"Sunrise," the guys say together.

Terrell rolls his eyes. "You'd think girls would be up for all this romantic shit."

Joey slurps her coffee dramatically. "Nope. We value sleep more than romance."

I smile. "Truth."

On the beach, sadly, there are no pancakes, but there is a boy in front of me, holding my hand and looking rather nervous. I can practically feel his hand shaking in mine.

"Are you okay?" I ask, walking with him along the shore where the waves tickle our toes and the sky bursts to life with pinks, purples, and lighter blues.

He runs his hand through his hair. "Yeah."

"You look like you did the day the trial ended." Fear pricks my skin and I curl into myself. I watch his facial features nervously. Is it me? Did I do something wrong last night?

"You know." He pauses and squeezes my hand. "When the trial ended, I thought, fuck, finally we can start our lives together."

My heart thumps wildly in my chest waiting for his words. "And now?"

"And now it feels like we're still waiting to start our lives."

I know exactly what he means. We're in college. We have no idea what the future will hold for us. Yeah, we want that happily ever after as much as the next couple, but what if we don't get it?

Asa pulls me closer, his warmth radiating into me. I lift my eyes to Joey and Terrell in the distance, walking the same path we are in so many ways. "I didn't say that to freak you out, Barrette."

I nod. "I know. I totally get what you meant."

"I guess I'm just saying that I'm nervous as to what the next year will bring for us. My career is an unknown and I want to go as far as to say I'm going to take care of you, but how can I do that when I don't know what my future holds for me with football?"

I lean in and press my lips to his. "If anyone can get through the unknown, it's us."

We keep walking up the beach and before I know it, we're in loose white sand away from the water's edge. With a smirk on his lips, he sighs, his breath blowing over my face and then he drops down to one knee. He doesn't look at me. No, instead, he sweeps sand away and uncovers a mason jar. It's glowing, like the ones he gave me when helping me through the darkest days.

His eyes drift to mine and he swallows as he holds the jar up. "I brought you out here at sunrise because this is our beginning. A new start to a life I want to share with you."

Tears sting my eyes. In the distance, I can see Terrell and Joey over his shoulder, watching us and taking pictures.

He's proposing and I'm sobbing. My hand flies to my mouth, my words caught in my throat when I read the note on the inside of the mason jar, purple and gold glitter surrounding his question.

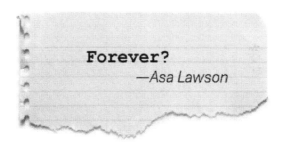

My heart twists in my chest as I look down at him, his eyes on mine, hair hanging in his eyes, and then the diamond ring he produces from his pocket. I nod, unable to say the words I so desperately want to give him. He reaches for my hand and places the ring on my finger.

I cry harder and stare down at it in disbelief. "Just so we're clear, you're asking me to marry you, right?"

His shoulders shake with laughter as he pulls me into him. "Yes, silly girl. I am."

I snort, and it's not pretty. I'm crying so hard snot is literally pouring from my nose. It's not romantic on my part. Placing my hand on his chest, the ring catches the morning sun bursting to life in the distance. In my other hand, the mason jar I will cherish just as much as the ring on my finger. "How long have you been planning this?"

Drawing back, he stares at me with a sudden serious edge. "Since we booked the trip. You wouldn't believe what I had to do to get a glow stick on the plane."

I laugh, remembering him freaking out and having Joey take me to get coffee when they searched his bag in customs.

Within a minute, Joey and Terrell return. "She said yes, right?" Joey asks, her hand in Terrell's.

I smile, nodding and showing them the ring.

"Perfect. Now we can eat."

"The buffet is half priced today," Terrell notes, dragging us toward the hotel.

We follow, hand in hand, only now everything is different. I don't fear the future. I look forward to it.

CHAPTER 31

The Call

ASA

TWO YEARS LATER
SEATTLE, WASHINGTON

"Steelers, Steelers!" Joey chants, parading around the house wearing her Steelers gear. Shirt, socks, hat, all of it she's sporting. I just hope the Steelers select Terrell in the draft or his fiancée is going to be pretty pissed off.

Our house is swarming with people. Cameras. Reporters. Family. Friends. They're all here for the day. Draft day. The exact moment in my, and Terrell's, football career that defines how our lives play out. I thought maybe I'd want to be in New York and see all this live, but it didn't feel right. Being here with family, in our own environment, that felt right.

Nerves? That's funny. They don't even begin to describe the gamut of emotions surging through me. I've never experienced anything like this before.

I breathe in. I breathe out. Nothing helps. I'm left with the same nagging feeling that today will change everything.

My life now? It's nothing like I thought it would be two years ago. Two years can change a lot about a person. It can change *everything*. I don't even know that guy I was two years ago sitting on the beach in the Bahamas with Barrette. The one fearing what the future would hold and afraid of change. I remember wanting to stay like that forever. I didn't want to leave that beach because everything was perfect for once.

That's not to say it's not perfect now, but I feared leaving, not knowing what change would happen. And our lives did change. Rather quickly.

I went from being a college junior who'd just won the Heisman Trophy, engaged, to a soon-to-be dad. All within a month of leaving. Turns out the Bahamas offered a little more than we'd planned for.

A baby.

I was teasing when I said I'd put a baby in her but apparently I wasn't.

Nine months later, Crew Warren Lawson was born. And he's the best fucking thing in the world. We never planned on having a kid in college, but you know, sometimes life just works out that way and you roll with it.

I'd never known the love a parent truly had until I held him in my arms. Do you want to hear something even crazier than me falling insanely in love with my son?

The day he was born, Roman was released from jail.

While I had mixed feelings about it, I felt like it was a blessing I had the distraction because, in my head, I had visions of showing up at the jail and putting a bullet in his head. Now, I clearly wasn't that irrational, but I guess you never know. I like to think my mom was watching out for me on that one. She was because instead of focusing on the past that day, Barrette and I were together, sharing the experience of bringing our son into the world. He gave us the strength to see that it didn't matter what happened, we could push forward. Yeah, it still fucking sucked that the judge was an ignorant bastard, but the outcome remained the same. We had to find the strength to accept that because the justice system failed us—and many others—it didn't mean that we had to stop living.

"Are you nervous?" Barrette asks, sitting next to me on the couch at my dad's house.

Nervous? Ha. I sigh, flipping my phone around in my hand. "No, not really. Terrified is more like it."

She laughs and rests her head on my shoulder. Crew pushes her head away. "No."

"I thought when I had a baby, he'd love me. This one just tells me no."

I kiss her temple. "I love you enough for the entire world."

Livia stands in front of me, fussing over Crew in my arms, constantly offering him toys he doesn't know what to do with. He's thirteen months old and Livia thinks they should be playmates by now. She holds up her hands, smiling around the pacifier in her mouth she refuses to get rid of. "Why he not play with me?"

"No," he says, clinging to the football in his hand and glaring at her. He doesn't say anything but pushes her away with his hand. He's not exactly the nicest kid. He's actually kind of moody. Joey says he's an asshole baby. Terrell thinks he's amazing. Barrette and I, we think he's the best baby in the world, but yes, an asshole most days. My dad likes to tease me that I was that way too, but I refuse to see it.

"He's shy," I tell Livia when she starts pouting, already making excuses for my kid being a dick.

She rolls her eyes and walks over to my dad where he looks probably as nervous as me. He winks at me and I give him a nod.

"Daddy?" Crew says, pointing to the television we're sitting in front of.

My heart swells at his word. He says three words. Daddy, no and ball. Barrette's not pleased by it. "Yeah, buddy. That's me."

His attention remains on the television above the fireplace. I can't look at the TV and the predictions they're talking about. It only makes it worse for me.

Barrette notices my distraction and reaches for Crew in my arms when he starts crying over Livia taking his football from him. I let her take him because yeah, I am nervous. My career, our future, it lies in the hands of others today. Today I'll get the call from a GM and asked the words "How do you feel about playing for our team?"

And I'll answer with "I feel great."

That's the answer my agent tells me to say, but in reality, I don't know how I feel about playing in the NFL. It changes a lot about our lives. For the past three years, we've been living in Seattle together with Joey and Terrell. We graduated last year, just five months after Crew was born. Since then I played in the All-Star League and entered draft eligibility in January along with Terrell. In February, on a rare snowy day in Seattle, I married Barrette Ann Blake.

I couldn't afford a fancy wedding, not like the one I wanted to give her. When you're in college, it's just not happening. Believe it or not, Barrette's parents actually paid for the entire thing and then refused to attend when we didn't want to serve tofu. They're still really fucking weird and haven't met their grandson yet, so I'll let you be the judge of their integrity there.

Since then, Barrette's been interning in Bellevue at a sexual assault victim's clinic and working toward her masters in psychology. What would today mean if I ended up on the other side of the country from my son and wife? For a long time, I thought about getting a job instead of football. I had my degree, but I knew if I didn't go for it, I'd always wonder. With Barrette's support, that's what's brought us to today.

When the draft officially begins, Terrell and I are much the same —our house teeming with people and the two of us on edge. After today, our lives will be completely different and this guy who's held me up and pushed me to be the best football player and human being, I hate that we're more than likely playing for different teams next year. He's pretty much a sure bet for Pittsburgh, and they're not in the market for a quarterback this year.

"Relax, man. It's good," Terrell says, bobbing his head to the beat of the music playing in his earbuds, an attempt to drown out the noise in the house. "We're solid."

"I'm trying to." And I am, but I'm pacing, tension rolling through me.

And then it happens. An hour before the official start of the draft, I get a call from the GM of the Arizona Cardinals, the team I knew was highly interested in me. My hands shake as I stare at the phone. Cheering erupts in the background. They all know what this call means.

I look to my agent and he smiles. "It's for you, A."

Barrette moves toward me, rubbing my back. "I love you. No matter what, I love you."

I want to say it back to her, but all I end up doing is nodding. I slide my finger across the screen and press the phone to my ear. "Hello?"

"Asa, this the Kenny Mann with the Arizona Cardinals. How are you doing?"

Reality smacks me in the chest and I struggle to push the words out. I swallow over the lump in my throat. "I'm doing good, Mr. Mann."

"Call me Kenny, son."

"Yes, sir."

There's more laughter from him, cheers next to me, and then "Let me ask you a question."

I wave at everyone to be quiet and press the phone harder to my ear. I can barely hear him in contrast to the noise around me. "Okay."

"I got you on speakerphone here, but what we want to know is how you feel about the heat."

I run my hand through my hair and then bite my nails. "I... uh, heat's good. I think I'm a little soggy here in Seattle," I tease, trying like hell to lighten the mood and steer the conversation away from how nervous I am.

More laughter in the background, and he says, "Well, Asa, let me ask you another question." He pauses, maybe for the dramatics of it all considering he knows we're being recorded today by dozens of news outlets. I wait with unnerving anticipation before he finally asks, "How do you feel about being the first pick of the draft?"

I push out a breath, tears stinging my eyes. I look at Barrette holding Crew, and finally a sense of relief washes over me. "That sounds good to me."

"Good, good. I have to go back to the draft room but welcome to the Arizona Cardinals, son."

"Thank you, Kenny." I hang up the phone and set it on the counter. I look at Barrette, Crew on her hip. They're both smiling. I'm sure Crew doesn't even know what today is, but the fact that I'm met with their smiles after that phone call, it means the world to me.

"It's looking like Arizona," I tell everyone waiting and then move toward Barrette. I watch her face, the happiness, the tears, the nerves, it's all there. It's a big day for our family. I press my lips to her forehead and wrap my arms around her and Crew. "How do you feel about that?"

"I go where you go," she says, repeating my own words back to me. I said that to her after her trial ended.

I breathe out a sigh and slide my lips to her ear. "I love you."

An hour later, it's announced to the world. "The Arizona Cardinals choose Asa Lawson, University of Washington, as their first-round pick in the 2018 NFL draft."

With the announcement, I look at up the ceiling and think maybe— No, I know my mom played a hand in today.

The remainder of the night is a blur. I'm serious, I don't remember a fucking thing that happens other than getting drunk. Terrell is chosen in the first round by the Pittsburg Steelers, and I think Joey is more excited than him, but you never can tell with Terrell. He does smile at me and knocks his knuckles to mine. "A, we're in."

"Looks like it." Statistically speaking, 2 percent of NCAA college football players make it to the NFL, and we did.

Not long after, when the majority of everyone is gone, I'm

holding a sleeping Crew in my arms. My dad's next to me on the back patio watching the flickering of the fireplace through the window.

He turns to look at me, smiling. "I know this might not mean anything now, because I should have said it a long time ago, but I love you and I'm sorry for all the times I didn't say it. I didn't show it the way I should have, and I fucked up over the years, but you were always what was most important to me. I wouldn't be half the man I am today if I hadn't gotten the chance to be your dad."

I smile at him and then look down at Crew, brushing his thick blond hair from his forehead before kissing him. I know exactly what he means.

IT'S AFTER ONE IN THE MORNING BEFORE EVERYONE LEAVES FOR the night and Barrette and I are alone in our room. I sink down to my knees in front of her at the foot of the bed.

She looks down at me, so sure, so happy. "I'm so proud of you."

It feels weird hearing her say that to me. I should be saying it to her. She's come so far since that night her life was destroyed. Now she's a mother, a wife, a friend, an amazing woman, and she's mine. All mine.

I wrap my arms around her waist, my head on her chest listening to the steady beat of her heart. It calms me in a way I hadn't been expecting. This girl, she's my future just as much as playing in the NFL, and without her, I don't think I would have gotten here. I wanted to quit so many times and give her a stable life. But just like I did for her, she pushed me forward and kept reminding me of the goal. I think about the signing bonus, the salary they offered me, and though I knew it wasn't a guarantee, finally I can provide her and Crew with a life we only dreamed of having. The life they deserve.

"I'm proud of you, Barrette," I tell her, hoping the intention of my words isn't lost in the moment. She needs to know that she should be proud of what she's overcome.

She ruffles my hair, winking. "Me too, Bear."

I snort at her use of her pet name for me and know that we're gonna be okay.

Epilogue: The life we deserved
BARRETTE

GLENDALE ARIZONA
STATE FARM STADIUM
PITTSBURGH STEELER VS. ARIZONA CARDINALS

"Holy shit, it's like an oven outside!" Joey says, closing the door to the suite.

"Try being here in August," I tease, handing Crew his snacks and then turning back to my pregnant best friend who I haven't seen in months. Not since their wedding in August. Not long after Terrell was drafted, they moved to Pittsburgh. Joey's back in school at the University of Pittsburgh working on her master's in neuropsychology. "I can't believe how much I missed you!"

Joey hugs me to her chest. "Not as much as I missed you." She grins and glances at my very pregnant belly. Yep. Baby number two on the way. "When you're pregnant, you look similar to a normal-sized person." I laugh, and her eyes drift to the rock on my finger. The one talked about in all the tabloids and gossip magazines. The one the star quarterback of the Arizona Cardinals bought his wife when he knocked her up the second time. "Can you even lift that finger?"

"Oh, stop. It's not that big."

"Yes, it is."

Between having Crew, Asa entering the draft and then signing with Arizona... let's just say I'm not sure I remember much from the last few years. Other than raising a baby. Is it weird to say I feel whole pregnant? I know, bizarre thought, but I do. I don't have nightmares. Not a single one while I'm pregnant. Asa finally made me whole again by putting his baby in me. I know, that sounds so completely wrong, but it's true.

Asa and I moved to Phoenix in late April right after training camp began and bought a house, and then I got pregnant. Again.

While I'm literally due any day now, I'm still going to school too, trying to get my master's in psychology. I had been volunteering at a local women's clinic where I assisted a sexual assault counsellor in Phoenix. I'd like to go as far as to say that I'm whole and healed and nothing fazes me anymore after five years, but every time I heard a victim's story, it brought me back to that night. I didn't want to relive it anymore. I wanted to move forward, but I also wanted the strength to know that just because it happened to me, it didn't define the rest of my life. For about three months I pushed through, but when my mood started changing and depression begin to hit, I knew I needed to make a change. Not only for me, but for my family. I couldn't go down that road again.

For that reason, I had to separate myself from it. I'm still pursuing psychology, but I've switched focus to developmental psychology. It helps with learning how my almost two-year-old son can be so sweet one moment and throw himself down on the floor next and scream bloody murder over his fruit snack stuck to his shirt.

Joey laughs and rubs her swollen belly. "He reminds me of Asa."

I frown. "Why, because they both throw fits over their food?" It's true. If Asa doesn't have food every two hours, he's the clinical definition of hangry, if that was a real word.

"I can't believe we only play each other once a year," Joey says, taking a seat next to the window overlooking the field where the Steelers are warming up.

"I know." Crew is at my feet, still crying over his fruit snacks stuck to his shirt.

Joey glances over at him and rubs her swollen belly. "I seriously can't wait to have this baby."

"Ha." I move to sit next to her, realizing how incredibly uncomfortable and hungry I am. I swear, I never stop eating when I'm pregnant. "Ready for nonstop crying?"

"He doesn't cry that much." She picks Crew up and places him on her lap. "I'm just really ready to be a mom, you know?"

I look at Crew, who's smiling, and I know exactly what she's talking about. I never thought being a mother would make me feel this way. The day I had Crew, Asa left me a mason jar in the hospital room with the quote:

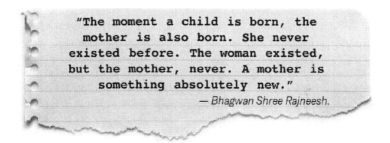

"The moment a child is born, the mother is also born. She never existed before. The woman existed, but the mother, never. A mother is something absolutely new."
— Bhagwan Shree Rajneesh.

Of course it made me cry because I feared being a mom. God, did I fear it. And I don't even know why I did. Maybe because of my parents' lack of... caring, I thought for sure I wouldn't know how to love the baby, but the moment I saw his face, I knew just like with Asa, I was born to love another brown-eyed boy.

"Are you guys still waiting to find out the sex of the baby?"

Joey grins and digs inside her purse for what looks to be two onesies and pulls them out. "We found out last week, but I wanted to tell you in person. I got Scout something from his baby cousin." Yes, we call our kids cousins.

Scout is the name Asa picked out for the new baby boy I'm carrying around in my belly. One of the onesies is pink and reads: Did we just become best friends? And the other is blue and reads: Yep!

"A girl!" I gush, hugging her one-armed. "Oh my God, how the hell is Terrell going to tell her no when she asks for money?"

Joey laughs. "I'm sure he won't even bat an eye to it. Nothing's breaking that man. I've tried. But hey, you never know. Maybe she'll crack him."

"Daddy!" Crew yells, jumping off Joey's lap and onto the ground. He presses his face to the glass. "Daddy!"

He doesn't say Mommy. He calls me M or you. But that's okay, I love him enough for the both of us and wouldn't change a thing about his stubborn, cranky butt. It's amazing to me how kids can be the biggest monsters and we still love them despite it.

My eyes follow Crew's tiny hand pressed to the glass of the suite we're in. Sure enough, the Arizona Cardinals are on the field and more importantly, my husband. It's different watching him play in the NFL. We didn't think he'd be a starter his first year on the team, but he beat out their current quarterback for the position in training camp and earned himself a spot. But the NFL compared to college is tougher in every way. His job depends on him giving 100 percent of himself to it and I have to be satisfied with that.

While it was definitely an adjustment, I've learned that the time he does give me is so worth it. Together, we've created an amazing life and I wouldn't trade it for anything.

The game starts up and I spend most of it catching up with Joey. That's when we land on the topic of Roman. I haven't forgotten about him or the way it all ended.

"Terrell said you and Asa went to his grave," Joey says, watching my reaction to it.

A punch of emotion hits my chest. Not because Roman died, but because Asa and I chose to say goodbye to him. At one time, he was our friend and there were some things I needed to say to him that I never would have in person while he was alive.

"We did," I whisper, rubbing Crew's back as he sleeps with his head on my extremely pregnant belly. "I think I cried the entire time. Not because I was sad, but because it still didn't feel like justice. I felt like he got the easy way out."

Roman died six months ago in a car accident in LA where he was living. His blood alcohol content was .60. I have no idea how he managed to get in a car, let alone drive it. The police report said he had cocaine in his system too.

When I heard the news from Remy, I was sad for her that her brother died. I hadn't spoken to her in over a year and to get that news, it wasn't easy. And then I thought about Roman, and if he ever felt guilty about what he'd done to me, and others, because there were others. Did he have remorse? Did he eventually regret it? Everything had always been handed to Roman and when I said no, he couldn't take it.

Asa spent most of the time at his grave cussing him out and telling him he deserved what he had coming. And I guess in some ways, I felt that way too. But, as I've learned over the years, change is inevitable, growth is intentional, and I'm not the same person I was the day that trial ended. I'm a mother now and we have a family. I have a lot to be thankful for, and just because my rapist got off easy, it doesn't have anything to do with my personal growth. Clarity is power, and I finally opened my heart enough to let love in. That right there was enough to keep me from breaking down completely.

As I stared at his headstone and his name engraved in it, part of me was thankful for the way it happened. Was it morbid for me to think that way? I absolutely love who I am and who I've become. I had scars on my body, but they told the story of my bravery.

I told Asa that and he looked at me like I'd lost my mind. At first, he was pissed at me, and then when he calmed down, he understood what I was saying.

He pressed his lips to my temple and whispered, "You are not what happened to you and I never want you to believe that."

I reached for his hand and smiled. "But in some ways, I am, and I have you to thank for pulling me through it."

We left the cemetery that day, and I can honestly say, I don't think of Roman anymore. If I do, it's a fleeting moment and I redirect my thoughts to what's important. Surviving.

Joey reaches for my hand when she sees I'm crying. I brush the tears away. "I'm not crying because he died."

She squeezes my hand. "I know, girl."

"Joey, can I ask you something?"

She nods, her expression one of amusement. "Is it at about..." She pauses and smiles at Crew. "...oral again?"

I snort. "No. It's not."

Her eyes soften and I know I still have that friend. The one I can count on to get me through anything, even if she lives two thousand miles away. I fidget with the onesie in my hand. "Do you remember when Maggie from our support group said it's my book and part of my journey. It's not his, it's mine?"

Joey nods. "Yeah, why?"

"I don't think it's my book. I think it's ours. Everyone's. Mine. Yours. Asa's. Terrell's. Even Roman's. We're all in it and we each have our own chapter written in it. I think that's why I went to his grave. I had to finish that chapter and the only way for me to do that was to bring closure to it and write his ending."

She starts crying. I've never known Joey to be a crier. Ever. But right here in the middle of that suite while holding my son, she bursts into tears. She waves her hand around when I try to comfort her. "I hate being pregnant. I'm emotional now."

Crew holds Joey's face in his hands and then kisses her nose. "No crying."

He can be a total turd most days but this boy of mine, he has his own chapter too. The one that's still being written and is full of life, love, footballs he sleeps with, Goldfish crackers, dirty hands, and orneriness most days, but he ties Asa and me together, completely.

The fourth quarter of the game is a nail-biter. I don't sit still the entire time and neither does Joey. We scream, laugh, and pray for our husbands. The game ends with the Cardinals winning over the Steelers 14-7. Both teams fought incredibly hard, and it was literally down to the last minute of the game when the Asa threw a fifty-six-yard touchdown to win the game.

Joey and I make our way down to where the locker rooms are to wait for the boys. "I know where the rest of the night is going. Asa is going to brag and Terrell is gonna be a grump."

"You never know." I fight to adjust my hold on Crew. It's around eight at night and he's out like a light again. Only trying to carry a sleeping two-year-old with a big belly in the way isn't easy. I stop many times and hold my stomach from cramping.

"Here, hand him to me. I need to get used to this anyways. I plan on having an entire football team of kids."

I laugh and give Crew to her, my arms shaking in the process. "Talk to me after you give birth."

It's another hour before Asa gets through the post-game interviews and showers. He and Terrell meet us in the lounge with the other players' wives. Surprisingly, they're both smiling and joking with one another.

We end up at a steak house in Phoenix in a private booth while

Crew eats his body weight in steak. Of course he's wide awake and it's freaking eleven o'clock at night. Product of living this life we have.

The conversation around the table doesn't center on the game like you'd think with two football players. Nope. They're talking about cars, hockey, and kids.

Me? I'm sadly... in pain. I'm not sure if it was carrying Crew down four flights of stairs or the excitement of the game.

Terrell notices first. "I've seen that look before," he says, chewing his steak slowly. It's true, he has. I went into labor with Crew while Terrell and I were Christmas shopping in downtown Seattle. I had been looking for something special for Asa, and four hours later, I gave him something far more valuable. His first son.

Asa's eyes slide to mine as he sets his drink down. "You okay, honey?"

I want to go as far as to say I am, but I know I'm not. I'm in labor. "I uh...." Just as those words leave my mouth, my water breaks at the table.

"Oh my God, yes!" Joey yells.

From there, it's a rush to the hospital and delivery room. Our son Scout Garrett Lawson is born two hours later with Asa, Terrell, and Joey by my side.

As I hold my new baby boy, his brother fast asleep in his uncle Terrell's arms, I have to smile. These people, they're mine. All of them. They got me through the last five years and gave me a perfectly imperfect life. One I never thought possible.

I stare at Scout, memorizing every detail of his precious face, and then my eyes drift to Asa, his face beaming with pride. "He's beautiful," he tells me, his lips pressing to my forehead. "Just like his mother."

I hand his son over to him. "He has your mom's eyes."

Taking Scout gently in his arms, he peeks at his face, tears in his eyes. "Wow. He does. He's a spitting image of her."

I like to think Asa's mom is watching over us and now we have a little piece of her here with us. I know he thinks about his mom more at times like these, wishing that she was sharing these moments with us. Asa was devoted to his mother and in his way, is fully devoted to his kids, to me. He shows us every day that he's here for us. Despite the pressures of the NFL, we come first. He's kept the promise he made the night that he saved me and has been by my side every day. I reach for his hand. "Thank you, for this life you've given me."

He smiles at me, his eyes lifting from the baby to me. He rocks the baby lightly in his arms. "Thank you for the life you give me."

His love, it's strong and loyal, and it saved me that terrible night and so many nights after. He's become my most trusted friend, my lover, my strength. He once said I saved him during those dark days when all he wanted was to throw away his chance at greatness, to give in to the temptation to lash out at Roman. But he saved me every day until I was strong enough to save myself. I don't know why I was lucky enough to have Asa in my life, but I am forever grateful that he is.

We are proof that out of terrible circumstances, something beautiful can grow.

Also by Shey Stahl

RACING ON THE EDGE

Happy Hour

Black Flag

Trading Paint

The Champion

The Legend

Hot Laps

The Rookie

Fast Time

Open Wheel

Pace Laps

Dirt Driven

Behind the Wheel – Series outtakes (TBA)

STAND ALONES

All I Have Left

Awakened

Everlasting Light

Bad Blood

Heavy Soul

Bad Husband

Burn

Love Complicated

ANCHORED LOVE

The Sea of Light

The Sea of Lies (TBA)

The Sea of Love (TBA)

Acknowledgments

All the credit for this book, which I wrote in about a week because I decided to take the characters on a very different journey than when I started, goes to my BETA readers. They read this book chapter by chapter and kept me going through it all. Without them, I don't think I could have done it in that amount of time.

Thank you Melissa for helping me with the last paragraph. I went over it and over it for weeks trying to tweak it to perfection, and you made that possible. I wish I could give you more than a thank you and hopefully someday I can.

Dawn, thank you for doing a final BETA read for more and catching all my crazy errors. I don't know why I accidentally type shit instead of sit.... *insert hysterical laughing*

Special thanks again, my editor and everyone at Hot Tree Editing. They always help make my novels shine bright.

Sommer, this cover! Thank you for giving me exactly what I never knew I wanted.

And finally, my family, thank you for always being there when I need you. You consistently give me the support I need. This author life isn't always easy. It's unpredictable, but the creative outlet it gives me is so good for my heart and soul.

About the Author

Shey Stahl is a USA Today and Amazon best-selling author. Rom-coms and sports romances with a unique writing style are her lady jam.

Her books have been translated into several languages, and if you haven't laughed, cried, and cursed in the same book, you're reading the wrong author. Shey lives in Washington State with her adrenaline-addicted husband, a moody preteen daughter, and their asshole cat.

In her spare time, she enjoys pretending to be Joanna Gaines while remodeling her house, iced coffee (only the good nugget ice), hiking in the mountains of the PNW, and hanging out at the local dirt tracks.